D0401762

CRITICAL
DAMAGE

ALSO BY ROBERT K. LEWIS

Untold Damage

CRITICAL
DAMAGE

A MARK MALLEN NOVEL

ROBERT
K. LEWIS

MIDNIGHT INK
WOODBURY, MINNESOTA

Critical Damage: A Mark Mallen Novel © 2014 by Robert K. Lewis. All rights reserved. No part of this book may be used or reproduced in any manner whatsoever, including Internet usage, without written permission from Midnight Ink, except in the case of brief quotations embodied in critical articles and reviews.

FIRST EDITION
First Printing, 2014

Book design by Donna Burch-Brown
Cover art: iStockphoto.com/19608991/dennissteen,
        iStockphoto.com/1124268/Ivan Chuyev,
        iStockphoto.com/8273903/Nathan Allred,
        iStockphoto.com/5479773/caracterdesign,
        iStockphoto.com/8147091/Kristina Stasiuliene,
        iStockphoto.com/15146577/Perkus
Cover design by Kevin R. Brown
Edited by Nicole Nugent

Midnight Ink, an imprint of Llewellyn Worldwide Ltd.

This is a work of fiction. Names, characters, places, and incidents are either the product of the author's imagination or are used fictitiously, and any resemblance to actual persons, living or dead, business establishments, events, or locales is entirely coincidental.

Library of Congress Cataloging-in-Publication Data

Lewis, Robert K.
  Critical damage : a Mark Mallen novel / Robert K. Lewis. — First Edition.
     pages cm. — (A Mark Mallen Novel ; #2)
  ISBN 978-0-7387-3623-5
1. Young women—Crimes against—Fiction. 2. Missing persons—Fiction. 3. Ex-police officers—Fiction. 4. Murder—Investigation—Fiction. I. Title.
  PS3612.E979C75 2014
  813'.6—dc23
                          2013027487

Midnight Ink
Llewellyn Worldwide Ltd.
2143 Wooddale Drive
Woodbury, MN 55125-2989
www.midnightinkbooks.com

Printed in the United States of America

DEDICATION

For Dawn, always.

ACKNOWLEDGMENTS

As with last time, you would not be holding this novel in your hands if it weren't for the hard work and support of a great group of people:

My loving wife and life coach, Dawn. So patient, so wonderful, so obviously crazy for sticking with this paranoid pessimist all these long years.

My agent, Barbara Poelle. It just doesn't get any better than Barbara. An agent that can slay enemies with one hand while never spilling a drop of vodka from her glass is the very definition of superhero in my book.

Terri Bischoff, Nicole Nugent, Amelia Narigon, and the rest of the crew at Midnight Ink. You couldn't ask for a more professional and wonderful group of people to work with.

My family: Sandy, Ed, Siobahn, Garrett, Sherri, Jim, Janet, and Ron. Their enthusiasm has been both incredible and humbling, and I love them with every bit of my soul.

The entire BP writing crew. Not only an amazing group of writers, but an amazing group of people that have given me their unflinching support, both emotional and professional.

And finally, to my parents, Roz and Steve. Mom gave me a love of reading and Dad gave me a love of bowling. What more could a kid ask for?

ONE

MALLEN STARED DOWN AT the hollow-point hypodermic needle poised over his arm, about a half-inch south of the crook in his elbow. The first needle he'd been around since quitting. The piece of rubber tied tight on his upper right arm was a sensation he hadn't thought he'd ever experience again.

But here he fuckin' was.

"Do it," he said as he looked up at the young nurse, who smiled and carefully slipped the needle into his arm, drawing out his blood. She deftly filled two glass vials and then pulled out the needle as she released the rubber tubing. Put a patch of gauze and some white tape over the pinhole.

"How long for the results?" he said as he rolled down his sleeve.

"A couple days. We'll phone them in to your doctor. If it's positive, we can recommend some great support groups."

He buttoned the cuff of his sleeve. "Thanks."

The day was warm, especially for this time of year. Mallen stepped out of the medical building and crossed the sidewalk to the 1965 Ford Falcon that belonged to Gato, his friend and companion. The small wiry man was behind the wheel, dark shades on his eyes, white t-shirt blazing.

"Anything hit the streets yet?" Mallen asked as he got in the front passenger seat.

Gato only shook his head in reply.

"Lupe's pimp will show, man," Mallen said. "You know those guys don't stay underground for long. Trust me: we'll find him. And if the trail should run dry? Well, I have some sources I can use if we need 'em."

"Sources," Gato echoed. "I've heard about some of your sources, *vato*. More like steel traps waitin' to trigger, if you ask me."

"Maybe. Sure. But let's not get too far ahead of ourselves, yeah?"

Gato replied with a nod of his head. "I don't like it though. None of Teddy Mac's stable has seen his ass for days. I don't like it."

"He'll surface, and we'll be there when he does." He knew it didn't sound as reassuring as he'd intended. Gato's sister's pimp going missing at the same time the sister did? Not a good sign, at all. "I'm sure Lupe's fine," Mallen added.

For an answer, Gato started up the car and put it in gear. "How'd the test go?"

"Like a blood draw. You know what?"

"What?"

"I don't like needles."

Gato laughed as he pulled into light traffic.

TWO

Tracy Goldman stared up into the sharp rays of the spotlight. White light, but not white hot. Reminded her of a doctor's light. She heard the soft *click-whir* of the old camera she'd seen one of the hooded ones carrying around. A ... Polaroid, he'd called it? Some sort of bullshit, old-school instant camera. She worked up a smile as she spread her legs wider. Rubbed herself, writhing a bit like she'd been taught by an old boyfriend during her last year in high school. Her new friends had just nodded when she'd told them about how she was going to work this scene. She was on top of it, she'd told them. A part of her had to wonder though: were they really your friends if *this* was the sort of stuff they thought was fun? Fun they seemed to almost push you toward? And then actually wanted a cut of your pay, saying it was a "finder's fee." That didn't really define *friend*, not in her mind.

But the pay was great. And at least it was from *her* work. Not her fucking dad's money. Money that was like a leash, used only to keep her tethered at the kennel.

At first she'd hesitated when her friends told her about this awesome opportunity to make some real dough. Just photos, they said. No fucking or anything like that. She'd thought they'd be photos in some bullshit motel room, but it hadn't turned out to be that. It'd *started* at a hotel, sure. A super nice one with a huge pool, and one of those refrigerators in the room that had tons of booze inside. Wifi throughout the place, and every cable channel you could imagine. The men she'd met had taken one look at her and smiled. Told her they wanted to do some *really* nice photos, they told her. The place they'd decided to take her was nearby too. Within walking distance of the hotel, they assured her. A real shooting studio, all set up for shooting beautiful, young women. She hadn't wanted to do it, at first. Leaving the hotel felt like leaving the shore behind as you went out to sea. But man … there was so much money flashing around! They handed her a roll of twenties, told her it was only an eight-hour day, if that. They just wanted photos of her. No guys. The man who paid for the photos didn't want to see *any* dick. Only pussy. Hot, young pussy … spread wide. She could do that, right? Spread her pussy wide?

Of course she could, she told them. Fuck it, these guys had money. Why not milk it? She'd told Jinky where she was. Jinky had her cell number, and she had Jinky's. It was all good.

It would be a lot of money just for a little posing in the nude. Just like Hollywood, she figured, or anything you see on TV. It beat going to college, or being prepped for some job she'd only get because her father was important enough. And she knew she'd hate whatever job it would turn out to be, anyway. She'd rather be here, making money on her own, turning some fucker on with photos of her body.

One of the hooded guys stopped shooting with the camera. Went over to an old leather suitcase. And yeah ... she thought the whole hood-wearing thing was fucking weird, but maybe they were bigwigs somewhere, right?

The studio had, as they'd told her, been nearby. And to top it off, they'd taken her there in a black limo. Had given her a drink. A vodka tonic, just like she'd asked for. The building looked from the outside just like any other small business office at night: five stories, no lights on. The limo drove down a ramp to the underground garage and parked near the elevator. They all got out and when the elevator came, they got in, one of the men standing so that she couldn't see what floor number was punched. It felt like they went to the fourth floor, but she couldn't be sure. The elevator stopped then, and the doors slid open with a hiss. As she stepped out into the large open space, she figured these guys must have a *lot* of money. It looked like a real movie studio. There were two sets: one was a posh bedroom, the other some sort of dungeon setup. *Weird.* One of the men moved her to the bed and indicated for her to undress. She did and then lay on the bed. That's when the filming began.

After awhile, the man with the camera mumbled something to one of the other men. That man brought over a suitcase and opened it. His hand came out with a large, flesh-colored dildo. She watched silently as he came over to her and held it out. There'd been very little talking the entire time of the shoot.

She tried to work up a smile. "Hey, um ... this wasn't talked about."

A shrug, then this man reached into his pocket and pulled out some more money. Threw it on the bed. Another thousand, it looked like. That blew her mind. It was just like a movie. She could feel the tension in the room...like they were waiting for her to make the first move, then the rest would fall into place.

She took the dildo. Figured that since it was a show, why not go all the way? She smiled as she took it. Spit on it, rubbing her saliva all over the head and shaft. Spit on it again. Wiped again. She could feel the tension fill the room to breaking point. She was turning them all on. She knew it. And she liked it. She heard the *click-whir* of the camera.

She lay back and spread herself wide as she rubbed the tip of the fake dick against her clit...

THREE

GATO'S FALCON CRUISED DOWN the street. Mallen stole a look at his friend out of the corner of his eye. Ever since Gato had helped him find Eric's killer, they'd formed a sort of bond. They'd both walked away that night, the night Eric's murder had finally been solved, turning their back on what had gone down by the north windmill at Golden Gate Park. Neither had mentioned it since.

Then a couple weeks later, Gato called him. Gato was angry, trying to hold it in though. Mallen could tell his new friend was wired to the breaking point...

"So, what's up, G?" Mallen had said. "What's buggin'? Hey, like I said back in the tank, if you need anything, anything at all, you just ask. I'll do what I can, you know that. If you need a bit of cash, I—"

"No, man," Gato said quickly, "I don't need no money. Nothin' like that. It's... it's about mi hermana."

When Gato wouldn't continue, Mallen said, "Your sister? What about her? Is she in trouble?"

"Yeah. She disappeared. A week ago. My madre is going crazy, and she's got her own probs, you know? She's not well."

Mallen nodded to himself, looked out the window of his office, the room situated in the loft of the floating home Officer Oberon Kane offered up as long as he took care of the place. Outside, the Richardson bay was calm and blue. He'd been lucky, he knew. Just like he knew he wanted to help people who didn't seem so lucky. He said quietly into the receiver, "And you don't want the cops involved?"

"Can't happen, man. My sister?" And here he spoke as if shamed. "She's a puta. Sells it for big bucks to wealthy bastards who ride into town on business. But my madre, she doesn't know that, see? I can't let her find out, Mallen. It would kill her. Word on the streets is that you were a good cop, and I've seen myself that you're a man blessed with a good heart. I thought . . . well, I don't know what I thought."

"I see." He took a sip of his drink. It was an easy decision. Gato had saved him, had been there for him. There was no other answer, and he was fucking well okay with that fact. "You know who her pimp is?"

"Oh yeah. I know that chingador. I'm sure you do too, come to think of it. He's the place to start, bro."

Mallen drained the rest of his drink. Put the glass on the top of his desk, next to a moss green paper kite he'd just finished making for Anna. "You mind coming and picking me up at my sinking, derelict home?"

"Already on my way, amigo."

FOUR

MALLEN AND GATO DROVE around the Mission area of San Francisco all afternoon, Gato asking everyone he knew if they'd seen Lupe. It was turning into late afternoon when Gato's cell rung. He checked the number, then answered.

"*Sí?*" Gato listened for a moment. Motioned to the glove box for something to write on. Mallen opened it up and found a pen, some .357 shells, a couple condoms, and a menu for a Chinese restaurant. He grabbed up the pen and menu. Nodded to Gato that he'd take down the address. "Bernal Heights. Corner of Jarboe and Bradford," Gato told him. "White house, ugly red trim."

Mallen wrote all this down. Not too many houses with red trim. Gato listened a bit more, then said, "Okay, thanks," and hung up. He grinned as he looked over at Mallen, saying, "Think we got him, bro."

"Him?"

"Lupe's pimp. Teddy Mac."

Mallen looked again at the location he'd just written down. "This is where he is?"

A nod. "That was one of his women, Diri. Told me this is a place he stays when he's burned out." He added with a slight smile, "Or when he's feeling the heat."

"Let's go then."

———

On the way over, while stuck in traffic, Gato silently pulled out his wallet. Flipped it open and handed it to Mallen. The first photo was of a very pretty, very young woman. Had the same shape face as Gato. Same smile.

Lupe.

Her smile was the kind that etched itself into your brain. The kind that would haunt you if she left you.

"I just wanted you to see her, *vato*. In happier times."

"How old is this?" Mallen said as he looked again at Lupe's photo.

"A long year and a half ago now, man."

Mallen handed Gato back his wallet. He knew people had to reveal themselves at their own speed and would take unkindly to any forcing of the issue. There were also the types who really only needed the opening question. He wondered which Gato would be. He knew very little about the man behind the wheel other than that he had a *very* strong sense of right and wrong, and that he was loyal to his friends. He wondered briefly if that sense of right and wrong had caused him problems in the past. Wondered if it would cause them problems finding his sister.

———

They pulled up to an off-white clapboard house with red trim, one in from the corner of Jarboe and Bradford. The freeway was only a few blocks away, and it was rush hour. The smell from the stalled river of metal oozing toward the Bay Bridge worked its way into Mallen's head, making him feel immediately short of breath. The house itself looked like it'd been permanently grunged by the chronic exhaust. Mallen wondered how many asthmatics lived in the neighborhood.

He was about to open the car door when Gato reached under the seat and pulled out a pearl-handled snub .38. "Wait a sec, man," Mallen told him, "What happened to fuckin' talking?"

"*Vato*," Gato replied as if explaining math to a challenged five-year-old, "Teddy Mac is a pimp and a thief. He's got a heavy rep for not takin' shit off anyone or anything. This isn't like the old days when you were *el policia*, right? When you could just walk into some dude's house and make him talk? You need leverage. Six shooter leverage, most times."

Mallen stared down at the gun. This was Gato's play, not his. "Okay," he finally answered, "But remember, G: this isn't the Wild West, okay? Don't go in there with a lot of attitude unless it's called for. We'll find your sister."

"I hear you, *amigo*. And I promise you that if things go bad, you won't be associated with this gun, okay?" Gato slipped the pistol into his waistband. Covered it with his shirt. "Okay. You have the cop knowledge. You call it, I'll follow."

They got out of the car. Checked the neighborhood. The streets were empty of foot traffic. They walked up the cracking concrete steps to the door of the house where Teddy Mac was supposedly staying. Mallen used his old cop knock, rapping loudly on the peeling, warped door.

"Who is it?" came a man's voice from inside. Deep in tone. Angry. Guarded. Guarded like Fort Knox. Mallen took a step to the side of the door. Motioned Gato to the opposite side. Gato's hand inched toward his shirt.

"We're friends of Lupe's," Mallen said. "She ain't been around. We need to find her."

"Why?"

"Hey man, it's about her mother. She's really sick. Heart attack."

There was a brief silence, then the entire world exploded as the door shredded apart in a hail of bullets. Sounded like an entire magazine was unloaded. Mallen and Gato dove for cover, Gato pulling out his .38, Mallen now wishing he'd asked if Gato had a spare. A door slammed at the rear of the building. Gato was on his feet instantly, bolting for the back yard like a pitbull on the chase. Mallen was up and after him a second later.

He watched Gato leap the back yard fence like a gazelle. He followed with more effort and less grace, but it was getting better with every day he stayed clean. Landed hard in a back yard filled with nothing but yellowed grass and forgotten appliances. Gato was well ahead of him, already at the back gate. His friend tore it open and was answered with a wall of gunfire. They both had to dive flat to the ground to avoid taking a couple in the chest. The squeal of tires ripping over gravel filled the air then faded quickly away.

Gato was already up, maybe ready to run into the street for a shot at the car, but Mallen got to him and grabbed him by the shoulder. "We need to get scarce, G," he said urgently, "and I mean like right now."

"But—"

"We'll find him again! You want to answer to your probation officer why you're involved in a shooting spree? Now, come the fuck on!"

They ran back to the car. Jumped in. Didn't see anyone around to mark their leaving. All the citizens were probably taking cover or still at their televisions. The Falcon roared off quickly. In a minute they were safely on the freeway, anonymous among all the heavy traffic. Mallen checked out the back window. Unless someone got a make on the car, they'd be all right.

He went over in his mind what the street was like right as they'd gotten back to the Falcon. There'd been no one. It was possible no one would associate the car with the gunfire. He felt 80 percent positive about that, anyway.

"Why you think that fucker opened up on us like that, man?" Gato said as he pulled the .38 from his waistband and shoved it under his seat. "That was some crazy shit."

"Don't know. But I know what you're thinking, and it's not an admission of guilt, okay? I don't think he would've blindly shot apart a front door if he'd thought it was just Lupe's brother knocking. No offence. Not if he's as badass as you say he is."

"I bet he would've. And I bet that piece of shit knows exactly what's happened to my sister, man. Exactly."

"Yeah, it's possible. But come on, the guy's a pimp, right? You said he's got a heavy rep. Guy like that could have any number of dudes after him, for any number of reasons." He thought hard as they sat in traffic, trying to figure out the best way forward. But the longer he sat there, the more he realized that he just couldn't figure one.

"You know, you just might be right, *vato*," Gato said, breaking in on his thoughts. "That was some pretty wild shit, right? Fucker just blasting the door like that? I mean, that *chingador* totally unloaded on us."

Mallen got it. Nodded. "Yeah. Teddy Mac was scared to death by who he thought we were, or might be."

FIVE

GATO STOOD IN THE living room of Mallen's floating home. He checked his messages, then closed the phone with a click. Said, "None of my *hermanos* report that a car matching mine is being looked for. I'm going to garage her somewhere out of the way for a while, just to be safe."

"You know a place?"

"Oh yeah, man. No sweat. I can even pick up a loaner," he said with a grin.

Mallen's phone rang and he pulled it out. It'd been the tone he reserved for anything from Chris. She'd sent him a text: CAN YOU COME BY? NEED YOUR INPUT. He couldn't help but feel good about the request. She was asking for his help. She must be feeling good about where he was, where they were, if she was going to do that. It was hard to suppress the smile on his face.

"Yeah, you should garage the car for a while," he said to Gato as he shoved his phone back into his coat pocket. "But can I hitch a ride back to the city with you? Chris needs to see me. You see if you can get a line on Teddy Mac. I'll call you when I'm done, and we'll hook up then, okay?"

Gato had a smile on his face the moment he heard Chris had sent his friend a text. "Hope it's all good with her, man."

"I'm sure it's about Anna, but yeah … she's trying to include me again. That's a good thing, right?"

"Most definitely, bro." Gato went to the front door, but then stopped and turned around. "Hey man," he laughed, "we sound like some private detective duo!"

"Yeah," he answered, surprised at the positive effect his friend's words had on him, "guess that's true." He paused then for a moment. Knew his next request might not make Gato so happy. "I think you should give me that gun, okay?"

The smile left Gato's face. "Why, man?"

"Because if for some reason your buddies are wrong, and you get stopped, they *will* find that gun on you, and then you'll be in the shit. Up to your ears. Give it to me to stash for a bit, okay? I won't hurt it. I promise."

Gato thought about it for a moment. Reluctantly he brought out the nickel-plated .38. Handed it over. "Only use the Remington 158-grain in that baby, okay? She likes to be fed on that."

"No worries."

Gato grinned. Followed it up with a shrug. "I got another at home, anyway."

"G, just be careful. We need you on the outside, okay?"

His friend seemed to appreciate the thought. "Of course, bro. I'm no hothead."

———

Gato had insisted on dropping him right at Chris's house. As it was the last time he'd been there, Mallen couldn't help but realize just how much he'd lost. Well, he thought as he stood looking up at the house, maybe he could get it back one day. He was clean now. Had no job, sure, but maybe that would come later. He could provide for his family again. Yeah, Chris had been dating, but still ... He couldn't help himself: he wanted it all back. Somehow. Another part of him then spoke up, saying that if he couldn't have it back in the way that he really wanted, then he would still be there for the both of them in any way they needed. If that's what it would be, well then that's what it would be.

He went up the tan-painted concrete steps to the dark wood door. They'd chosen this house because it was in the Mediterranean style, painted in a happy, light blue color. He could tell it'd been painted recently, and he was happy to see that Chris had not changed the color. He knocked and waited.

After a moment, the door opened and there was Anna. Her hair had been cut in a short bob, one that matched her mother's. She wore a bright yellow sundress and tan sandals, and looked like the prettiest thing in the universe. "Daddy!" she yelled as she threw herself at him, and he grabbed her up and hugged her tightly.

"Hey, A," he said. "You stayin' out of trouble, Little Miss Criminal?"

"Are you?"

"Yup."

She laughed then. "I'm not!" Like she'd won a game. He hugged her again and then put her back on her feet as Chris came down the hall. She looked worried, but smiled when she saw him.

"What's going on?" he asked.

"Thanks for coming so fast," she replied. "I'm sorry if the text sounded dramatic. It's just that a friend of mine, well, she…" her voice trailed off.

"No need to apologize. What's up?"

For an answer, she glanced back down the hall. Toward the kitchen. "You remember Liz Goldman? I went to Mills with her? She was a year ahead of me."

"Sure. Of course. You were Architecture, she was Poly Sci. You married a cop; she was married to Richard Goldman, who is now Mr. New Mayor." And it had been a landslide too. Goldman had captured almost 70 percent of the vote, even running on the standard bullshit: clean up Market Street, bring in new businesses and jobs, convert old hotels into condos. The usual, but it had worked. Mallen had to admit it helped that the man had charisma. Charisma in spades.

"Don't they have two kids?" he asked. "Older kids. I think I remember reading about the son. Thomas? Living in New York, right? Being a big-time stockbroker or something?"

"Right. Then there's the younger daughter, the one who was in kindergarten when I met Liz."

It was the way she said it that made him answer with, "What's Tracy up to?"

"That's why I texted you." She led him to the kitchen. There he found Liz Goldman, sitting at the round, mid-century kitchen table. She huddled over a cup of coffee, and he noticed a bottle of Baileys near her right hand. She'd been crying. Chris sat down opposite her. He took one of the spare seats.

"Hi Liz," he said. "Something going on?"

She looked over at him. "Hi Mark. Been awhile. You doing okay?"

Everyone of course knew about his past. He nodded. "Yeah. Every day's a victory now."

A nod. Silence filled the room, and he looked a question over at Chris. She urged him on with a look back at Liz.

"I hear Thomas is doing well in New York."

"Yes, and as to your next question, no, Tracy's not doing well. In fact, she's—" Liz took a drink of her coffee cup. Wiped away a tear. "She's gone."

"Gone?" he said.

"Took off a week or so ago."

Man, he thought, *is everyone's daughter going missing?* Made him think of Lupe, and of Anna, and how he'd feel if she had gone missing. Shuddered at the thought. He knew nothing really about Tracy, figured she would be about eighteen, maybe nineteen tops. And man, kids were so impulsive nowadays. Anna came into the room at that moment. Smiled at him as she went to the fridge. Opened it and pulled out some roll-up snack that Chris kept in the house. Trotted out like the world wasn't a bad place, and even if it was, it couldn't hurt her here, in her house. He had to admit: he envied his daughter then.

"Took off," he said. "For parts unknown? Or someplace closer to home?"

A shrug. "I think she's in the Mission. Maybe Hunters Point. Those were the last places she mentioned to me, anyway."

What would she be doing there, he wondered. People didn't usually go running around Hunters unless they called it home. He could understand Liz's worry.

"Why did she mention those neighborhoods?" he asked.

19

"She said she was looking for a place there. Told me she might be rooming with friends there." She broke down then. Pushed aside the coffee mug and began to cry. "My baby, my baby, my baby…" was all they could get out of her for a moment.

Mallen wondered why exactly he'd been called over, but knew Chris enough to know that if she'd summoned him here to listen to this woman, there was a good reason for it.

After Liz composed herself, she continued on in a halting, hoarse voice. "She's a legal adult, but she's still so young. It's not like when any of us were kids, right, Chris? Back then, when you went to college, you were expected to be an adult. Act like an adult. Now? Now it seems that college is just an extension of high school. You're *not* expected to act like an adult. Maybe it's the world we live in? Bad behavior isn't looked at as being, well…bad. It's something like *outrageous* or *epic*. I don't get it." She shook her head, looked over at Mallen. Her eyes were very sad. "Tracy's suddenly left home. Moved out, and in with a couple of her girlfriends about ten days ago. I was okay with that. Why shouldn't I be? She didn't want to go to college right away, and no, I wasn't okay with that. Tuition wasn't a concern for us, which we told her, but she has these new friends. I don't know where she met them, but I didn't like them when I met them. They weren't like the other friends she has. She only met them a month ago."

He automatically reached into his coat pocket for a pen and notebook that weren't there, and hadn't been for some time. He caught Chris's slight smile at his movement, recognizing it immediately. They both knew what he was going to do. Chris pulled a pad and pen from a nearby kitchen drawer and handed it to him with a look of gratitude.

"What are those girl's names? Do you know?"

"Only their first names. Jinky and Minta."

"Jinky?" he said to himself as he wrote it down. Definitely a street name. Maybe Gato could help him track one or both down. "What did 'Jinky' look like when you met her?

Liz thought for a moment, then said, "Tan to dark skin. Short. Only just over five feet or so. Dyed purple hair when I saw her with Tracy a few weeks ago. She was wearing a pink tank top and very short shorts. Both arms were tattooed. Completely covered, from wrist to the shoulders."

He wrote all that down. "And Minta?"

"Full figured. Young-looking black girl. Dyed red hair, all done up in these short braids. Same kind of clothes as the other one. Average in height, I guess. Same height as Tracy."

"Either of them carrying bags that might stand out?" Clothes you can change daily, but women tended to stick with purses.

Liz thought about that. Nodded then. "Yes. Minta's bag was a huge, knitted sack-like affair. Jinky had nothing like a bag that I saw."

As he sat there, his mind formed images of what these two girls might look like. Maybe it was his history in law enforcement. Maybe it was his history of shooting dope in the Tenderloin. Whatever it was, all his mind could conjure was an image of two young prostitutes. *Man*, he thought, *Mallen? You're gettin' old.*

He glanced again at Chris, then back at Liz. It was time for the million-dollar question. "Why no cops?"

And now the two women exchanged glances. Liz took up her mug. Kept her gaze on the dark liquid inside as she said, "Richard doesn't believe that she's in trouble. Thinks I'm overreacting."

"Ah." He wondered if that's what Goldman really thought, or if he just wanted to really keep it quiet. Keep it on the down-low. He'd heard of this type of shit going down before. Some guys he'd known, back in his SFPD days had done a little digging into private matters for the local politicos, on their own time. It was the way of the world, or so it seemed.

"Yes, 'Ah'," Liz replied. "We don't expect you to do it for free, Mark."

The statement alone was fine. It was the glance at the crook of his right arm that told him exactly what she was thinking. Even though Chris had probably filled her in on how he was doing, Liz Goldman obviously thought otherwise. Man, but the world was filled with cynics. "The cynics are right nine times out of ten," was a famous quote, though he couldn't remember the guy it was quoted from. Something that Dreamo used to say to him from time to time as Mallen stood there in the bathroom of the Cornerstone, buying balloons of H to fill the emptiness of his right arm and soul. He knew now that the saying was a fun play on itself. Very meta. This saying about cynics was itself cynical. Well, Mallen knew every day that he didn't shoot dope he was proving that saying wrong. He was good with that fact too.

"No worries, Liz," he said as he folded the piece of paper he'd scribbled his notes down on and shoved it into his coat pocket. "I don't want any pay. I'll see what I can find out. If I can help you and Richard, I will. But, if it looks bad I'll tell you immediately and you should really then go to the police, husband's opinions be damned, okay?"

Liz nodded in reply. He would help her, but because of Chris. Any parent who didn't want to go to the police out of appearance sake bugged him. And Mayor Goldman now officially bugged him. He said his goodbye to Liz after getting her cell number, telling her he would contact her in a couple days. Chris followed him back down the hall and as they got to the entryway, he heard a voice from the stairs behind him.

"Freeze, Daddy-O," Anna said as she lay in wait, ready to pounce.

He scooped her up off her feet, a squeal erupting from her lips. He hugged her tightly, telling her they would fly a kite soon, that he was just about done with one. Chris told her it was time for a bath and she should get upstairs. Once she was gone, he turned to Chris and said, "You okay with this? Her using me to find their daughter?"

She didn't look sure, at all. "We go way back. And she asked."

"I'll do what I can. You know that."

A smile. "Thanks, Mark." Then after a moment. "Everything still okay?"

"Yup. Even went for a test. Should have results very soon."

She hugged herself, ever so slightly. "You think … think it'll be negative?"

If he could remember every needle he ever shot into his arm, he'd be way ahead of the game for sure. As it was, he knew he was clear on about 85 percent of them. "Odds are that … yeah, we're good. I never got into sharing needles, and that's a biggie," he said. Shrugged then. What else was there to do? "It never got like that," he told her quietly. "I always kept it clean … thinking I was like Keith Richards or Jimmy Page, yeah? Shooting clean. Sure, we won't know until the results, but I'm willing to bet you a dinner that the results will be negative." He smiled then.

And she smiled back. "How about ten dollars instead?" That hurt him, and she could tell. She added quickly, quietly, "Come on, Mark … our history? What do you expect?"

"Yeah … I know. And you're right. Sorry." Held out his hand then, the smile on his lips as genuine as he could work up. "Ten goddamn dollars, lady."

She shook his hand, then pulled him close and hugged him. Whispered into his ear, "Deal, asshole. You're her father, and I want you around for her high school graduation, her senior prom, and her graduation from college. Don't fuck it up again, okay?"

And he answered back in the same whisper: "Deal."

SIX

HE WOULD'VE ASKED CHRIS for a ride downtown so he could catch a Golden Gate Transit bus back to his side of the bay, or to the Ferry Building for a ferry, but since Liz was there, that was obviously out of the question. Instead, he took the 38 Geary bus back to the Loin, the land of the sometimes helpless and the sometimes hopeful. His intent was to go see Bill and have a drink at the Cornerstone. He hadn't seen Bill for a while, and he'd always enjoyed the man's company. And, sure, there was a part of him perverse enough to think of it as some sort of test: could he get in and out without copping from Dreamo?

The street seemed quiet. Felt like a Sunday instead of a bustling Saturday; no one was really hanging around. Only saw a couple people sitting on stoops. Noticed a drug deal going down on the corner in front of the liquor store there.

Pretty much a light day.

He was only half a block from the Cornerstone when his phone went off. He checked the number: Gato.

"Yeah, G," he said.

"*Vato*," Gato said, "I found someone who can tell us where Teddy Mac might be."

"Who?"

"You'll see," came the reply, hot with humor. "A homie of mine found him coppin' over on Mission. He put the brakes on him until we could speak with him. You'll want to hear this for yourself. How soon can you be at the end of Illinois, at the ICC."

The Islais Creek Channel. "Why are you there?"

There was a slight chuckle on the other end. "Just come on, man. I'm gettin' hungry."

He sighed. He was getting hungry too. *And can I get a Scotch double neat with that, please?*

"Yeah, well, I'll have to cab it from the Cornerstone, which is where I was goin'."

"That place?" came the reply. Mallen knew that Gato always thought he might fall back to shooting dope the longer he hung there.

"Don't worry, G. I'm good."

"Then stay outside. I'll have a ride for you stat, bro." And with that he hung up.

Mallen looked longingly at the doorway to the Cornerstone. A drink was oh-so-close. But if Gato had told him to stay put, that's what he would do.

The ride showed only ten minutes later. A *very* cherry 1974 Chevy van. An airbrushed mural on the passenger side depicted some sort of warrior riding a white, winged horse. The man in the passenger seat waved him over as the side cargo door slid open. Mallen wasted no time as he jumped inside

The three men inside the van were big. Bordered on huge. Looked Samoan. One had braided rows of long hair. The other had a shock of ponytail. The third was bald, his head completely covered in tats that reminded Mallen of some sort of Maori design. Even back in the day, he would never have been able to take them. Well, he might have been able to send them to the emergency room, and he probably would have accompanied them, but that was a bathtub full of horse ago.

After they'd driven a few blocks in silence, the largest one, the one with the frizzed-out ponytail that would cause any ten shower drains to quake in fear, smiled at him. "Bro," he said in a deep voice, like some ancient church bell over in England, "Big doings, bro. Big."

"Thanks for the ride," he replied. Glanced over his shoulder. Noticed that the back of the van was carpeted. A single mattress was there, too, with a pile of blankets, along with a couple old World War II ammo boxes.

"Gato said we're to take you to the south pier side, just past the last pier," said the bald one who was doing the driving.

"Yeah, that's what G told me," he replied. "You know anything about why?"

The man only shook his head. "Figure it's important. He know we don't like comin' out until after ten or so." The driver's phone rang, Hendrix's "Voodoo Chile" the ring tone. Pulled it out. "*Talofa*," After a moment, he continued, "*Ioe*, mission accomp'd, *amigo*." Listened a bit longer, and then hung up.

They pulled up to the corner of Illinois and Cesar Chavez. Gato was there, pacing, hands in the pockets of his large gray hoodie. No mistaking the excitement in his movements. Something big had gone down, or was about to.

Mallen got out of the truck. The air was cold, moving toward freezing. "What the fuck are we doing here?" he asked as he got within speaking distance of his friend.

For an answer, Gato indicated the end of the street. Mallen noted the crumbling sea wall to the east. He shrugged. "And?"

"Come on," Gato said with a smile as he took off in that direction. "There's an old ship container there. Interesting cargo inside, *hombre*."

Ahead of them, just past the end of the street, was a rusty orange shipping container lying among tall weeds. How long it'd been left there was anyone's guess. He quietly followed Gato over to it. "You can keep my baby thirty-eight for a while longer, by the way," Gato said as he pulled up his shirt to show the butt of a nickel-plated after-market automatic sticking out of his waistband. "This avenging wolf has new teeth now."

Mallen shook his head with wonder. Said, "G. Where and how do you manage all these guns and cars, man?"

"Mallen," his friend said with a slight smile, "did I ask you where you got your *la heroina* back when you were using? Or what it was like the last time you were with your wife?"

"Okay. Point taken."

"Then let's go, bro." Gato dragged him forward. Took him to the far end of the container. The hinges had rusted off long ago, the doors long absent. The inside stank of urine and mold. Inside were three men. Large Mexican-looking dudes. Gato's friends. In the middle of them on the floor sat a young, rail-thin guy. Looked twenty-two, twenty-three at most. Dirty blond hair. Ravaged, pockmarked face. Dressed only in a filthy flannel shirt and torn jeans. A dark raincoat was tossed nearby, obviously having been gone through. Almost ripped apart at the seams. The guy needed a fix bad and was also scared to death.

Mallen looked over at Gato. "Who's this?"

"Teddy Mac's younger brother. Name's Carpy."

"Pimps have brothers?" Mallen inquired as he turned to Carpy. "You're Teddy Mac's brother?"

A nod in response.

"He's not a nice guy, to not take care of his brother, is he?" Mallen said. One of Gato's pack kicked Carpy hard in the back when he didn't respond. Mallen glanced over at the man. Shook his head. The man backed off a step.

"I got nothing to say about Teddy," Carpy said in a hoarse voice. Cleared it. "Haven't seen him in over a month."

"Did this guy have a score on him?" Mallen asked Gato, who nodded. "Hold it up so he can see it." Gato did this. Carpy's eyes riveted on it. Metal to a magnet. Mallen had to fight not to do that himself. Briefly wondered what inner strength Gato had that he lacked. Faith in God? Wouldn't that be fuckin' crazy, if it were so?

"Well, Carp," Mallen said, "you're in what they call 'some shit' here. I'm surprised you could cop anything from anyone, lookin' like you do. Anyone would think you'd roll over at the first whiff of trouble, am I right?"

"C'mon, man," Carpy whined, "give it to me. I paid for it."

"Well, just tell us what we want to know, okay?"

"What's that?"

"Your brother took a shot at us earlier. Just laid off and blasted away through a door, man. Without even knowing who we were, or might be. Why's he so scared?"

Carpy looked around at them. Shook his head as he glanced away. "Don't know, man. We don't talk."

"You know something?" Mallen said quietly. "When you look away like that, it makes me nervous. Makes me think you're lying, Carp." It felt like ages since he'd done just this thing: shake someone down for information on a case. Had to admit he'd missed it, and that was a fact.

Carpy just shook his head again, never bringing his gaze up. Gato spit on the ground. "Let's just kick his ass. Toss him in the water and be done with it."

The other men grabbed Carpy up. Held him by his shoulders, like guys holding up a sack of laundry. Gato sighed. "Sorry to bring you out for nothing, man," he said to Mallen. "I hate wasting my homie's time, you know that." Gato pulled a set of brass knuckles from his pocket.

"You're a one-man arsenal," Mallen said to him with a shake of his head. Turned to Carpy. "Look, Carp, my guy here is pretty steamed at having your brother shoot at us, especially being your brother is his sister's pimp. You read me on this? Now, you're going to tell us where he goes when he goes to ground. That's the bottom line here, okay? And not that shithole over on Bradford, either. That's where he shot at us."

"I don't know anything!" Carpy moaned, alternatively eyeing the drugs and the brass knuckles. Mallen knew the guy was lying. Could tell he knew more. It was the eyes—the way they blinked and shifted when he'd said it. The amount of times Mallen had seen that reaction on the streets was legion.

Mallen shrugged then. "Wow. Never met a guy before so eager to take all his nourishment through a straw." Indicated for Gato to get to work, winking at him without Carpy seeing. He knew he wouldn't need Gato to do anything more than threaten. Gato pulled his fist back, the brass knuckles glinting in the faint light.

"Wait! Okay!" Carpy said, panting with fear. "He goes to a place south of City College. On Lakeview. Tan building, with a lawn gnome and one of those green plastic overhang things for a car. There's a shack out in back. If he's really hiding out, that's where he'll be."

"Why do you think he's hiding in the first place?" Gato said.

"I don't know, man. He's always looking to fucking get over on people. Might've gotten over on the wrong ones, I don't know."

"Address?" Mallen said.

"I don't know the exact address, but it's right off Majestic. Tan, with the lawn gnome in front and the car thing. Only one on the damn block like that, man."

Mallen sighed. Looked over at Gato. "You believe him?"

Gato shook his head. "No. Let me pound on him for five minutes. He'll tell us the truth, trust me."

"No! I swear!" Carpy yelled in panic. Mallen would've put down a ten spot that the guy was about to wet himself.

"Look," Mallen said, "just go and get the fuck out of here, okay? And if you warn your brother about us, I swear the next time we meet will be the last day you live with all your limbs intact, got me?"

"Can I ... can I have my junk?"

Mallen indicated for Gato's friends to let Carpy go. Glanced over at Gato. Nodded. Gato tossed Carpy the powder. "That shit'll kill you, man," he said softly.

Carpy nodded absently as he pocketed the junk and took off at top speed. Gato put the knuckles back in his pocket as he chuckled. "See, man? That guy was easy."

"Yeah, he was," Mallen answered. "Let's hope the rest of them are that way too."

SEVEN

Mallen and Gato drove around the block a couple times before they got a bead on which house it was that Carpy had squealed about. The moon was high in the night sky now. A few backlit clouds hung heavy above. Somehow, and Mallen figured it was better not to know, Gato had replaced his old Falcon with a 1971 dark green Camaro Z28. The engine sounded like a purring dragon. The black interior was mint. The only nod to the modern day was the CD stereo with MP3 jack. A fit rig, for sure.

The house matched perfectly with the description they'd gotten out of Carpy, right down to the lawn gnome. No lights were on inside. Gato parked a block away, and they made their way back quietly in the direction of their destination. Stood across the street for a moment. Checked the place out. It gave off a very still air. Mallen was about to light a cig but thought better of it. Glanced across at the house. "He said in back, yeah?"

Gato nodded.

Mallen felt in his coat pocket. Gato's gun rested heavily inside. He'd tried to leave it in the car, but it'd just been too hard to do. Would King Arthur leave Excalibur back at the ranch? Not a chance.

"Look," he said to Gato, "let's not have a repeat of last time. This time we go in expecting all Hell to fucking crash down upon us sinners, okay? I take the high road, you take the low. But remember: we want to shock, not to shoot. There are too many windows around, and this time of night, citizens are all cozy in their beds, yeah? Also, remember that we need him to be able to converse."

"I hear you," Gato said as he took off across the street. Mallen followed.

There was a driveway ahead of them, complete with green fiberglass carport. Like something usually seen in Florida. Past that was a tall, wood-slatted fence, painted white, blocking off the back yard. A gate was situated right in the middle. They crept low as they moved forward, hugging the wall of the house, moving quietly under the blank, dark windows. When they got to the gate, Gato reached up and tried the latch. It was unlocked, the gate swinging inward, giving off a faint squeak of tired hinges. The two men exchanged glances. In unison pulled their guns. Gato nodded at his pearl .38 in Mallen's hand. Grinned with what looked to be an almost paternal pride. Mallen moved forward, every nerve wired tight. He couldn't remember the last time he'd been creeping along the side of a house, armed, with death on the line. Was surprised at how much of the old feelings and sensations he remembered. Wondered if this was how a once-sick, old dog felt going back out on the hunt.

The back yard was beyond dark, heavily sheltered by a couple large maple trees growing in the yard next door. In the far, northwest corner was a small, ten-by-fifteen wooden shack. A small light faintly glowed crimson behind red curtains. The two men moved forward silently, stopping only when a dog barked a couple houses away. After fifteen long seconds, the barking stopped, leaving a large vacuum of silence. Nothing else stirred. Mallen gave it a ten count, and only then continued on, Gato right next to him.

At the shack, Mallen stood to the right of the door, back to the wall. An old habit, choosing the right side. Gato crouched low on the left. It was then he noticed a thin strip of red light glowing in the darkness of the doorjamb.

The door wasn't closed.

He tensed. The air was still. Cold. His old entry training took over. Using the muzzle of his pistol, he inched the door open. Through the crack he could see a dark splatter on the maroon carpet. Blood. He went in, Gato staying at the door, fanning the room with his pistol. The blood was tacky to the touch.

The contents of the single room were meager at best. A bar fridge. A hot plate. A chemical toilet behind a shower curtain. The rectangular window in the back wall had been completely broken out. The blood pattern indicated that someone had been shot as they crashed through it. The gunshots would've meant noise. And that would've meant cops camping out on the doorstep. Why weren't they here?

The answer set the hairs on the back of his neck on end. Stood them straight up.

A silencer.

He wondered why Teddy hadn't shot back. It looked like the man had taken a quick-ass powder. Mallen noted that there was nothing else in the room but an army bag half-filled with clothes and a handful of cooking utensils near the hot plate. Some blood had spattered over by the wall, and also onto the carpet. The crimson liquid had fallen on something small that was no longer there, as evidenced by the cut-off droplet pattern. Something rectangular. No bigger than a shoebox, by his best guess. He led Gato out of the shack, closing the door without touching the knob, using the barrel of his gun.

"You think what I think, *vato*?" Gato whispered.

"Yeah. T-Mac got jumped. Shot. Not bad enough that he couldn't get away, though. I'd say it happened a couple hours ago, judging by the condition of the blood. Come on."

They were returning to the back gate when Gato tugged at his sleeve. Mallen's stomach tightened when he saw the open rear door to the house. The glass pane in the top half had been shattered, the few remaining shards glinting in the night like silver. He took a deep breath. This was getting sticky. Nodded to Gato. Mallen went in first, careful not to make any noise on the broken glass.

They found themselves in a large, old-fashioned country kitchen. Felt like they were alone, the house still, but his gut kept screaming at him that something was up. Impulse drove him to the nearby hall, a hall that in this type of house would lead to the bedrooms.

They found the two bodies on the floor of the master bedroom. A man and woman in their late fifties, maybe early sixties, both African-American. The man lay on his side, facing toward them. The moonlight streaming in from the nearby window illuminated the brutal beating the man had taken. The woman lay close by on her stomach, the back of her head exploded by a bullet. The same silencer, for sure.

"We gotta get out of here," he said quietly, "but we need to check the rest of the house first." Gato nodded as he said a silent prayer. His friend looked shaken by the finding of the two bodies. Mallen figured he was thinking what it might mean for his sister if killers who would do something like this were tied up with Teddy Mac.

The rest of the house told a bleak story. A blood trail led from the center of the living room back to where the bodies were found. A couple bloody footprints stepped in and out of the crimson liquid. Mallen couldn't be sure, but it looked like the killer, or at least one of them, had followed behind the beaten man as he dragged himself along the floor back to the bedroom. For what? A gun? Maybe to stop what was happening to his wife. A coldness crept over him. Whoever had done this were some cold-ass motherfuckers, no lie. Who had these people been that they would take a beating like this— risk death, even—for Teddy? It didn't make any sense. There was the muffled sound of a car driving by the house, but it was like an alarm going off in the room.

"Let's split," Mallen said.

"No *quejas* on this end."

They left carefully, at Vietnam War patrol speed. Checked first from the shadows of the house before moving out onto the sidewalk. The street was quiet, oblivious to the violence that had happened. As they made their way to Gato's car, Mallen wondered just what the hell they'd found themselves in.

Gato started up the Camaro. Drove away slowly and casually. Shook his head and spoke quietly to himself in Spanish as they rolled down the street and away from the house of death. Sounded like he was trying to reassure himself that it would all work out.

"Just because she's gone doesn't mean she's dead," Mallen told him.

"She was into something, man. It must be the reason she took off."

"You don't know that. Maybe she found out something. Maybe *that's* why Teddy's after her. Maybe she realized that what she knew would get her in trouble with the same people that are after Teddy."

"You think he got out of that?"

Mallen thought back to the scene. There was no sign of anyone being carried or dragged away. "Yeah, I think so actually. I think he made it over the back fence, without shooting his gun this time. Otherwise, the street would be a cop convention."

Gato didn't look like he believed it, but wanted to with all his heart. Crossed himself again. "Lupe," he said softly, "what have you done, girl?"

"You need to be home, G. Home with your mother. Try not to worry her. Just be with her."

"True, *vato*. You're right. I'll drop you at your place first, though." After a moment Gato added, "What's our next move?"

"I have no idea, man. No damn idea, at all."

EIGHT

TRACY WOKE UP SORE and tired, and very hungover. She looked around the posh hotel room, still unbelieving that she got to stay in such a cool place. She'd never seen anything so killer in all her life, except in the movies. And she felt a little like that one movie she'd seen on cable, about the prostitute and the rich guy. Of course, she wasn't a prostitute. Was just having some fun.

The previous night started to come back into focus. The good coke after all the photographs were taken. The money there in her hands had been sweet. Way more money than her father had ever, ever given her. But that wasn't the main thing and she knew it. What it came down to was that it was *her* money. *She'd* made these dollars, on her own. It felt sort of ... empowering.

She rolled over onto her back and rubbed her stomach, low down below her belly button. A frown crossed her mouth then. The total blackout of all the lights as that one big dude that always seemed to be around had left the room. Then the two men who'd entered wearing the masks was definitely freaky, but they assured her they were just into that kind of kink. She shouldn't have let those two men fuck her, but the coke had taken hold of her, and she'd said yes. Wondered if they were handsome underneath those masks. They definitely had been older men, judging by their guts and hairy bodies. She'd never imagined doing it with someone so old. It'd been a little freaky when the second one joined in, the one missing part of his pinky. She'd never done anything like that before, but then again she'd never posed for pornographic photos, either. At least they'd used a lot of lubricant. The coke had turned her on, but not to the point where she'd wanted to do two guys at once. Still, once they all got started, it hadn't been that bad. She felt sorta worldly now, just like her friends told her she would. The extra money would help, now that she was on her own.

On my own, she thought with a smile. That felt good, to be out from under daddy's shadow, and hands.

She tasted the inside of her mouth and frowned. Got out of the bed and went into the bathroom. There she found a wealth of brand-new toiletries, just for her. She opened the toothbrush and got it wet under the fancy-looking faucet. Spread some toothpaste across the bristles and started to brush the taste of old cum out of her mouth. As she brushed and rinsed she tried to remember if they'd used condoms or not. She couldn't, though. *No more coke for you*, she thought to herself. Thought back to the money they'd paid her. A couple grand. Pictured herself riding in sports cars and being flown around the world as maybe the mistress of one of the two men. What had that one said his name was? Jack? She was sure that wasn't his real name. The shorter one, he'd been the one who'd been rougher with her, jabbing his finger in her ass as he fucked her doggie-style. He'd had that strange tat on the back of his hand. Like a spider. That was one of the reasons she hurt, that guy's finger. The other reason was the size of the other man.

She thought again of the money they'd paid her, and the fact they told her she could stay all day in the room, at their expense. Order up whatever room service she wanted, they'd said. She'd have to call Mint and Jink and have them come down. They'd all have lunch, here in the room. It would be very, very fuckin' cool.

She finished brushing her teeth and went back into the main room. Went to her clothes and bag. Funny. Her cell wasn't in her bag. She checked her pants pocket. Nope. She checked her bag again, wondering if she'd left it back where they'd taken the photos...

NINE

MALLEN HAD CALLED IN the 911 on the old couple once they were about a mile from the house. They pulled onto the freeway that would lead them to the Golden Gate, and Gato pulled out his phone and got in touch with his homies to see if there'd been any other sightings of Teddy Mac. There hadn't been. Teddy had probably gone to ground again, or was busy putting miles between him and the city. If he was smart, it would be the latter.

Mallen found it hard to concentrate. What they'd found at the house had turned everything upside down in his mind. He rolled down his window and took a long breath of air. It was hard to get the image of the dead couple out of his mind. Who could do something like that? But just as important, *why* would someone do something like that? The people responsible were definitely into not leaving anything to chance. He hadn't been up against people like that in a really, really long time. He'd have to dredge up all his old skills and training if he and Gato were going to survive whatever it was they found themselves in.

He shook his head and rubbed his eyes. Had to switch gears or he felt he'd leap out of the car and throw himself off the bridge. Turned to Gato, saying, "G. I know you have a lot on your plate, man, but I need help tracking down a couple names if possible, and the girls they belong to."

Gato shrugged. "Of course, *vato*. What's up?"

He told Gato about his meeting with Liz Goldman. About Tracy, and how the Goldmans didn't want to make waves. Gato snorted with disgust as he shook his head. "*Pendejos ricos*. Whatever you need, bro, but she has to handle it that way ... because he's mayor?" Another shake of the head.

"I hear ya. Chris asked me, as a favor." He left the rest unsaid.

"Okay, *vato*. I get you. You said the names were 'Jinky' and 'Minta'?"

"Right. I'd really appreciate it, man. Thanks."

The two men rode the rest of the way back to Mallen's in silence. Gato dropped him right at the gate that led to the pier where Mallen's home lay floating. Mallen thanked his friend again, then got out and took off to his place. Checked out the parking lot for any strange cars or people as he turned the gate lock, thinking back to a couple of dead people in a house down by City College.

When he got inside his place he went to the fridge. Slim pickings. Only a couple pre-made sandwiches he'd bought from the nearby liquor store. He'd bought a fifth of whiskey too. Grabbed one of the sandwiches from the fridge and the whiskey from the counter. Figured such was dinner for a man on the job.

————

Mallen spent his mealtime out on his deck, listening to the water lap against the hull of the houses around him, watching the winking lights of passing oil tankers. He was trying to work on the problem of what Teddy Mac was into, how it tied in with Lupe's disappearance, and what could be in that container the blood outlined back at the house by City College. He just didn't have near enough information yet. Carpy knew something more than he was saying, and that was the *only* thing he was sure of at this point.

Then there was Tracy Goldman and her friends Jinky and Minta. Was that just a case of two street-wise girls exploiting a sheltered rich girl? Could fuckin' be. He'd seen it before. Some of the girls he'd seen during his time in the Loin had come there on some demented journey, thinking they were being cool. But the real inhabitants always could smell them out, and would exploit them any way they could. He remembered one girl he'd first seen early on during his time in that hood. She'd obviously come from a good home, had money, but for some reason wanted to run the streets of the Tenderloin, hanging with street kids and crack heads. The drugs got her, bad. He hadn't seen her for a couple of years, and when she walked up to him outside of his building, he didn't recognize her at first. It was only her washed-out blue eyes and the pale scar over her right eye that made him realize this was the same girl. She was thin, almost a rail. Eyes red and haunted. Asked him for a cigarette, which he gave her, and as he lit it for her, she asked if he wanted a blowjob for ten dollars. Ten dollars. She looked so desperate and scared and tired and strung out. It tore at him. In the end he just gave her twenty bucks and walked away. He never saw her again. That was life in the Tenderloin.

———

His cell phone rang the following morning. The ring tone he'd chosen was "Under the Bridge" by the Red Hot Chili Peppers. The sharp jangle of Frusciante's guitar was like shards of glass in his mind. Reached over to the neighboring chair where his coat lay draped and pulled the cell from the inner coat pocket. Read the screen. Gato. Answered it before it went to voicemail.

"What's up, G?" he said.

"Bro," Gato said. Sounded like he was in his car, and it wouldn't surprise Mallen at all if his friend had been on patrol all the hours since he'd dropped him off. "There's been no sign of Teddy Mac and I'm checking all over this town. Nothing. Fucker's gone, man."

"We'll find him." An idea came to him then. "Why not put someone on Carpy? If T-Mac is in trouble, he might turn to family. Even a piece of work like his little brother."

"That makes sense. Okay, I'll have one of my boys do it." He then added, "I've got feelers out for that Jinky and Minta you told me about. Names like those? I'll get something."

"Thanks, Gato. Appreciate it."

"Hey," Gato said with laugh, "maybe we can get you back with your woman and kid, bro! Could happen, right?"

"Right," he answered, but didn't really believe it. He *wanted* it, sure. Badly. But really, he knew that was a dead issue. *Maybe just for now*, said a voice inside his heart. He ended the call and went downstairs. What he needed was a hot shower, followed by some good, hot food. No more sandwiches if at all possible.

———

It was forty-five minutes later when Mallen passed the dock gate, figuring to walk up the street to this little place he knew that catered to the local boat workers and more "blue collar" crowd. He'd always felt more comfortable among people like that than he ever did among people like Liz Goldman and her mayor husband.

He'd just left the parking lot outside the dock and was on the sidewalk when someone spoke up behind him. "You know where to get some H, man?"

He turned around, instinctively bringing his hands out of his coat pockets, ready to defend himself. He was two seconds too late, and too many years out of practice. A fist that felt like a sledgehammer crunched into his cheek. Sent sparks into his eyes. He went down on one knee. Something that felt like the sledge's big brother slammed into his kidneys. Was sent flat to the ground, on his stomach. Legs were numb. He tried to shake the pain out of his head. Barely felt anything as he was dragged to his feet, arms pinned behind him. It was like being in a vise. His vision cleared. The guy standing in front of him was African-American, about his height, but with very big fists and very red eyes. Definitely hopped up on something. No citizens were nearby. It was like the entire area had cleared out.

"You must have me mistaken with some other recovering addict, friend," he said through a mouthful of blood. The guy smiled. Shook his head, then laid a good one into Mallen's stomach. Felt like being kicked by Chuck Norris. A groan escaped his lips. Managed to rasp out, "I've been home, nursing your sick mother, man." Caught his breath a bit, then added, "Sorry, I meant nursing *on* your sick mother."

There was another sledgehammer to the cheek. Mallen felt blood running down his chin. This was followed by many more punches, punches he no longer felt, then he was jarred by the sidewalk as he slammed to the ground, barely conscious. Vaguely heard someone say to him, "Don't fuck with Carpy again. Ever. Or we come back for reals and put you under the ground forever."

The last thing he remembered was needing badly to call Gato and warn him before it was too late.

———

Mallen woke to an older man bending over him. It took him a moment to recognize the man who looked after the pier, sort of a groundskeeper, if such a thing existed for floating homes. The man's name was Mr. Gregor. He'd been in the Vietnam War, but Mallen only knew that by the tattoo the man had on his forearm. It was of an eagle with the dates he'd served, late sixties. Other than that, he'd had very little to do with the man in the time he'd been living there. Only the occasional nod and brief greeting. A groan escaped his lips as he forced himself into a sitting position.

"You're Mallen, right? Berth two-zero?" Gregor said to him. Mallen nodded his head in response. Gregor had grizzled hair and a long, gray beard, braided all over. Wore a Stevie Ray Vaughan t-shirt with the sleeves missing, military shorts, and flip flops. And the weather wasn't above fifty-five.

"You took some fuckin' beating, Mallen. Mrs. Jenson in one-four told me that she heard you were a cop once. I guess that's true, unless you were a Marine, because you sure can take a beating and keep on ticking. Guess it's true at that," he added with a slight grin.

"Yeah. I was a cop. Some years ago now. Lots of road between then and now, though."

"Lots of road between *lots* of places, son," Gregor answered as he helped Mallen to his feet and over to a bus bench. Mallen felt his nose. Wasn't broken. Checked for missing teeth. A sorta loose molar, way back on the left. Left cheek was sore as hell already and his kidneys were on fire. Pissing would be a bitch, and his head pounded like it was being beaten on by a heavy metal drummer. But he'd live.

Gregor smiled. Like he was proud that Mallen could take such a beating and live to sit up on a bus stop. "Mallen, you think you want an ambulance? You look like shit."

"No, I'm good, thanks."

"You see who did this to you? Did they jump you?" Gregor asked.

Mallen nodded. "Yeah, jumped me. Got a look at one. I'll never forget that face, trust me. Not until I've put my fist through it, anyway."

A nod and another smile from Gregor. "Good to hear that."

Mallen got to his feet. Gregor didn't offer assistance. Mallen figured the man knew to let him do it on his own. He needed to clean up, but first call Gato. He lurched back across the lot, Gregor next to him. Gregor opened the gate for him, and Mallen went through. He did follow Mallen back to his home though, and even opened the door to his place when he saw Mallen was struggling with getting the key in the lock.

"You *sure* you'll be okay, son?" Gregor asked.

"Yeah, I'll be fine. Just gotta clean up and get a drink to numb some of the pain. Thanks for the help, Mr. Gregor. I won't forget it, trust me."

"Take care then, Mallen. Keep on keepin' on." And with that Gregor turned and walked back up the pier to his own home, the last one on the right just before the gate.

———

First thing he'd done after Gregor had left was to call Gato. No answer. The call went immediately to voicemail. He didn't like that. He kept trying every five minutes as he got out of his bloodied clothes and stalked to the bathroom to wash away the blood and apply some first aid to his body and face. There was a lump forming on the back of his head, and it hurt to take a deep breath. Tenderly felt around his rib cage. Didn't seem like any were broken. Once cleaned up, he put on a fresh shirt and pair of pants. Tried Gato's phone again, and again immediately got voicemail. He figured it must be either turned off or smashed.

Shit...

He needed to find out if his friend was okay, and sooner rather than later. But how to get back to the city sooner rather than later? Couldn't afford a cab ride, and to bus it would take forever. Damn, but he would need his own fuckin' ride again. Decided there was only one thing to do. He gathered up his coat, checked the bullets in the .38, and went back out, locking the door behind him.

Mallen made his way to Mr. Gregor's. Gregor's place was all shingles and crazy-angled windows that opened outward, never up or down. Like he'd raided some boat graveyard. Mallen knocked on the thick wooden door. After a moment Gregor answered. Had a beer in his right hand despite the hour. "Mallen. What's up?" Gregor said to him, seeming a little surprised, but pleased. Mallen figured it might have to do with seeing him up and around so quickly,

"I know this is probably a bad time to ask," Mallen said, "but I'm in a bit of, well ... the shit."

Gregor looked up and down the dock. Like expecting to see either killers, gang members, or police. "Ya think, son?"

"Yeah, but not about those guys earlier. What I need is to get to the city. Fast-like. I'm helping out a friend, and he may be in trouble. Another trouble is he lives in the city. I'll pay ya at the top of the month if you can drop me off out there. I'm really sorry to—"

Gregor cut him off. "No, can't do that. Steelers are playin' Balt. Can't miss that. Sorry, man."

"Oh," Mallen dug out his phone to call a cab. Hell, he'd just eat Ramen for the rest of the month before his pension check came.

"Stop," Gregor said. Grabbed up a key ring by the door. Lots of keys there. Tossed a small ring of three keys to him. They were car keys on a Steelers key ring. "That's to my spare truck. You'll find it parked in slot nine-nine. Just fill it up before you bring it back."

Mallen looked from the keys, to the man, then back again. Stunned. "You sure? I mean—"

"Yes, I'm sure," Gregor answered. "I trust ya. Hell, if you fuck it up, then I'll make sure you have no electricity or plumbing, right? You think you'd risk all *that*?" Laughed. "Just bring her back in one piece, and let me get on with my fucking game, son!"

"You got it," Mallen replied, wondering at the way life worked sometimes. "And I'll bring it back in one piece."

Gregor nodded and shut the door with a definite air of "conversation closed." Mallen walked out the security gate and over to slot ninety-nine. Stopped dead in his tracks. Looked back once at Gregor's place, then back to the old Toyota Land Cruiser, painted the very familiar 1970s taupe with the white roof. It was in pretty good shape, given the number of years it must've been on the road, and off. Tires looked good. Climbed inside and started the truck up. Yeah, sounded like a truck. Turned on the stereo. It was tuned to NPR. Again, he looked back at Gregor's place. Wondered again at how people were just a fuckin' mystery, and that was a fact. Put the truck in gear and headed for 101.

The drive over the Golden Gate, in the truck, was better than he'd thought it would be. Loud, sure, but very smooth. Gregor obviously kept up his vehicles.

TEN

MALLEN WALKED UP TO the old, faded green, two-story row building where Gato and his mother lived. Found the front door propped open by a small chunk of wood. The last time he'd been here, he'd been beat to shit too. Laughed silently at that. Made his way to the back of the first floor and knocked softly on 1B.

"Yes? Who is it?" Esperanza, Gato's mother said from behind the door.

"It's Mallen," he said.

The chain and locks were undone in short order. The door was pulled open and there she stood, one of the most beautiful women he'd ever seen. Her white hair framing her strong cheekbones, her eyes outshining the sun. She hugged him, then looked at his face. "Ah, Mallen! *¿Estás en problemas otra vez?*"

"Just a little trouble, *Mamacita*, trust me. Have you seen Gato today? He's not answering his phone."

"That's because it got smashed, man," he heard Gato say as he came down the hall. His lip was split like a ripe melon left way too long in the sun. There was a bandage just above the right eye. Jaw looked swollen, too, like he'd taken a nasty uppercut. Gato grinned when he saw Mallen's face in the dim light of the room. "See you met them too."

"Yeah, out by my place."

Gato smiled then. Like it'd all been expected. All just part of the game. Gato led Mallen to the couch. As Gato did so, he turned to the old fireplace mantel where images of Mary and Jesus stood. A small white candle burned there, cupped in an ornate, silver holder. A photo of Gato's father hung behind and above the candle. Gato crossed himself once. Said something to the photo under his breath that Mallen couldn't catch.

As both men sat on the dark red velvet couch, Esperanza said to both of them, "Remember what the Bible says about fighters, *mis pequeños*," and then left the room. Mallen heard the door to her bedroom close.

As soon as she was out of the room, Gato turned to him. "A black guy, right? With a big white friend?"

"Never got to meet the friend, but yeah, a black guy. Warned me off Carpy."

"*Pendejos.* They're toast. Try and put me on the sidelines? You're meeting your maker, bro."

"No, no killing. But yeah ... Carpy knows more about Teddy Mac than he let on. He's gotta be covering up something. I want to find that little fucker, and that's a fact, G." Thought for a moment about what had happened to them, then added, "You know, Carpy is pretty well-connected for a strung-out shooter."

"I hear you, brother, I hear you. I was thinking that too."

"I'd really like to find out how he got those guys onto us so fuckin' fast. Only someone with some juice could've done that, you know?"

"You think it was his brother?"

"Could be, but if that's true, then Carpy is a *way* better liar than I gave him credit for. I won't make that mistake again, man."

Gato clenched his fists. Brought his right hand down on his leg like a hammer. "Man, those assholes broke my phone! I liked that phone too."

"I have some money if you need it, G."

"No, bro, but thank you. You're a generous soul. Jesus would be happy with you."

Mallen looked back to the hallway. Said quietly, "How's your mother doing?"

"She's had some bad headaches lately. Getting more forgetful. They gave her some pills to make the headaches go away, but they also make her ... cloudy."

"Sorry to hear that, man. Is that all they can do?"

A shrug, followed by a slight nod of Gato's head. "I need Lupe back. I can't look after her like Lupe could." Gato thought for a moment, looking sad. Abruptly changed the subject. "I put the word out on those girls you wanted found. Jinky and Minta? Only thing that came back was a bar down in Bayview. My info giver says someone named Jinky hangs there a few times a week."

"They say why? Buy drugs? Raise money?"

Gato shook his head. "Don't know."

"Which bar?"

"Shithole named Shang-Gri-La. That's a bad place. You go in there armed, or you don't go in, got me, Mallen?"

"Got you," he replied. "Wouldn't do to lose it all, right when I'm getting it all back together."

"Word," Gato replied. "So, what next? I haven't heard anything on Carpy, man. I'm out of ideas, too, *vato.*"

Mallen thought for a moment, then answered, "Well, let's go to Shang-Gri-La."

"Okay," his friend said, "but only after I get me a new damn phone."

———

After Gato kissed his mother goodbye the two men left. When they got to the street, Mallen suggested they take Mr. Gregor's truck. Gato took one look at it and shook his head, but got in after checking up and down the street first. Like he didn't want to be seen riding in such a ride.

They drove down 3rd, and near the corner of Shafter, they found the bar. It was moving into evening. If they were lucky, and if what Gato had been told was true, then Jinky might show. If not, then maybe they could at least figure a way to get a line on her place or where she stayed. They parked a few doors up from the bar and Mallen put the steering wheel lock in place.

"*Vato,*" Gato said with a scoff, "don't worry about that. This ride is safe, trust me."

"Thanks," Mallen laughed. "You're a car snob, yeah? Who woulda guessed."

They got out, walked back toward the bar. The outside was nondescript stucco. He couldn't tell what color it was supposed to be, but the closest Mallen could come up with was Basic Puke. The only thing that told them it was bar, aside from the smell of cigarettes coming from the front door, was the old neon sign, half burned out so it read, "S ang- r -La".

"Remember what I told you," Gato said, "this junk hole can explode. Lots of assholes drink here from what I've heard."

Mallen nodded as they went inside.

It was worse than he'd figured it was going to be. Dark and depressing. Old cone lighting from like the seventies. Noticed a couple hookers in the corner, making time with a couple guys that looked like they couldn't afford a hand job but were enjoying the attention. Maybe it was a drug thing. He briefly wondered if he would run into anyone from his undercover days. That would be a clusterfuck, and then some.

They went to the bar and stood. The bartender, a huge black dude missing his left ear, came over and asked them what they wanted with a jut of his jaw. Mallen ordered scotch, Gato had a beer, bottled. Told Mallen under his breath, "In this place you get beer and water if you don't do a bottle." Mallen wondered how watered the scotch would be. The bartender brought the drinks and as soon as Mallen took a sip, he realized how much he missed Bill and the Cornerstone. It was like drinking the dregs of a scotch on the rocks, and the rocks won.

He sighed and looked around the bar. Didn't see anyone he figured to be a "Jinky" or a "Minta." Guess he would have to throw out a line, see what bit. When the bartender passed by, he finished his drink and ordered another. But when the 'tender came with the drink, he asked the man, "Hey, I need Jinky. She been in today?"

The man looked at him for a moment. Then looked at Gato. He could feel Gato tense at his side. Like he would reach for his gun at any hint of trouble. The man eyed Mallen again. "You don't look like one of hers, man. You just leave it, and I'll forget you asked."

Mallen downed his drink. Hell, wasn't hard to do, being how much water was in it. "Can't do that, Bubba," he told the man. "I need her. Bad like." He slipped a twenty across the bar. "Just want to know if she'll be in, or maybe I can go to her?"

"Hey man, why you want Jink so bad? She's nothin' special. Far from it, man."

"I hear different."

The man glanced over at Gato again. "What? You guys into tag teams?"

"No, *vato*," Gato replied, "I'm just into watchin' is all."

The bartender grinned. Thought it over. Shrugged then walked away, taking Mallen's twenty with him.

"Dude," Gato said to him, "you gonna let that sack of shit take your money like that?"

"Give it a moment, G. Just a moment." He figured the bartender couldn't be seen giving over information. Not in that place. Either all his customers would vacate for good, or he'd end up with a snitch label, which would eventually put him in the ground. After a long three minutes, the man came back with another drink, this time on a bar napkin. Silently put it down in front of Mallen, then went to dry glasses. Mallen took a sip of the drink. On the napkin was scrawled an address only a couple blocks over. Mallen finished his drink. Shook his head sadly like he didn't get what he wanted, then he left, Gato in tow.

Outside, Gato looked back at the place. "Man, I'm glad I have some standards, bro. Can you imagine drinking there for reals?"

"Not in this life. I'd rather drink in an alley," Mallen said as they climbed into the truck.

They drove the couple blocks over to the address. Scoped the place out: an old, mid-sixties looking building. There was a walkway on the upper level, accessed at both ends with concrete and stone stairs holding up rusty metal railings. Large picture windows faced out onto the walkway, either covered with drapes or showing black empty squares with no one seeming to be home. Mallen glanced at the address in his hand. "Says number ten," he said quietly. He didn't like the look of the place.

They parked and got out. Went quietly up the stairs and walked toward the back of the building, where Mallen figured the apartment would be. They passed the picture window that belonged to number ten. The drapes had been pulled together, but not tightly. It was dark inside. Mallen stopped to look. His breath caught in his throat.

There had been some sort of struggle or fight here. Chairs were overturned, broken glasses could be seen on the floor. The screen on the TV looked like it'd been kicked in, or someone's head maybe had broken it. Who knew? He indicated for Gato to take a look. His friend gazed inside for a long moment. Looked over at Mallen. "What the hell happened here, man?"

"I have no idea," he replied quietly. These girls were the only lead he had in trying to find Tracy Goldman. And now? He was pretty sure that a couple girls didn't just trash the joint before bailing. He was curious about something, and needed to get inside to satisfy that curiosity. He glanced up and down the walkway, and looked at the downstairs. The area was quiet. He went to the window, where the lock was. It wasn't hard to jimmy open with his ID card. "Wait here,

G. Keep guard," Mallen whispered as he pushed the drapes aside and entered the apartment. Went quickly to the bedroom and looked through the closet. Two sets of cheap clothes were still there. Two sets for two girls. There was also a knapsack on the floor. He went to it and opened it. These clothes were nicer, like stuff someone would buy in the Haight if they wanted to look "street" but didn't want anything too cheap and junky. He rifled around in the bag but came up with nothing that would for sure link the bag to Tracy. He closed it back up and left it where he found it. Scanned the room quickly, knowing he couldn't take all day over it. Found nothing. Lots of candle wax and some dead flowers in a vase. He went back out into the living room and checked out the walls and carpet.

That was when he found it. A bullet had lodged in the floor. That was what he'd been curious about: would there be any signs of a gun. Someone with the silencer.

The similarity irked. Badly. Mallen knew he couldn't take the bullet because the cops would be here at some point. He was torn about whether to call this in, or just leave it. He crawled back out through the window, ignoring Gato's whispered question about if he found anything. He closed the window back up, wiping down the glass for any of his prints. Quickly walked away then, Gato close on his heels.

Only when they were back in the truck did he tell Gato what he'd found, and what it might mean. Gato let out a low whistle. "*Vato*," he said, "what the hell is going on?"

"I don't know, Gato, but it's getting deeper and darker and I don't like that fact, not one bit."

And that was when Gato's new phone rang. He checked the number, instantly answered it. It was business, that was for sure. "*Sí?*"

Looked over at Mallen and smiled. "*Gracias, mi hermano.*" Closed the phone. Said, "That was one of my street brothers. He saw Carpy. Twenty-Fourth and Capp Street, right in my hood. Followed him to an apartment building nearby on Lucky Street."

"Let's get going then," Mallen replied as he put the truck in gear.

"Stop at my house first, yeah?" Gato said. "We need better wheels."

"What's wrong with these?"

Gato looked like he'd been slummin'. "Nothing, I just think we need ... faster wheels, is all."

ELEVEN

MALLEN SAT BESIDE GATO as they drove down 24th, heading east toward Lucky Street. After they'd returned to Gato's place, his friend had changed into his "work clothes": all black. Mallen knew he'd be happy with any catch tonight: Teddy Mac, Carpy, or maybe one or both of the men who'd jumped them.

Gato had left him at the curb outside his apartment building. Was gone for about ten minutes after telling him to wait. He finally showed up with a new set of wheels: a 1970s honey-yellow, metal-flake Dodge Challenger. Wouldn't say where he got it from when Mallen asked. Probably guzzled gas like an alcoholic guzzles vodka, but it was also probably as fast as anything on the road. Carried a 440 six-pack under the hood that growled a deep, throaty rumble that Mallen could feel through the padded leather seat. Gato'd assured him it wasn't stolen. They then headed out to the building Gato's contact had told them about.

They were cruising over to Lucky Street when Gato said suddenly and quietly, "That's him." Indicated a liquor store down the street on his left. "I just saw Carpy go inside. I'm positive. You want to follow him when he comes out?"

"Yeah. But pull over and park as soon as you can. He got there on foot, so we'll also do it on foot. Wait for him to come out." The parking gods were with them: Gato was able to park the car almost immediately. He pulled out a blue handicapped placard from the glove box and hooked it behind the rearview.

"Hey, bro, it comes with the car, okay?" Gato said in response to Mallen's expression.

From where they were, they had a good view of the liquor store door. After a few moments Carpy came out, shoving a bottle into his coat pocket. In his other hand was a box of donuts. *A junkie's dinner,* Mallen thought as he watched Carpy amble off down the street toward them.

"Shit," he said to Gato, "get down!" Both men hunkered down as far as they could, the darkness of the car's interior and the color of their clothes hiding them. They waited until Carpy got to the end of the block before they quietly got out. "I'll stick behind him," he told Gato, "you follow across the street. We'll switch up every three blocks. He knows us, so don't get itchy and try to push it, okay?"

"Got it," Gato replied as they took off after their quarry.

It was an easy tail job. At first. However, Carpy seemed to get more and more careful as he went. Would quickly check over his shoulder. Would stop suddenly and tie his shoe. Mallen figured he was getting closer to wherever the fuck he was staying, so was getting more worried about a tail. The junkie also started to take sudden turns, only to turn back after a block. It was then that he realized Carpy was doing wide circles as they slowly moved in a southerly direction. He hoped Carpy was leading them to some bolt-hole of

Teddy Mac's. Fuck man, he'd be pretty damn happy if it were just Carpy's digs. At the least, he was going to take Carpy's bottle from him. *Consider it payment, you little piece of shit.*

After another four blocks of useless meandering, Carpy turned left on 26th. Headed east. Gato and Mallen switched sides of the street. He watched as Carpy went another few blocks and turned north onto Lucky Street. Mallen smiled at that. Hoped it would be lucky for them, not for Carpy.

Turned out it was lucky for Carpy. They came around the corner only to see Carpy approach two men who sat on the stoop of a dark, quiet three-story apartment building. Even with the low light, Mallen recognized that one of the men was the guy who beat on him. He motioned across the street for Gato to hang back. Stepped into a dark patch near the entry to a closed-up business. Carpy and the two men talked for a moment, then Carpy went inside while the two men stayed where they were.

So, Carpy had guards. A junkie with bodyguards.

Mallen snuck back down the street. Crossed over to the other side, using the traffic on the street for cover. Made his way to where Gato was stationed.

"Fuckin' Carpy, *vato*," Gato said, "what kind of world do we live in where even junkies have bodyguards?" He grinned then in the darkness. Made Mallen think of the Cheshire Cat. "*Vato*, we need to pay those *dos pendejo de mierdas* back for my lip and your face."

"We do, but we need Carpy more. Those assholes can wait, if at all possible. If they alert Carpy, we're dead in the water, yeah? That loser would really go to ground. I'm sure the only reason he's staying around is because all his connections are here."

"So, what's your plan?"

"Workin' on it, workin' on it." Mallen wracked his brains for an idea. It took about a minute, but then it came to him. "Look," he said, "we gotta draw 'em off. Once they leave the stoop, we'll be ready to enter the building."

"How do we do that? Man, you sound like some guy in a gangster flick."

"Get the car alarms going," he replied. Gato smiled, obviously enjoying the plan. The street was little more than an alley, but there were cars parked along its entire length. They went to the two nearest cars, glad they were newer models. Kept low. Each man took a car. Put his back up against it. Mallen then nodded and they rocked the cars back and forth. The alarms cut through the night as they moved forward and set the next two alarms going. Then they went on quietly, keeping low, maneuvering up the street. Kept their eyes on the two men who were now standing, wondering what the fuck was going on.

"I don't think it's going to work," Gato whispered to him. He picked up a nearby bottle. "This might help," he said as he threw it back near the cars they'd just set off. The bottle smashed to the sidewalk, barely audible above the noise, but high enough in the sound range to stand out. The two guards moved forward, wanting to check on things. They slowly prowled to the opposite side of the street, one pulling a gun. As soon as they had the chance, Mallen and Gato whispered across the pavement and made their way into the building's dark lobby, quietly shutting the door behind them.

"Dude," Gato said, "that was fucking killer."

"Yeah. Nice work there," he said back, smiling with the energy of a mission going well.

"Which apartment do you think he's in?"

"Dunno, let's start at the top, and—" Stopped when he heard the two guards already coming back up the steps. Mallen grabbed Gato and dragged him to the stairs that led to the basement. They huddled there in the darkness, out of visual range.

"Man," they heard one of the men say, "some shit is up. I'm sure of it."

"Yeah, most probs. Go tell him, man. Stay up there near him for a bit," answered the other man. Mallen recognized the second voice. It belonged to the man who'd beat on him. Heavy footsteps trudged up the stairs over their heads, then after a moment, went up another flight. *Two flights up.* The man in the lobby was alone now. The front door opened, then closed. Mallen crawled up the stairs. Peered out from around the railing. He could see the man through the front door glass as he stood there, lighting a cigarette, back to the door.

He leaned close to Gato. Spoke quietly. "Move to the door when I do. Quietly. I'll rip it open, and you handle him any way you want, but non-lethal and silent-like, yeah? We need to speak to him."

His friend nodded in reply. Pulled out the brass knuckles. Shoved them tight onto his right hand.

Mallen stepped out into the lobby. Padded over the carpet, Gato behind him and to his right. They easily reached the door. Mallen gripped the knob. Nodded at Gato, who hunkered down, ready to pounce. The door opened with only a faint creak of hinges and Gato leapt out in a flash before the man could turn. The brass knuckles slammed into the man's kidneys as Gato gave the punch everything he had. The man groaned and collapsed into Mallen's arms. He put the man's right arm in a brutal twist. The guy could barely stand from the punch, and they had trouble keeping him on his legs. Fucker's kidneys were probably bruising a deep purple right about now. They dragged him back inside the lobby. Took him down the stairs to the basement. It was a labyrinth of halls and boarded-up doors. Found a secluded corner toward the back of the building and threw their prisoner to the ground.

The guy looked up at Mallen with glazed eyes, still dumb from the pain. It was indeed the guy who'd attacked him. Mallen bunched up his fist, thinking back to the beating. Slammed the man in the nose. He hadn't hit anyone that hard in over four years, easy. There was the crack of cartilage as the nose broke. For a moment he thought he'd popped a knuckle. Blood poured from the man's smashed nose. The man went to put a hand up to his face, but Gato slapped it away.

"Choke on your own blood, motherfucker," he said.

"Yeah, but not before you talk to me," Mallen added.

The man weakly shook his head. "Not talkin' to you, man. You dead men," he said weakly.

"Yeah? Carpy that connected, huh?"

"Ain't sayin' shit, asshole."

Mallen looked at Gato. Shrugged. "Hurt him."

Gato took the man's left hand. Gripped the middle and ring fingers. Pushed the fingers slowly backward until the air was cut by a soft popping sound as the bones broke. The man groaned in agony, tried to stop Gato by reaching out with his free hand, but Mallen pushed it to the ground. Shoved it under the heel of his boot. Stood on it. "It'll be a year before you use your hands again if you don't answer questions, fuckhead. Where's Teddy Mac?" he said.

"Go fuck your mother," came the strangled reply. There was a harsh snap, and the man cried out as two more fingers broke.

"Oh, sorry," Gato said. "I lost control, *pendejo*. But that's not a nice thing to say. I always seem to lose control when people tell me to fuck my saintly *madre*."

"Where's Teddy Mac?" Mallen said quietly. "We want to talk to him, is all."

"Don't know, man. I swear I don't!" Gato took hold of the last unbroken finger on his right hand. The thumb. Their prisoner looked ready to piss himself.

"Carpy knows though, doesn't he?" No response to this. Mallen leaned more weight on the man's wrist with his boot. "Look, asshole, I'm through fucking around. If you don't tell me, I'll have my friend here cut your thumbs off. Try jackin' without a thumb, fuckhead."

The man got it then. Nodded wearily, "Okay, okay . . . Carpy knows where his brother is. There's some trouble goin' down. Bad trouble. Lots of guys after Teddy Mac. What I hear, he took something that don't belong to him. There's only two ways out of it for him now: cops or dead."

"What did he take?"

"I don't know. Think Carpy does."

Gato leaned in, gripping two of the broken fingers in his hand. "Look, man, you hear anything about one of Teddy's stable? A girl named Lupe? Nobody's seen her for a long time."

The man thought for a moment. Shook his head. Gato squeezed the fingers together. The man bit his lip against the pain, a low painful moan escaping through like the hiss of a teakettle. "You sure?" Gato said quietly. The man nodded, the veins on his forehead standing out. Gato released the fingers, then looked over at Mallen.

"Good night," Mallen said and clocked the man in the temple with the butt of the .38. The man was unconscious before his head hit the cement floor with a dull thud.

"Were you really going to tell me to cut off his thumbs?" Gato said as he pulled the brass knuckles off, flexing his fingers before putting them back on.

Mallen shook his head in response. "I'm not about that. But *they* don't need to know that, right?"

Gato crossed himself. "Like I've said: I knew there was a good heart beatin' in that chest, *vato.*"

They left after Mallen took the man's cell phone and the clip to his gun, and had thrown a dirty tarp over him. He'd be out for a while. They went quietly back up the stairs. Mallen knew the other man had gone past the second floor. Sounded like he stopped on the third. At the second level, Mallen stopped and opened the cell phone he'd just taken. Checked the call log. The most recent call was marked "Pit." He dialed it. They heard a ringing upstairs. The man was indeed standing guard.

"Trav, what up?" Pit said, his voice coming from both upstairs and the phone.

"Pit," he said into the phone in a hoarse voice. "Man! Fuckers... knifed me. Help me, man! Downstairs!" He cut off the call, pulling the .38, waiting for Pit to make an appearance. Pit didn't disappoint. He could hear Pit saying upstairs, "Trav? Trav? I'm right there, bro!" There were heavy steps above them, and then there was Pit, stopped dead in his tracks at the top of the stairs, Mallen's gun pointed right at his face. He was a large guy, built heavy, but not thick. Most of it was flab, either way.

"Hi, Pit. Don't move while my friend here frisks you, okay?" Gato was up there and expertly frisking the man. Came away with Pit's phone, a switchblade, and a Beretta .96 Vertec.

Gato pushed Pit back, giving room for Mallen to come up. He held the .38 level, right at Pit's stomach. "Okay man, we're gonna go talk to Carpy now. Come on." He let Gato put the man in an arm lock and push him forward down the hall. When they got to the right door, Pit was about to knock, but Mallen stopped him.

"Color me paranoid, but I'll knock, thanks." He rapped softly. He'd rather be wrong with the knocking than let Pit warn Carpy outright. Guys forget secret knocks sometimes.

"Yeah, what is it, man?" came Carpy's voice from behind the thin door. Mallen put the gun to Pit's temple. A bead of sweat ran down the side of the man's face, and he said softly, "Carpy, man. I . . . I need to piss, man."

"Oh, fuck me . . . whatever." There was the sound of the chain being pulled back. Then the door was opening. "What are you a fuckin' bitch you can't piss in the—" He never got to finish his sentence because Gato shoved Pit in through the door, knocking Carpy back onto his ass. Then they were inside, Mallen's gun trained on the two men. The junkie made a move to get up, but Mallen shook his head.

"I wouldn't, if I were you."

Carpy looked around the room like a trapped cat. "Where's Trav?"

"What matters is where Teddy, your brother, is. See how it all goes now? You fucked up, man. You sent some guys after us. That made me question just what was going on. If you'd acted like any other junkie, taken his lumps and gone away, then I wouldn't have thought anything. But you didn't. You know, I know about that stuff. Being a junkie. One junkie can't fool another." He leaned closer, the gun held so Carpy couldn't help but notice it, the muzzle a black hole as big as a baseball. "Now, where is Teddy? I'm not foolin', man. I want to talk to him. I don't care what trouble he's in, that's not my business. I just need info. I'm not here to blow the whistle on him or alert anyone to where he's at."

"If you go after him, they'll find him," Carpy said, never taking his eyes off the gun. There was something in Carpy's voice that made Mallen believe him.

He motioned for Gato to take Pit into the other room. "Make sure he doesn't hear anything," he said. Gato winked, pushed a suddenly very scared Pit into the bedroom. There was a moment of silence, followed by a heavy sound, as if someone had dropped a large bag of grain onto the floor from a very tall ladder. After a moment Gato came back into the room, a smile on his face as he placed his brass knuckles back in his pocket. Smoothed out his shirt.

"He's resting in a very comfortable way, bro."

Mallen nodded. Turned back to Carpy. "See? It's all good. No one will know what you said now. Where's your brother?"

"Why do you guys want to see him so bad?"

"No questions from you; only answers. I promise you though, we aren't gunning for him. Just want to talk with him."

The struggle going on in Carpy was not fun to watch. He scratched at his arms, mumbled to himself, glanced at Mallen's gun. "I . . . can't," he whined, his eyes pleading.

Gato stepped forward and grabbed Carpy by the neck. He pulled the man off the floor. Punched him hard in the stomach. Carpy groaned, trying to double up, but Gato held him straight. Mallen tried to gauge his friend's mood: he figured some of it was for show, but he also knew his friend was frustrated at their lack of information about Lupe.

There was a cry of pain as Gato grabbed Carpy's left hand and twisted it around. "I'm gonna fucking break your *brazo* in four fucking places, *pendejo*, if you don't tell me where your brother is. *Le mataré si no nos ayudas!*"

Carpy struggled but it was no use. Finally, he relaxed, his body sagging. "Okay, man, okay. But I'm trusting you mean it when you say you only want to talk." Carpy looked over at Mallen. "I've heard some things about you, of course. That you were a cop, but you didn't fuck with people that didn't deserve it. Hope that part's true."

"It's true," he said as he put his gun back in his pocket. "I just want to talk to him, okay? About one of his girls. Lupe." Motioned for Gato to release him. Carpy fell to his knees, rubbing his wrist.

"Man, if it was only 'bout one of his girls..." Here he paused, then said, "Teddy's into something bad. Like I said, I'm not sure what. We don't talk much, but we still care about each other. Family, right? Anyway, after the house in the south was hit, he took off for Half Moon."

Half Moon Bay was down the coast about thirty to sixty minutes, depending on traffic. "Why there?" Mallen said.

"It's where we grew up. No one really knows that. I'm pretty sure he went there."

"Man, that's some lame-ass shit," Gato said as he stepped forward, slipping his brass knuckles back onto his right hand. "So we go all the way down there, wasting our fucking time, and you get away to tell Teddy to go somewhere else. What the hell do you think we are, man? Stupid like you?"

"Yeah, that's asking a lot of trust," Mallen said.

"No, man! I swear!"

He considered it for a moment, then came over and frisked Carpy. Removed a cell phone, Carpy's rig, and a small vial of heroin. He stared at the vial for a moment. It wasn't easy ... hell, it was fucking hard ... but he gave the vial back to an amazed Carpy. "Gato will keep the rig. I'll keep your phone."

Gato accepted the rig like he was accepting a bag of dogshit. "Why, man?"

"Because we're *all* going down to Half Moon. Together. Once we get what we want, then you'll hand the rig back to Carpy, and we leave him to find his own way home."

"Hey, hey ... man," Carpy said, "C'mon, man. How'll I get back?"

"Well, if your brother is really there, I'm sure he can arrange passage for you. The alternative is I flush the rig and your scag right fucking now and tie you up in the trunk. You want to take the drive down there in that manner, instead?"

Carpy frantically shook his head in response, freaked out at the mere thought.

"Well then," Mallen said as he and Gato escorted Carpy out of the apartment, "let's have a nice, mellow drive down south."

TWELVE

"Turn on Poplar, then right on Main," Carpy said. They were the first words that had been spoken in the last hour since the three men had gotten into Gato's car and headed down 280. They'd taken the 92 turn-off and were now in the small town that Janis had sung about on the last album before she died.

"You still got my rig, right?" Carpy asked.

"Yeah, yeah, yeah," Gato said, "I got your fuckin' rig, dude. What's the address?"

"Ninety Arnold Way. Small house. Light blue."

They found the house but didn't pull to the curb. Instead kept driving, taking in the lay of the land. The house looked abandoned. Overgrown grass, peeling paint. Gato went around the block one more time, then parked a couple houses past their target.

Mallen pulled Carpy out of the car. "Look," he said, "it's like this, Carp: You're going to help us get into that house to talk to your brother. If you try to fuck us up, I will make it so you will never shoot another load of H into your arm again, okay? And how will I do that? I'll take a rusty kitchen knife and saw your fucking arms off. Are we clear?"

Carpy nodded, believing every word of it.

"What's the signal?" Mallen asked.

"What you mean?"

"The lord hates a liar, *pendejo*," Gato said. "What's the coded knock you have so that Teddy Mac would know it's a friendly?"

"Oh, that. Three short, two long."

Mallen studied Carpy's face. The addict looked desperate enough to be honest, knowing it would be the only way to get back his rig. "Okay, come on."

They walked Carpy down the block and up to the door. Gave three short knocks, followed by two with a longer interval between them. Mallen had his hand in his coat pocket, thankful for carrying a weapon this time should Teddy give a repeat performance of their last meeting. Gato pressed himself against the wall on the opposite side of the doorframe, shirt tucked back behind the butt of his pistol, hand resting there, ready to go.

A voice answered the knock. The same one heard from behind the door back in the city. "Yeah?"

Gato nudged Carpy. Indicated for him to say something to his brother. "It's me, man. Carp."

"What are you doing here? I told you to stay the fuck away!"

"I know, I know! There's some guys after me. I have to dig in. Open up, man." Mallen heard the chain being moved back, the door unlocking. When the knob turned, he used Carpy as a battering ram into the room. Carpy yelled out in pain as his face crunched into the door, which slammed back against the wall. Gato leapt in after them. There was Teddy Mac, pulling a .357 from his waistband. He was well-muscled, with long red hair tied up like some samurai refugee, the effect heightened by the slight slant of the man's eyes. He wore nothing but faded jeans and a blood-stained bandage wrapped around his stomach. Mallen dove forward, hitting him right in the gut, right on the bandage. Teddy howled in agony as he crumpled to the floor before he could completely draw the gun. Gato corralled Carpy, clopping him in the back of the head with his gun, making him lie on the couch, face to the back cushions. Mallen yanked Teddy Mac's gun the rest of the way from the man's waistband. Went and locked the front door. The entire episode had taken less than eight seconds.

Mallen pulled Teddy over to a nearby dining room chair and sat him in it. Teddy was still focused on the agony in his bullet wound. The living room and dining room were decorated with secondhand-store furniture. The only new things in the place seemed to be a large flat-screen TV and a PS3. He was about to send Gato to check the rest of the house when Teddy Mac spoke to him in a harsh voice filled with pain.

"Who the fuck are you? You're not what I expected."

"Yeah? What were you expecting?"

Teddy Mac studied him for a moment, dark eyes boring into him. Then he looked away. "Nothing. I don't know. Nothing."

Gato put his gun in his waistband. Cracked his knuckles. "Where's Lupe Calderon?"

"Who?"

Before Mallen could stop him, Gato slapped Teddy Mac across the face. Not too hard, just enough to get his attention. "Lupe, man! *Mi hermana!* Where is she? What did you do to her?"

Teddy glared back at Gato, and Mallen had to give the guy props. Even wounded like he was and flat in a chair, the guy showed no fear. He and Gato may not have been who Teddy was expecting, but Teddy sure wasn't what Mallen had expected in a pimp, and that was a fact.

"Oh, yeah," Teddy Mac finally said, weak smile playing over his lips, "I see the family resemblance. You're *Paloma's* brother. Ah, I get it now." He chuckled, tired. "Man, the world we live in."

Gato's hand moved like lightning, cutting Teddy hard across the mouth. "Her name is Lupe!"

It was feeling wrong. Teddy's reaction was wrong. *Not what I expected.* Mallen took a harder grip on the gun in his hand. "So who were you expecting, Teddy?"

Before Teddy could answer, Gato stepped in and slammed Teddy again, right in the mouth. The man's head rocked back. "If you don't fucking tell me what you did to my sister, I'm going to fucking kill you. Right here, right now!" Mallen grabbed Gato by the arm, pulled him back.

"Gato! Come on, man. Think. Keep your mind focused, brother," he said quietly.

Teddy Mac studied Gato for a moment. Spit a glob of blood onto the carpet. "I believe you would," he said. "I didn't do anything to her, man. She took off, is all. Said she wanted to start over. Clean up her life. Go somewhere where nobody knew her pussy."

There was a sudden, quiet stillness in the room. Gato shook himself free. He began to swing on Teddy, but caught himself, yelling, "You *pinchero*," Gato said. "*Pinchero!* You're lying! She'd never leave her mother! Never!"

Teddy Mac looked up at him. "Well, it's true, anyway. She was tired of it all."

"Teddy," Mallen said, "my friend here is going to kill you because you are his missing sister's pimp, and... well, you know how that goes, yeah? It looks bad for you, man."

Teddy laughed under his breath. "You don't know nothing, fucker."

There was fear now in Teddy's eyes, but Mallen realized it wasn't them he was afraid of. "What's going on, Teddy? We know you took something you shouldn't have." He glanced over at Carpy, still lying on the couch, face in the cushions. Man hadn't moved a muscle, but Mallen could swear he was quaking with fear. "It's those guys who are after you, yeah? The ones that went for you in that little shack. What'd you take? Drugs?"

"I wish it were drugs," came the reply. Teddy was a man who had been running for a long time now, and he was running out of energy. Mallen could sense that, having seen it in other criminals many times.

"What happened?"

"*Vato*," Gato harshed, "why the fuck are we even listening to this fucker?"

"Yeah," Teddy yelled back, "just fucking shoot then, wetback! Go ahead! And *then* see how you get to your Lupe. Go ahead! Fucking do it!"

Mallen stepped between Teddy and Gato. Gato had his gun out now, eyes slits as he stared at Teddy. "G," Mallen said to him, "We're not like this. I repeat: we're not like this. This doesn't fit with the guy who helped me out in jail, yeah? Not with the guy who loves his *hermana*."

Gato's eyes never left Teddy, but after a tense few seconds, he stepped back, nodding at Mallen. "Okay. You're right... you're right."

Mallen turned back to Teddy. "What was it, Teddy? What'd you take?"

Teddy thought for a moment, then shook his head. "No, man, I can't say. Trust me, you don't want to know. I guarantee you that."

"That's not good enough," Mallen replied. "Is it because of the shit you're in that Lupe left?"

A nod. "She got scared. I *think* she went down to Los Angeles. It was hard, but I let her go. Told her to, actually."

"Oh, you let her go?" Gato said. "You're her pimp, and you just let her go? You'd say any fucking thing right now to save your ass, *pendejo*!"

"She's alive!" Teddy yelled back, wincing in pain. Looked down at the ground. "It was hard to let her go, not cuz I wanted her to work for me, but... but because I loved her, man."

Mallen watched Gato carefully. He thought Teddy was telling the truth, but would Gato believe it? Gato stood there, staring at Teddy, at his eyes.

"It's true," Teddy said again, quietly. "I fell for her. Her smile. Her laugh." Looked right at Gato as he said, "She only worked for me a little while, man. Then I took her off the streets and made her my girl. She was for me, and I was for her. Exclusive-like."

Gato shook his head, mumbled a prayer in Spanish and crossed himself. "Okay," was all he said, then went and pulled Carpy off the couch and sat him on a chair next to his brother. Looked over at Mallen. "So now what, bro?"

Mallen stood there, thinking hard. "Teddy, maybe we can help you with your problem?"

All he got was a shake of the head. "Not if I have to tell you all about it, you can't."

"Look, Gato has resources. Good ones. Guys, guns ... if it's good protection you need. We can do that, but you have to let us in on what's going down."

Teddy sat there for another minute, chewing on it. Mallen had seen that look before: a guy who's in trouble and wants help, but is afraid to ask for or accept it, for any number of reasons. "I can't," he finally said. "I can't tell you. It's too hot for me if I do. It's already fucking bad, but that would only make it fucking worse. As it rides now, I can get out from under it, taking some steps to ensure my future, and Lupe's." He glanced at Gato. "I don't know where she is, man, because I told her not to tell me. She needed to get anonymous. Like a ghost. I told her right before she left that she'd know when it was over, one way or another. If she's anywhere, I figure she's probably south. When she wasn't talking about her family, she was talking about how much she missed Los Angeles. But you can't, *can't* fuck'n' go after her, man! You can't. You'll draw the dogs down there with you. I swear to you, I'm not lying, man. Leave her be. She's safer that way."

"I can't do that," Gato said.

"Yeah," Teddy replied, the tired note creeping back into his voice, "I figured you'd say that. She told me once how stubborn her brother could be. Said you got it from your father."

Mallen could see the look in his friend's eyes: he wanted to be out of there, rescuing his sister. Mallen said to Teddy, "Okay, if you don't want help, there's nothing I can fucking do, yeah? You've told us a lot, and I appreciate that. But"—he stepped up to Teddy then, put the barrel of his gun right up against the red patch on the man's bandage— "if I hear you lied to us? I will follow you to wherever you go to hide and I will make sure that you pay, okay? Only fair, right?"

Teddy nodded. Not afraid at all. A pimp of a different color, that was for sure. "I hear you. I'm not lying. And I appreciate you wanting to help. Like I said, man, you don't want any part of the shit I'm in."

Mallen stepped back. Gato tossed Carpy back his rig, and the two men left quietly.

Once outside, Gato said, "You know, bro, I wouldn't be leaving if I got one sniff of a lie from that *pendejo*. He was telling the truth. I don't know what the hell he's into, but I really think Lupe ran for her life, just like he said."

"I know, I felt it too. A junkie can sniff a liar out better than anyone, because he lies all the time. To other people. To his dealer. To himself. Teddy was being straight." They made it to Gato's Challenger and got inside.

Gato was about to start up the car when he paused. "I can't believe my *hermana* would fall for her pimp, man. That girl needs serious help."

"Love's a weird thing. Like the song says, people look for love in all the wrong places." Mallen looked back at the house. "I want to know what he's into that would make him run like he did. He seems like a brave sort of fucker, especially for a pimp."

Gato shrugged in response. Started up the car, the engine roaring to life. "I have a feeling it'll come out one way or another, man. All we have to do is wait."

THIRTEEN

By the time they got back to the city, it was late. Past midnight. They went directly back to Gato's mother's house. They turned the corner onto the street where Gato lived and pulled up next to the borrowed Land Cruiser. Mallen watched his friend. It looked like Gato was struggling with something, and he could bet he knew what was coming.

"What's your plan?" Mallen said.

"I gotta talk to my *madre*. Somehow let her know Lupe is still alive without letting her know too much, you know? I have to go down to L.A. man. Very soon."

"I get ya. I'll try to have a fuckin' plan by the next time we talk. Watch your back," he added as he got out of the car and went quickly over to the Land Cruiser and got in. Watched as Gato drove down the street and made the left at the corner.

He turned the ignition key and got the engine going. Drove for the bridge. There was virtually no traffic. He rolled the window down, the night sea air invigorating him, making him feel that he could come up with a plan that would solve the puzzles he seemed to find himself confronted with. He certainly hoped the fuck so.

It was just after one a.m. when he parked the Land Cruiser in the lot outside the dock where home was. Mallen wondered how long Mr. Gregor would let him use the truck.

Had to admit, as he walked down the pier to his home, the smell of the sea and the slap of water against the pier pilings was quickly becoming music to his ears.

FOURTEEN

SHE LAY ON THE opulent king-sized bed, watching cable, a nice buzz going from the drinks she'd been sipping all night. There'd been no sign of anyone all day, so she'd just chilled like they'd told her to do. The only contact she'd had with anyone all day was a phone call from a man who didn't give his name, but he said he'd been at the shoot and they'd love some more photos tomorrow. Told her to stay put until she heard from him again. She'd glanced around the room and then said into the phone that it would be no problem to hang. He told her that she'd get a nice raise out of the deal, so just be patient.

She took another sip of her rum and coke. Smiled to herself. It was fun and empowering to be doing stuff like this. Way better than living with her parents. So Dad was mayor, big whoop. Fuck that. That was for old people. She'd had enough of old, white people.

She focused back on the TV, but after awhile it was hard to do. She wanted to get some fresh air, and she'd always loved the night air. She got off the bed and grabbed up her bag, realizing she would need a new phone but man, she had the dough for one now. A top-of-the-line iPhone was definitely in her future. That was a kick-*ass* piece of communication, for sure, and she'd get it totally tricked out.

Tracy checked once more around the room as she wondered one last time about her old phone. No go. Grabbed up the room key, then went to the door and pulled it open. Stepped into the hall and made for the elevator, hearing her room door click closed behind her. Heard another click behind her, but barely registered it. Found the banks of elevators and pushed the down button.

She suddenly heard someone behind her. Went to look over her shoulder but felt a slight stab in the right side of her neck. A pinprick, really. Then it was like God himself slammed the lid down on her.

FIFTEEN

EVEN THOUGH MALLEN GOT home after one a.m. and had been running around all of yesterday, he found it hard to sleep. He was already awake before the sun came up. First thought that came into his mind was, *What the hell. I'll just try to take my rehab to another level.*

Decided to try jogging. Found some old, very worn sweatpants. Found a very stained t-shirt. Couldn't find a hoodie, and it was fuckin' cold out, judging by the coldness of his home. The place was only heated by the fireplace, and he loved the simplicity but wondered if he would find himself wishing for a real heating system. Wondered if he'd ever have the money to put one in. Well, fuck it, right? He'd be sweating within a quarter-mile anyway, so maybe the cold would be good. He needed to do something, remembering back to how winded he'd been when they'd chased Teddy Mac from the house by the freeway. Did he even have tennis shoes? Dug through his closet. Found a pair he'd moved with him when he'd packed to leave the Loin. They were filthy, and the right one even had a cracked sole.

Well, he reasoned, its owner had a cracked soul too. Slipped them on and tied them up. The lace on the left one snapped, so he had to make do with tying it minus a hole. It would do.

Grabbed his keys and left. The outside air was indeed cold, hitting him like a wall of ice. He did some stretching and didn't like hearing the creaking in his joints. Had to laugh though, at the thought of what he was about to try to do. Walked down the pier to the security gate and then started to jog. Figured he'd head south along the waterway, toward downtown Sausalito.

If he didn't get picked up for vagrancy first, that is.

————

He'd managed, he figured, about three miles between the walking and the "jogging," which ended up being like speed walking. But hey, it was a start, yeah? Or so he told himself. He was drenched in sweat by the time he made his way back to the dock gate. Had to admit that his lungs felt cleaner than he could remember them feeling in the last five years or so, even if the rest of him throbbed from yesterday's beatdown.

As he entered through his front door, his cell went off. Checked the number. It was Gato. "G," he said as he sat on the couch, his knees screaming at him.

"Bro," said Gato, "where are you?"

"My place, why?"

"I think I have a new line on Lupe."

"What a sec. She's *not* down in Los Angeles? How'd you get this line? Where'd it come from?"

"One of my homies just called me. Told me he found a friend of hers. A girl called Tamara. Roomed with Lupe. Knows where she's staying, and it isn't Los Angeles at all. I knew that fucker Teddy Mac was lying his ass off. Next time I see him, I'm putting a bullet in each knee cap then throwing him off a pier."

"Hey, keep steady. We don't know any of this is true yet, yeah? Tamara say why Lupe is hiding in the first place? Any sniff of anything different from what Teddy said?"

"Just that she was scared about something Teddy Mac was into. That sort of works with what we know, right?"

"Yeah, it does. Okay, where?"

"Near the Chinese cemetery in Daly C. Meet me at the south entrance as soon as you can. I'm almost there. I got a couple of my platoon with me. If some shit goes down, we'll be ready."

"Gato, this feels wrong. I don't like it, man. Right after we see Teddy? After what both he and Carpy told us? I believe them, G. I do."

"Mallen, I have to go. Look, I know, okay? But we'll go in all careful like, okay? Just get over here, and as fast as you can."

"Leaving now. Hang tight." He ended the call. Wished he had time to shower as he got out of his soggy jogging clothes and into dry street ones. All he had time for was toweling off and drinking a bunch of water to go with a piece of bread he found in his fridge. Quickly ran out and down the dock to where the truck was. As he got inside the vehicle, Mallen couldn't shake the misgivings his gut was feeding him over the bout of intel Gato had just laid on him. Didn't feel right. No way. Why would some roommate of Lupe's know the one piece of information no one else seemed to know? Maybe if they were real friends, then yeah, but two hookers just sharing a squat? Felt too easy.

He gunned the engine and put it in first gear, thankful there was a gun in his coat pocket.

———

The sun had barely begun to break through the fog when he pulled up at the entrance to the cemetery. Rows of stark, white slabs of granite. Acres of dark green grass. The occasional tree, bent and twisted. Gato was at the entrance, pacing back and forth. Came over to greet him. Mocked looking at his watch as Mallen rolled down the window. "Bro, you call this 'leaving now, hang tight'?"

"Nice. Whose vehicle are we taking?" For an answer, Gato opened the door and leapt inside.

"My guys are already in position. They've been staking the place out. Say that no one has gone in or out. Turn around and take this road down to Morton Drive, then hang a right."

Mallen got the Land Cruiser turned around. "This is sounding like a wild goose chase," he said.

"Ah, I don't know about that. My buddy told me that Tamara seemed on the level about it."

Mallen didn't want to say, but it was really feeling like Gato was desperate to grasp at any straw he could find. "There's something wrong with it."

"Well, what? What do you think is wrong, *vato*?"

"I don't know."

They took the right on Morton. Gato instructed him to stop behind a dark van. "The place is up the street. The green one."

Mallen looked up the street at the house for a moment. "Well, how do you want to play it, G?" He was determined to let his friend do it his way. Had to remember that this was about Gato's sister, not his. The only thing he was determined to do was not let Gato get hurt rushing into something.

His friend thought for a moment. "Let's wait a bit more, just to see if anyone goes in or goes out. Then we stalk in and see what we can see."

"Look," Mallen said quietly, "just be prepared for it to be nothing. I can't imagine your sister would be sitting right out in the open like this. We're only fifteen minutes from the Mission."

Gato looked around the neighborhood. "Dude, this is like Anonymousville, you know? She's in there."

"Then why are we waiting?"

"Because I'm not sure who else is in there with her," Gato answered as he pulled out his gun and checked the clip.

They waited an hour. The house remained quiet and still. Mallen thought he saw lights going on in one room, then another. There must be more than one person at home. He looked up at the sky. The fog hung overhead, making the day gloomy and dark. Made sense to have lights on inside the house.

Gato looked over at him, nodded, and got out of the car. Mallen followed. Two other men, Gato's friends, quietly exited the van they'd been parked behind. Both men wore black hoodies and baggie jeans. Mallen hadn't had any idea the van had been occupied. The four of them stalked their way down the street. Gato explained the plan: two go in through the back, two through the front. And they were going in full throttle too. No fucking around with knocking. Mallen didn't want it that way, but Gato said his sister's safety may be on the line. Gato wouldn't listen to any other viewpoint on the matter. Against his better judgment, Mallen let it go.

The other two men went around to the back of the house. Didn't even make a whisper as they moved. He and Gato padded up the steps to the porch. A light went on in the front room next to the door. Mallen pulled his gun, every fiber inside of him screaming to stop the whole thing. His gut was telling him it was wrong. All wrong.

Gato took out his phone, sent the signal. Waited three beats. Kicked the door in with all his might, and there was an echoing answer from the back of the house. They flew into the room, but it was empty. Mallen and Gato quickly made a search of the front rooms. The floor lamps were plugged into timers; that's why they'd gone on and off like they did. Mallen knew that was super bad news, and no doubt. He was about to tell Gato they had to get away, and fast, when one of Gato's friends suddenly shouted from the back of the house, "¡Madre de Dios, entra aquí!"

They ran down the side hall to the bathroom where the two men were standing just outside the doorway, guns at their sides. In the tub was a young woman. Looked about nineteen. There were deep cuts and bruises all over her body. Mallen pushed his way in. Even though he knew it was pointless, he checked for a pulse. Body was cold. For a brief, sickening moment, he thought it might be Tracy Goldman, but then he realized this girl looked like a Latina. He turned to Gato, who stood rooted in the doorway. "This..." Mallen said, voice tight with emotion, "this isn't Lupe, right?"

Gato shook his head. "No."

"Tamara," said one of the other men. "I saw her once, and—"

As if on cue, sirens cut through everything like steel blades through bodies. They were right there, right on the street.

"Get out! Go!" Mallen shouted as everyone piled for the back door. He knew the cops had been called *before* they'd ever kicked the door in. He'd heard at least three cruisers outside, all Code 3: lights and sirens blaring.

All he could think of as he blasted out of the back door and across the back yard was, *Who had set the trap?* They heard dogs barking, men shouting. It was now every man for himself. He swore under his breath as he leapt over the back wall and charged through the neighbor's yard. He'd known it was a bad setup. His insides, all his years as a policeman had told him that fact, but he'd allowed himself to go along with it anyway. The four men went separate directions over neighboring walls. The only goal now was to ditch the weapons and get the fuck out of Dodge.

Mallen bolted to the front gate. Heard a man shout out what the fuck was he doing in their yard, but then he was leaping over a wall, not waiting to check if the gate was even unlocked. He heard someone running behind him. Hoped it was Gato.

"Split!" he said, "I'll call!" He knew Gato well enough to know that the guy would make it out of the area somehow, even if it were hiding in the back of a garbage truck. Right now he was more concerned with his own skin.

Got to the end of the block. Danced the gun down a storm drain without even slowing. Ran across the intersection as he heard the roar of a big engine. Police cruiser, no doubt. Had to get off the street. As he ran, thinking of what the hell to do, he couldn't help but come back to the fact that whoever had set that trap for them didn't mind using a young murdered woman as a frame for the picture.

This was bad, and getting worse.

———

He waited out the cops for about two hours. Watched as the yellow tape went up around the street and the news teams reported on the death "from the scene." Then there was a moment when most of the cops were inside the house, along with the forensics team. That was when he rolled the dice and calmly walked to the Land Cruiser, which was just on the safe side of the crime scene tape. He got in and drove away like he hadn't a care in the world. His hands were shaking the entire time, ready to see a black and white in his rearview mirror. He drove out of Daly City, up 19th Avenue to the park, where the road turned into Park Presidio Boulevard. Couldn't get it out of his head that a trap had been laid for them. That wasn't Teddy. That sure as shit wasn't Carpy. So it had to be the men after Teddy, and that meant those men knew about him and Gato and what they'd been up to.

And he had never seen *anything* that had given him even a whiff that there'd been anyone lurking about, tailing the two of them. *Shit*, he thought, *these guys are good. Really fucking good.*

———

The first thing he did when he got inside his home was fill a glass half-full with scotch and sit in what was becoming his favorite piece of furniture: a derelict wood and leather chair he'd put by the fireplace. What the fuck were they getting close enough to that someone would kill a young girl and leave her in a tub and then call the cops? And he realized that these people, or at least one of them, must've been there to see them enter the house and spring the trap.

The cops had been there just too damn fast. It was possible the cops had been called as soon as they'd left their cars.

Mallen lay his head back on the couch and closed his eyes. Let out a sigh. This storm was growing in intensity.

———

A sharp knock at his front door shook him awake. Mallen rubbed his eyes. Glanced at the empty glass, and the almost-empty bottle of scotch. Just couldn't remember drinking that much. Bad sign, but then again maybe not given what he'd just been through. Another knock got his attention and he went to the front window to steal a glance at who it might be. He was completely prepared for it to be the police, or some dudes he'd never seen before, armed to the teeth.

It wasn't either. It was Gato. He went quickly to the door and opened it. He wasn't surprised to see that Gato had shaved his head in an attempt to not be recognized by the SFPD or any other hostiles out there in the big bad world. He'd also trimmed his Fu Manchu down to a smaller, more-conservative looking 'stache. Sorta Billy Dee Williams–looking.

"Nice disguise," he said.

Gato made a face. "Had to do something, bro. You should consider it too. Gotta be safe."

"I got away clean. I'm sure about that. Did you get the chance to go back for your car?"

Gato shook his head as he went and sat down on Mallen's couch. "It's still there. My uncle will pick it up tomorrow."

"Your uncle?"

"Yeah. He runs a junk-n-tow. Owns the yard too. That's how he's got all these cool rides for me to use, bro. He's *loco* for old muscle cars."

"So, how about your friends?" Mallen said. "They get out, too?"

"No, man. They got Stephan."

"Shit. How bad? Can I do anything to help him out?"

"Appreciate it, but not necessary," Gato replied as he picked up the almost-empty bottle off the coffee table. Looked over at Mallen for a moment. Put the bottle back down as he sat on the couch, saying, "He'd ditched his sidearm. Was a couple blocks away when they picked him up. They got nothing on him, but held him anyway, because of his history with law enforcement. He's good, *vato*. Be out later today, probably."

Mallen went to the kitchen sink and splashed cold water on his face. Came back rubbing his face dry, saying, "Still, I'd like to do something for him. He got picked up helping us out."

"That's nice of you, *vato*. I'll let him know." Gato leaned forward, hunching over his arms, looking intently at him. "Mallen, that was some hairy shit they tried to pull on us, man. What's up with that?"

"I wish I knew," he said as he returned to his chair. "Whoever it was used that girl like a hunter would tie a small goat to a tree and wait above in a blind for a tiger to come by. What they did took balls, G. Big ones. And a stone-cold iron will to match." He thought a moment before continuing. "Obviously not Teddy Mac on a double-cross, yeah? I mean, you ever hear of a pimp so willing to kill just to set someone up? Pimps are about beating up women or johns that don't pay. Not killing girls as window dressing. Women are their stock-in-trade."

Gato nodded emphatically. "And no way was it that hypo-hound brother of his."

"Right. So, gotta be the guys after Teddy. They know we were looking for him. Just like they are. And they can't be tracking us all the time, or Teddy would've been dead when we got down to Half Moon. So, they're not 'all-knowing', but probably pretty damn close. Worse, G, is that these guys formed a plan to crash us out and executed it as cold as scientists in a fuckin' lab, man. We *have* to find out what the hell Teddy was into. We also need to gain some space between us, and the people after us and him."

Gato nodded. "Agreed. But how?"

Yeah, how? "Look," Mallen said, "we knew it was something he took with him. That's obvious by the shape left on the carpet from the splatter pattern back in the shack. A bag of some sort? But more structured. A box, maybe? And he must've either had it with him in that house, or he's got it stashed away so safe he felt good enough to leave it behind." He stopped then, thinking hard. What the fuck could it be that a pimp could get a hold of? Something that was that big, importance-wise. Must be *way* off the scale, that was obvious. Mattered the world to the guys hunting him. What would be so big nowadays that you couldn't just carry it around on a fucking flash drive? "What the hell could it be?" he said mostly to himself.

Then an idea came to him. There might be a way to learn more. It was a hard choice, though. Could be like kissing an atom bomb. Could be there was no other way. "You're probably using up all your points with your crew, yeah?"

Gato considered this for a moment. Shrugged. "We're family, this crew and me. We all know that it could be any one of us needing the help, at any time. They're with me for now."

"Okay. Good to know, because we're gonna need 'em. I think we have to start back with Teddy's girls, man. Maybe one of them heard him talk about something. It could be just a plain, everyday sentence, who knows? But it might mean something." After a moment, he added, working up to that A-bomb, "Remember the sources I told you about? The ones I mentioned that day I went to get that test done on my blood?"

"Yeah, I remember," Gato answered dubiously. "What about them?"

"I think it's time to call one in. I need to see Ali."

Gato looked at his friend like he'd just announced he was going to fly to the moon on golden wings of joy. Gato said, "You remember what I told you then? *That* particular source is a steel trap, bro. Remember back when I first did some digging on you? When I first helped you after you'd gotten clean? I learned about her and you, what happened. Everyone on the street had heard about what happened between you and her." He shook his head emphatically. "That woman's not going to talk to you."

Mallen went to pour himself another drink. So what if it was before noon? It was already after twelve on the East Coast. He made it a short one, then tossed it off. "I think she will. If it's about her brother? Yeah, she'll talk even to me."

SIXTEEN

TRACY WOKE TO THE rag tied over her face being violently ripped away. Everything that led up to that moment had been a hazy nightmare dream that she could barely recount. She was at the hotel elevator, then ... nothing. She'd opened her eyes, fighting her lids, only to find blackness. There was the sound of a car motor. She was in a moving vehicle. From the exhaust fumes, she figured she was in the trunk. Then she'd fallen back into unconsciousness.

Then there was another brief moment of awareness. She was still tied, only partially aware she was being stripped of her clothing. Her hands were briefly untied, and then she was bound again, this time hands behind her back. That was when something inside her finally woke up and she started to struggle and scream out for help. That netted her a punch across the jaw that shot agony down her neck. There was another pinprick in her shoulder, and she didn't really go out of consciousness as much as she felt ... out of focus. She imagined she could see everything through a haze, but it was like watching a movie of it happening to someone else.

Then she was dragged to a bed and tossed down on it, face down. A part of her told her this was bad and that she should struggle, but she couldn't. She had to piss, and did so.

"Fuck," she heard from a long way away, "bitch pissed herself!"

"Quiet, fuckhead! Remember: no talking," came another faraway voice. Sounded like someone from Russia?

Then the pain struck her like being split in half by lightning. It made her vision go white, and then she was rocking back and forth, her face hitting and hitting the mattress. She passed out soon afterward. And was vaguely thankful that she did . . .

And now she was here, wherever *here* was. Everything on her hurt. Her bones, her skin, her vagina, her asshole. All hot and sore. Her left eye felt swollen and the vision wasn't that good out of that eye. She looked around her as best she could. She still felt dazed and more tired than she could ever remember.

At first it didn't make sense. Looked like an empty warehouse. She turned her head and saw that in fact there was something like a movie set around her. Like a hotel room somewhere. She heard movement. A man in a black leather jacket, black combat pants and boots, with a black ski mask over his head pushed a chrome silver cart up next to the chair where she was strapped. The top shelf was covered with a white cloth. But she could tell there were things under that cloth. And she knew they wouldn't be good things. Sweat broke out on her forehead and she began to shake. Another man, dressed like the first, came and forced each of her feet back to the chair so the other man could bind them to the chair legs. It spread her legs wide.

"Please," she pleaded, hating the slur of her words. "What's going on? Why are you doing this?"

The only answer she got was a slap across her face. It stung, and made her swollen eye start to pulse. One of the men removed the white cloth over the top shelf of the cart and she couldn't help it: she whimpered with fright when she saw that there was a tray there, a tray filled with medical-looking instruments. Scalpels of different sizes. She recognized a speculum, like what her gynecologist would use on her when she went for check-ups. There were other implements she had no idea what they did, but they looked like they would cause a lot of fucking pain.

"Please! Let me go! I swear, *swear* I'll never say anything! Please, for God's sake!" she screamed out. She was met with another slap, then another. Her head lolled on her shoulders from the force of the blows. Her mind was once again slapped blank. When she was able to gather her wits enough to see and process information again, she saw that one of the men was now standing in front of her with some sort of movie camera resting on his shoulder. A big sort of thing. He was filming her; only then did it come to her that these men had something to do with the photos taken earlier. It crept into her mind, like a rat chews through the wood lathe of a wall, that she was going to be filmed and would be dead by the end of that film. She struggled the best she could, but it was impossible. Her young mind reeled at the thought of dying. She was just starting out! She cried more. Pleaded. Begged. Cried some more, but the man in front of her said nothing. Only filmed her through the entire episode. The second man came and stood next to the first, arms across chest. She begged him. Pleaded some more.

Nothing from either of them.

Then she heard a door behind her open and close. A third man walked into her field of vision. She screamed when she saw he wore nothing but a black bathrobe and full head mask. It took her a moment to realize the mask was an old president: Bill Clinton. All she could see of the man were the burning eyes through the mask holes.

"Let me go! My father will pay! He's got a lot of money. He's the mayor of San Francisco, for fuck's sake! He'll pay you a lot if you let me go! I haven't seen anything! I'll stay quiet. Please? Please? Just … just let me go!"

The man in the Clinton mask only stood there a moment, then took the tie away from his robe and opened it. He was an older man. White hair on his chest. But he must've taken Viagra, because as he came toward her, he grew quickly. He wasn't big so much as thick. He stepped near her and grabbed up one of the scalpels. She was shaking violently by now. Sweat drenched her entire body. The man leaned over her, resting the scalpel just on the inside of her ear canal, point in. He then forced her head toward his penis with his other hand, and she realized she had to suck it or get the scalpel rammed into her head. She opened her mouth.

———

Had she passed out? Tracy slowly opened her eyes. She was still tied to the chair, everything below her waist numb by this point. The man with the camera was still there, filming the entire episode. She couldn't even tell if she still had feet. The man in the mask got to his feet from crouching on his knees in front of her. Tossed the speculum onto the tray, dripping blood over the other implements there. He picked up a large knife. Like a kitchen knife. Walked behind her and she closed her eyes, knowing this was it. They'd never find her body. She'd never be held by her mother again. Never see anything, ever again. Felt the knife blade rest against her throat but it didn't move. She felt rather than heard the man lean in close next to her left ear.

He whispered when he spoke. Whispered in a monotone, "Your father knows what to do."

And with that she felt another sharp sting in her right shoulder. She looked at her shoulder to see a hypodermic sticking out of it. It was the last thing she saw before the black rush of oblivion washed over her and she swam away down a waterfall of black blood.

SEVENTEEN

MALLEN PUSHED THE BROKEN-LOOKING buzzer next to the rotted wooden door of the warehouse where Ali held court. He'd parked the Land Cruiser nearby, hoping it would still be there when he came out. If he came out. Either way, this wasn't a friendly hood at all. The warehouse reminded him of an abandoned, derelict ship dropped from above. He knew from his days back on the force that the place had been many things in the past. Shooting gallery. Gang headquarters. Even a dog-fighting club. The listed owner was a front company called Intellectualized, LLC. The real tenant was Teddy Mac's sister, Ali McCane.

All he needed was to get into the same room with her so he could plead his case. It was, however, a good fuckin' bet they wouldn't even let him through the door. That was okay. He was ready for that possibility. Ready like back in the old days. Ready for it to go either way. He pressed the buzzer and waited. Glanced up at the camera stationed above the door, carefully made to look like it was broken.

The door lock buzzed. He pushed inside, instantly confronted by a large, white bald dude, Louisville Slugger in his hands. Both naked arms were completely sleeved in jail and prison tats. Took Mallen a moment to realize that it was Griffin himself who stood there—the guy who'd tried to kill him more times than Mallen cared to remember, the last time punctuated by a dive into the frigid San Francisco Bay.

Griffin stepped forward, heavy boots scraping over the dirty concrete. *You fucker*, Griff's eyes said.

"Griff!" Mallen said. "Love your new look. Who does your hair, man?"

Griff grabbed up a handful of Mallen's collar. Mallen could swear the guy's face turned a deeper shade of red he was so fuckin' pissed. It took a long moment for him to come back to his senses. There was the crackle of a hidden speaker. It worked on the man like a dog whistle.

"Lady says for you to hand over your weapon, Narc."

"Didn't you hear? I'm an ex-junkie now."

"Can the comedy. Just hand it over, man."

"Ain't got one." And it was true. He'd decided that to come in this way, without a gun or knife or anything, might resonate with her. He wanted Ali to see he'd come for information, not for war. Open palmed, as they say in Buddhist circles. It was a roll of the dice he hoped would land him a seven.

Griff thrust him against the wall. Frisked him. "Well, goddamn," the man said to himself. "What a dumbfuck you turned out to be, hypo-head." Mallen was then grabbed by his collar and pushed down the hall like a homeless pussycat.

"Easy on the threads," Mallen said as he straightened his coat, "they cost me a day's wages."

They went down a short hall that ended abruptly in a large, open space. Dirty windows let in a hazy light two stories above. He counted six other men in the room: four sitting on a large couch and loveseat setup, complete with oak coffee and side tables. Two other men were at a bar that looked like it was taken right out of someone's home, complete with marbled mirrors behind it. The whole fuckin' thing reminded him of a movie set on a soundstage. The soldiers on the couch were rewatching a football game on a nearby big screen TV. Oakland against New England. Guns were everywhere, as was weed.

"Well, my love has returned," said a deep, husky voice. Ali appeared from behind a harshly painted screen that sat in front of what he remembered was "the office." She was living well, he figured, evidenced by the amount of diamond she had on her fingers and ears. Her hair was still raven black, still worn swept up into a long top-knot, like her brother's.

"You got balls coming back here," she told him.

He could feel Griffin behind him move in closer. Stood just to the left. Setting up for a take-down. All eyes were on Mallen now, the air filling quickly with a thick tension. He heard an inner voice in his head tell him he'd been an idiot for leaving the gun in the car and now "ha ha ha" on him, as he was about to die. The voice scolded him that he should've come with a bat, not an olive branch. *Oh well. That can be fixed.*

"I need to talk with you, Ali," he said to her, "about your brother, T-Mac."

"Miz McCane to you, junkie."

"You're behind the times. It's ex-junkie now, just like it's ex-cop."

She strolled over. He could smell her expensive perfume. Didn't know which one it was, but it smelled good enough to be high-priced. She looked into his eyes. Laughed.

"*You* want something? And after what you did? You come here, wanting something? Fuck you, Mallen." Spoke then over her shoulder to the men at the bar, harsh and loud. "Send this guy out on a stretcher."

It was the cue he'd been waiting for. Even mostly out of practice like he was, he still remembered the moves drilled into him during his time at the academy. No way he could've done this a couple months ago, but ever since getting clean, he'd felt better than he could ever remember feeling. The running, the homemade lifting, the yoga—all had gone to help him get slowly back into shape. And along with that shape came the muscle memory of defensive moves pounded into him since the first day he signed up to be a cop.

He stepped back and twisted, blasting his knee into Griffin's groin. The guy groaned, dropping the bat in favor of his slammed sack. Mallen managed to snatch the bat before it even hit the ground. Swung around behind the man, pulling the yard of maple hard under the thick neck for a chokehold. He felt a little like Jet Li then, and he really had to admit that he didn't mind that feeling. Nobody moved. He could see stunned expressions on just about everyone in the room. That alone made it worth it.

"Everybody take it easy," he said loudly. Knew his chances of actually getting out of the place were for nil if the shit went any more south. Looked right at Ali as he said, "I'm not looking for trouble, okay? Just need to talk to Miz McCane here." She hadn't lost one bit of her beauty. He added quietly, straight to her, "I'm sorry about what happened before. I was trying to do my job, but I fucked it up. I'm sorry. I didn't mean to hurt you."

"You didn't!" she said, her eyes flaring up in anger. She lunged toward him, but he pulled back on the bat. Griff gasped, struggled for breath. Mallen pulled on it even more.

Ali looked him in the eyes. Could read his intentions clearly. "Stop. Everyone relax." Retreated a step. Nodded at him. "Okay, talk."

"Okay, but first just tell your pack to step back against the far wall, hands in view. *Then* I'll let Hulk Hogan here go."

"You will?" she said, eyeing him, not believing.

"If they do that, yeah, I will."

She motioned for the other men to get up and go stand against the wall. They weren't happy about it. Acted like pit bulls barely on the leash. Mallen moved forward as they moved back, until he was near the coffee table laden with handguns. Before anyone tripped to it, he let Griffin go and grabbed up a nickel-plated Colt automatic. Trained it right on Ali. An angry murmur rose from the other side of the room. Griffin, whose balls he'd sent north, slowly got to his feet, eyes slits of anger and vengeance.

"Just relax everyone," he said to the room. "Man, you guys are way too fuckin' high strung. I just need to talk to Ali. Alone." She never took her eyes off of his as he stepped closer. He couldn't tell what the hell was going on inside her. Never could. "I just need an answer to one simple question," he said to her. "Where would T-Mac go if all the places he could think of that he thought were safe, weren't safe anymore? That's all I need. See, there's some shit brewing. And not the regular strain, either. Big wave of it. Big enough to wipe him the fuck right out, leaving no trace behind."

"Why the hell would I tell you?" she said.

"Like I said: someone's after him. And I mean a *big* someone."

"Who's this 'big someone'?"

He glanced around the room. Needed a better place to have the conversation. One less crowded. "Come on. We're going for a walk."

"And I'm going to say yes to that because ...?"

"Because maybe *both* of your brother's lives are stake, that's why."

She stood there for a moment. Weighed options. In the end she nodded. Instructed her men to stay put. He walked her outside, never putting his back to the room.

———

They walked to the end of 25th Street. The air was cold. Strong with salt and impending rain. The gray sky above seemed the color of loss. They found an old concrete bench, worn by the decades of wind and the elements. There was no talking for a few minutes as both of them just looked out at the bay. A slow-moving freighter made its way to the Oak's yards. A couple sailboats were out there, flashes of white on a somber canvas.

"I lied back there," she said as she gazed out at the water. "It hurt, what you did."

"I know. I'm sorry. It was a hard job."

"Did you ever do that with any other women?"

"No. That's what made it so hard."

"You're the only one to ever get away with lying like that."

He nodded.

"I could've had you killed. Any time I wanted, Mallen."

"I know. I appreciate that you never tried."

She smiled then, but there was little warmth in it. "It made my heart happy knowing you were out there just shooting your life away. Wasting away. Kept me warm on cold winter nights."

He chuckled at that. "Sorry I ruined it by getting clean."

"Fucker." After a moment, she said, "So, what's this about Teddy and Carp?"

"Bad people, and a lot of innocent blood." He told her about the dead girl. About the setup. About all of it since the day he and Gato had first gotten a line on her brother. She shook her head sadly the more he told her.

"That stupid asshole. Assholes, I mean. My brothers don't have a brain between them. Pimping, shooting dope. Jesus, but my mother would be proud of her boys," she said, bitter tone heavy in her voice. "Why you so hot on this? So much you'd come into the lioness's lair?"

"Has to do with a friend of mine. His sister is one of Teddy's girls. Or maybe was, if what Teddy told me was the truth. The deeper we got into it, the more we found out. Teddy's into something really bad, and I think that Carpy's in it now too. And like I said, it looks big. Big, dark, and full of guys in suits not caring about collateral damage." He then told her about what Teddy said in Half Moon.

She grew more and more concerned the more she heard. Sighed. Stared up at the gray ceiling of the sky.

"I'm not sure where he would go, if it was as bad as you say," she finally said. "He's no hero, but he's no coward, either. Not him." Added, "But he can be a vengeful fucker when he wants to be."

"Ali," he said, "have you heard anything at all about who he pissed off? What it could be over? It might be a big help to me. I know I don't have a right to ask, but I am." Shifted on the bench. "Whoever they are, they're coming after me now. I'd sure like to know what I'm up against."

"Isn't the trap they set for you enough? If I were you, I'd fucking drop this and forget about it. Tell your buddy to have a funeral for his sister and move on."

"Can't do that."

She studied him. "No," she said finally, "that's not you, is it?" She stared out at the bay, and finally said, not looking at him as she said it, "I'd heard a little whisper that Teddy'd made some bad enemies. Very bad. I didn't want to believe it. He's usually more ... cunning. Did some checking anyway. Low-like, so no one would know."

He rested his elbows on his knees, hands clasped. Gazed down at the ground. "What'd you get?"

"Did I ever tell you that my brother wanted to be a filmmaker? That's what he wanted to be, back when he was a kid. Would shoot video of Carpy, dressed up like a Star Wars character, doing all sorts of Star Wars crap. Teddy wanted to be like that guy that did E.T. Did I ever tell you that?"

"No."

"He's always had a thing for movies." She got up then. "But," she added with a smile, "you didn't hear it from me. I know how to read the signs, and I'm not afraid to keep my nose down. You could learn from me, *Marcos.*"

Mallen winced at the use of her old nickname for him. "Maybe so. Thanks."

She walked off. Heading back up the street. He thought long about what she'd just told him. So that was it: Teddy Mac had some camera content that someone was willing to kill to get back.

EIGHTEEN

MALLEN WAS ONLY HALF a block away from his car, turning the corner onto Cesar Chavez, when he noticed a dark BMW parked up the street. There was nothing outstanding about it. Looked just like any other dark-colored, late-model BMW. Thousands of them in the city. Couldn't be sure, but he thought he saw someone behind the wheel. Noticed the red glow of a cigarette cherry. Maybe it was just one more facet of the old sixth sense kicking in after years of being doped into slumber. Maybe it was his mounting paranoia at what Ali had laid on him. Whatever it was, all it took was a look at the car, and he just knew: that car was there because he was there.

He went on past the Land Cruiser. No way he'd be able to outrun them in that. No, he'd have a better chance on foot. As he passed, he cemented the vehicle in his mind: a BMW e5 sedan, smoked windows, trick rims included. Just to make sure, he crossed the street after he passed the car and headed around the corner. He wasn't sure but he thought he heard an engine start up. There was a liquor store up ahead, on the opposite side of the street. He jogged across to it.

They'd have to make a U-turn then, or park somewhere close by. They might even circle back to the truck and lay in wait. And how to handle that possibility? He tried to come up with a better plan as he stood there and bought a pack of Marlboro Lights and a pint of Seagrams. Paid and then checked out the magazines by the door. Glanced up. Yeah, they'd parked on this side of the street, one building to his left. He exited the store and walked in the direction of the car. Shoved his left hand into his empty pocket and now really cursed himself for not being armed. Wondered if they had orders just to follow him, or to grab him up, or just to put a kink in his head to make him paranoid. If it was that then it was working. In fucking spades.

He passed the car and turned at the next corner. Then went right at the next one, never looking for the car. Sure enough, the BMW always seemed to appear on the street somewhere. Sometimes behind him. Sometimes going the opposite direction. He'd see it sitting at a red light, or maybe turning onto a side street right ahead of him. Whatever he did, the car was always there. Whoever was driving was good, and that guy must be feeling pretty fucking assured in their position if they were going to be so obvious. That thought made him wonder how many guys were actually in that car. At least two: one to drive, one to be the eyes. And here he was, without a weapon. *Shit,* he thought, *God is just not looking out for recovering junkies today.* Quickly pulled out his cell and dialed Gato.

"Bro," Gato said, "glad to hear your voice. How'd—"

"Later man. Got a problem right now. Get someone to Ali's warehouse. I don't have a number for her. Tell her I think she may have been seen talking with me. Could be a lot of trouble comin' her way."

"Okay. Where are you?"

"I'm about to try and lose a black BMW that's taken an interest in me. Call you back."

"Be safe, bro. I'll go to Ali's myself."

"Thanks. Tell her sorry for me, okay?" There was the click as Gato ended the call.

Ahead was a 99-cent store. Right there. He moved toward it just as he heard the growl of a high-performance engine. Looked over his shoulder to see the BMW sweeping to the curb. Like they'd fuckin' read his mind or had maybe just tired of the games.

He bolted inside the store, ignoring the looks of the young Asian man behind the counter. Mallen knew from back in his working days that the buildings around here all butted onto alleys. And that's what he needed right about now: a back door. Ran through the store, pushing aside the curtain that hid from the rest of the world that the owner and his family were also illegally living there. A baby and young wife were there on the bed, but he just ran through, ignoring the woman's protests. Could hear yelling coming from the front of the place. Found the rear door. So many locks. Sweat broke out on his brow with every passing second as he undid them all, but then the door was open and he was bursting through and into the back alley.

No time. Ran to a nearby dumpster. Dove in, pulling the top down on him. The odors worked together to make him wretch, but he covered his nose with his sleeve and tried to breathe through his mouth. It was Hell. A dark, putrid Hell. Could hear the store door bang open. Footsteps as they paced the alley. After a moment he heard them head away toward the street. And that was the hardest time, the waiting. The not knowing where his enemies were. But then they came back, this time slower. Careful now. Like they'd guessed they'd been outmaneuvered. He heard the bang of a couple other dumpster lids going up. It felt like a clock ticking: either he was gonna get caught outright or puke loud at having to lay on a mound of rotting Indian food remains.

He heard an angry voice. The store owner. Of course he'd be pissed at people running through his store. One of the honest ones, the type who gets riotously indignant at crime if it slams into their world. They pay taxes, vote, have rights. Even in the face of a gun, they'll argue for those rights. Well, some of 'em will. The brave or dumb ones, anyway.

The voices went away then. Faded into the smells and odors that were about to overwhelm him. *Fuck Indian food, man.* If he ever smelled tandoori chicken again, it would be too soon. After he heard the alley go quiet, he counted slowly to sixty, then crawled out of the dumpster. Wiped off or dusted off what he could. And man, he didn't even own another coat. He decided to wait until dark to go back for the truck. He didn't think they'd gamble and sit on it the rest of the day. If they were waiting for him when he got there, well, that was just something he'd have to deal with on the fly. Otherwise, it was high fucking time to go do some laundry.

——————

Mallen approached the corner onto the block where the truck was parked. He'd spent his time waiting for the sun to go down by hanging out in a Laundromat, drinking the pint of Seagram's as he washed and dried his coat, shirt, underwear, and socks. Just had to wear the pants as is. He would change when he got home, but at least he now smelled more of dryer sheets than curry.

He stopped just before turning onto the street and peered around the corner of the old, large factory Ali headquartered in. Scanned up and down the street for a long while. Tried to be as thorough as possible. No black BMWs were in sight. In fact, the truck was the only vehicle on the block. A part of him was surprised it was still there. *Maybe you're lookin' out for recovering junkies after all. God.* He pulled out his phone and called Gato as he quickly went to the truck and leapt inside.

"Bro," Gato said, relief in his voice, "glad you're still among the living. Where are you? I'll come get you."

"Don't worry about it. I'm still in the city but about to be leaving for home. How mad was Ali?"

A chuckle. "Oh, *vato* ... like the sun exploding. Fuckin' ouch, bro."

That would be another thing he'd want to clear up. Didn't want her pissed at him again. Not at all. "I learned something interesting in my conversation with her," Mallen said. "Ali mentioned that she'd heard that Teddy'd been into video and film. She was trying to say something without saying it, man. She was that scared."

"Video and film?" Gato replied. "Could be, *vato*. Could definitely be. I know a couple of the women in his stable have done movies. They're not bad, either."

"Real Academy Award stuff, I bet."

"Oh man, for sure!" More laughter. "This one girl? She took this one guy's—"

"Another time, G. I gotta get home. Dig into what she said, okay? I'll call you tomorrow. Oh, hey! How's your *madre*, man? She handling the news of Lupe leaving town okay?"

The line went quiet for a moment, then Gato said, "She's... well, *vato*... I don't know. I'm not sure she got it. You know, what it might mean for her and me if Lupe never comes back."

"G, we'll make sure your *madre* is taken care of, any way we can, okay? I promise you that, man."

"Thanks, Mallen. I appreciate that, *desde el corazón, mi amigo*. Stay safe, bro."

Gato ended the call. Mallen turned the key in the ignition and drove quickly away. He wanted to be home in Sausalito as soon as humanly possible. Even being in the truck, he was feeling very exposed. Like his enemies could look down from some satellite and see right into his vehicle.

He drove up Van Ness and headed for the Golden Gate. He was now swimming in much deeper waters than he'd at first imagined. What sort of videos or films could Teddy Mac have made, or run off with, that would bring down so much fucking heat? The answering list quickly became longer than John Holmes's legendary member, so he gave it up. He needed more information. Badly. And he vowed never to go anywhere from now on without being armed. Damn the consequences.

———

It started to rain as he pulled into the dock parking lot. He made it inside his house before it really let loose. Once inside, he went and retrieved his pistol and, even though he knew it was probably a bit on the paranoid side, he went through his entire place, looking for any hidden enemies. Found no one, and no sign of anything being tampered with. He changed clothes, and then went to the kitchen to make himself a double scotch. Neat.

It turned out to be a night straight out of a disaster flick. The rain got more and more heavy, feeling like the Heavens themselves had opened up. Just like the rain the day that Oberon had come to tell him about Eric's murder. He stood at the sliding glass door of the office, watching the sheet of water pelt the back upper deck. Had it only been a couple months since he and Oberon had sat in those very deck chairs, reveling in the end of the case that had helped bring him back to the living? Back from the pit of the needle and the spoon? Took a sip of the scotch. He couldn't hide the fact that at that moment, he really just wanted to shoot and make it all go away. Teddy Mac. Carpy. Liz and Tracy Goldman. Unknown enemies coming after him. Just shoot the skag into his vein and call it a night. Maybe call it a year. Yeah, that would be very fuckin' okay right about now.

But then he looked over his shoulder to the worktable where the soda kite he was making (and not finishing) for Anna rested. He took a long pull of his drink, following that up with a long breath. After a moment of resting his forehead on the cold glass of the sliding door, The Need slowly receded. And he realized then he'd won another round. That was something to celebrate, no doubt. Went over to the kite and ran his index finger over a part of the frame. It could be done very soon, if life would quit fucking intruding.

And that was when his phone rang. *Yup*, he thought, *straight out of a disaster flick.*

However, it was Chris.

"Hey," he said, "anything wrong?"

Heard her soft laughter. "That's still the first damn thing out of your mouth whenever I call, just like back in the day."

"Well," he replied with a soft laugh, "there usually *was* something wrong, remember? With the plumbing. Or the wiring. Or the credit card. What do you want from me, right? I'm a creature of habit."

"Yes, yes you are," came the reply. Then the line went silent. "Sorry. I didn't mean it like that, Mark."

"It's all good, Chris. We can't pretend it never happened, right? I have to accept my past. Learn from it. That's all I can do."

"Very true." A pause, then she said, "I called because I heard from Liz. She's upset."

"Yeah? She say why she was upset? If it's because I haven't called, it's only because I haven't had any real success." He didn't think telling her about what he found at Jinky's apartment would do Tracy's mother any good. He *would* tell her, and the cops, but not just yet. There were still too many questions. Questions that he wanted the damn answers to. "I'm working on it, though," he continued. "But then... well, something else intruded. Something I'm doing for a friend who helped me out once."

"That sounds like the old Mark."

"Guess it does, at that. I am working on helping Liz, though. Tell her that. She say anything to you about what upset her?"

"No. But you know, I got the feeling that maybe her husband had told her to call or something. Almost as if it were *that* that made her so upset. I'm not sure... just the way she put some things. Bottom line, Mark: she wants you to drop it."

He chewed on that for a moment. Could be the new mayor didn't want to risk a story that involved a recovering junkie ex-cop working for his family under the table. "What do you want me to do, Chris? You think I should drop it?"

"Very funny. Like you would, right?"

"Right. Seems to be my night for stand-up. Look, just tell her you talked to me, and leave it at that. Tell her I was … ambiguous as to what I would do, okay?"

"I won't have to tell her. You'll have that opportunity yourself. She wants to meet with you again, here at the house. Tomorrow morning at eight, if you can make it."

"I can make it. I'll be there." It was strange, though. Why have him come all the way to Chris's house just to fire him? She could do that over the phone. Or hell, just have Chris tell him. Why the need for the meet? He couldn't come up with any answers.

Chris was silent for a moment, and then said, "You get the results back?"

Shit. He'd totally forgotten about the blood test. "No. I need to call them. I mean, that's a good sign, right? If it were bad, they'd be calling me, sending me pamphlets in the mail, all that shit."

"You need to find out for sure, Mark. You can't base the rest of your life on the absence of a positive. You have to call and find out for sure. Okay?" Then after a moment, in a quieter voice, she added, "I want to know too. For Anna's sake."

And that hit home. How could it not? "I'll call first thing in the morning. I promise."

"Thank you."

There was real warmth in her voice when she said that. Maybe it was the phone connection, sure, but then again …? Fuck it, he'd take it and run with it. Drained his drink before continuing. "Tell Liz I'll be there."

"I'll have breakfast waiting for you."

"You sure? I can stop on the way."

"Oh shut the hell up and prepare for a hearty meal, sailor," she said and hung up.

He stood there for a moment longer, staring out at the bay. He knew he'd have to keep it real, knowing that Chris was putting a lot of chips on the table, opening herself up to him again, hoping that he'd stay clean.

He would prove to her that she'd made the right decision. Even if it took his last breath.

NINETEEN

AFTER A NIGHT FILLED with nightmares, Mallen quickly washed and brushed his teeth the next morning. Slipped into some clean clothes. Through what felt like an act of a gentle God, he found some clothes he hadn't seen in awhile. Clothes he must've packed back when he thought he was going to go north to Mendocino, not north across the bay to his floating home. The black hoodie that he wore now under his leather jacket was something he'd not seen in years.

There was a knock at his door. He stopped at the sound, glancing over at the gun on the table. Grabbed it up and moved quietly to the front window. Peered through the crack of the curtain. Just enough to give him a view without being seen. It was something he'd rigged so he'd never have to move the curtain and draw attention. Call it something from his junkie days. There was a man standing there, dressed in a well-tailored suit. Slightly gray at the temples. It took him a moment to realize that Mayor Richard Goldman stood at his front door. His next thought was, did Liz know? Why had nobody called to tell him this was going to happen? He could make a good guess as to why the man had come here. Mallen was going to be told to stay away. Well, he wouldn't find out for sure just standing there. He went to the door.

Goldman didn't smile at him. Oh, he worked at it, but it didn't quite get there. Now that he was closer, Mallen could tell the man hadn't slept in some time. Worried about Tracy, probably.

"Mr. Mallen? My name's Richard Goldman. Liz told me what you were doing for us. I want to thank you for your effort."

"I haven't done that much yet. Still early days, Mr. Mayor."

"Please, call me Mr. Goldman."

"Okay, Mr. Goldman. Come on in."

Goldman seemed reluctant at first, but then smiled and came inside. He looked around. Seemed to approve. "Reminds me of Quint's house in *Jaws*. You see that movie?"

"Who didn't? Sure. I saw it like thirty-two times on cable. I used to know every line of dialog, back when I remembered things like that. Can I get you a drink?"

Goldman shook his head, obviously figuring it was too early. Sighed. Forehead wrinkled up a bit, as though concerned. "I'm going to get right to the point, Mr. Mallen, just like they say in the movies. I know Liz felt she was doing the right thing in going to you, but I don't. No reflection on your abilities, of course. I've looked at your record as a police officer . . . back when you were one. It's very impressive." Here he cleared his throat, like he'd brought up a terminal illness Mallen suffered from. "What I'm here to say is that I think we can handle this in-house."

"Oh," Mallen said. "*We*? You mean the police, right?"

"Of course, if need be. Liz agrees with this now, once I really explained it to her. She's behind this decision, a hundred percent.

Anything else she may have said was born of her own imagination, trust me. I still believe that Tracy will come back on her own. Look, she's young, right? Brought up fairly privileged, if you will. Not surprising she'd search out new experiences and people for friends. And, she *is* a legal adult."

"Well," Mallen replied after a moment, "I wish you'd been *my* father, Mr. Goldman, that's all I gotta say. Look, if you don't want any involvement that might draw bad publicity or cause you worries at City Hall, just say so, man. That's all."

Goldman stood there, hands in pockets, staring at Mallen. After a moment, he nodded. "If that's the way we feel about it, I'm sure you can understand that, right?"

"Sure. I just wanted to help. Liz asked, and so—"

"I realize that. Liz was just being a good mother. Just like I'm now being a good father." He moved to the door. "Thank you for understanding," he said as he opened the door.

"Right. By the way, who'd you draw down at the police?"

"Excuse me?"

"The man in charge of tracking down your daughter. I still know people down there. Like to share with them what I've found out so far." He was lying, sure, but something inside him had told him to ask. Something deep down inside. And Mallen always tried to listen when it came from there.

Goldman blinked once. "Wong. Detective Wong. And if you have anything to share about my daughter's disappearance, you better share it with him and me immediately."

He thought back to his cop days. Couldn't come up with ever meeting any cop named Wong. But he'd been off the reservation for a long time. Never hung out where cops hung, never spent time down at Central Station once he'd made undercover. Maybe Oberon would know the name. What he said to Goldman was, "Yeah, of course." Here he grabbed up his keys. "I was heading into the city when you showed. I'll for sure go and tell Wong everything."

Goldman didn't move from the door. Almost as if blocking Mallen from leaving.

The mayor smiled then and said, "Just a moment. I said to share information with us both."

"Right. Well, I found that she had a couple friends, one of which, based on her description and places she hangs, seems like a prostitute. But I haven't made any progress regarding finding a name, or where she lives." Under any other circumstances, he wouldn't have lied to this man. But there something he hated about the new mayor. Was it the fake grin? The feeling that the man was lying about his concern for his daughter? These things worked on Mallen's mind enough that he decided to keep information from him.

"We'll let Chris know when Tracy comes home safe and sound," Goldman said. Turned to the door and opened it. Stopped and looked over his shoulder. "And I'm a man who expects that what he says doesn't have to be repeated. I hope I'm clear on that. Have a good day, Mallen."

He watched Goldman leave. Waited a moment then went outside and stood just past the gangplank that led from his place to the pier. Watched the mayor walk down the pier and over to his dark limo. Waited for it to drive off and then went back inside. He was about to call Chris, then remembered their conversation from last night.

He dug out the paperwork from his blood draw and called the number on the sheet. He couldn't help it: he found himself shaking a bit as he spoke with the nurse. She said they'd been trying to contact him. That set his heart racing, but it turned out they just hadn't been able to read the number he'd written down. She put him on hold so she could get the results. Kept him on hold long enough to have glaciers form.

When she came back on the phone she said, "Mr. Mallen?"

"Yes, I'm still here." Why the fuck wouldn't he be? His life hung in the balance.

"Well," the nurse said, almost like she was relishing drawing it out, "your results came back negative."

"Negative," he echoed. Relief was a wall around him that just crumbled. He was okay. He was going to be okay. "You're sure you have the right guy, right?"

He heard her smile now. "Yes. We have the right Mark Mallen."

"Thank you," he said, then ended the call and dialed Chris. Got voicemail. Left a message that he was on his way and asked her to call him if Liz had not shown. That was all he said. Wanted to tell Chris the results face to face. He grabbed up his gun, a spare clip, and his pack of cigarettes. He figured it would be almost thirty minutes with traffic into the city.

As he pulled onto 101 south, he thought back to his conversation with Goldman. The guy was the new mayor of San Francisco. People like that had to guard every aspect of their lives like a lion guarded his kill from a pack of jackals. Still . . . it felt all wrong.

124

TWENTY

HE'D JUST STOPPED FOR the light at Lake Street when his phone rang. It was Gato.

"Hey *vato*, I got a report for you."

"Yeah? Doesn't sound like good news, from your tone."

"It's not. It's Teddy. Some buddies tell me he heard about you involving his *hermana* in this shit. He's pissed."

"Well, I'll tell him I'm sorry next time I see him."

Gato's response was a laugh. "You kill me sometimes, bro," he said. "Keep watch over your shoulder."

"You too." He disconnected the call. He needed someone else to look out for like he needed a hemorrhoid. Made his way to Chris's using as many side streets as possible. Seemed there were more and more people out there with the ability to find and track a lone recovering junkie ex-cop.

He got to Chris's in just under thirty. As he approached the familiar front door, it opened and there was Chris, shaking her head in disbelief.

"I can't believe it. Seven forty-eight. I think this is the first time you've ever been early," she said, a smirk on her lips.

"Yeah, well … you said breakfast, yeah?"

She smiled at that as she stepped aside. Then looked back at the kitchen as he entered. Told him quietly, "Liz is already here. She's pretty upset."

So she *had* showed up. As he'd crossed the Golden Gate, he began to feel that she wouldn't come. Wondered what her doing here really meant.

Chris looked at him for second, then said, "I know that look, Mark. What happened?" He gave her a quick, hushed rundown of his conversation with Goldman. Chris looked like she couldn't believe it and said as much.

"I know," he told her, "it's weird, and very wrong. Have to wonder if Mr. Mayor really put the whack on her."

A nod. "I don't like it, Mark. And I think you're right, I—" she stopped as Liz appeared in the kitchen doorway, cup of coffee clenched tightly in her hands. He wondered if there was a lot of Baileys in that cup, given how she swayed this early in the morning. Could tell immediately that she hadn't been sleeping, at all. Dark circles under her eyes. Could swear she looked even thinner than last time. Whatever the fuck was happening, it was taking a toll on her.

He put on his best smile. "Liz. Heard you needed to talk to me." Came forward and put his hand on her shoulder as he guided her back to the kitchen. Offered her a seat at the kitchen table where they'd met only a couple days or so before. "You all right? You look beat," he told her.

Chris went over and poured herself a cup of coffee. Fixed him one. "You always know what to say to a woman, Mark," she said with a slight laugh as she handed it to him. He could tell she was trying to lighten the heavy mood in the room.

Chris's attempt didn't work for Liz. She ignored Mallen's remark. Took a drink from her cup. "Mark," she said as she kept her eyes down, "I owe you an apology."

"Really? For what?"

"For wasting your time. I shouldn't have involved you in all this. I . . . I panicked. I should've known better. Richard has the police involved and they'll take care of it. They can do things that you can't, even—"

"Liz," he said to her, "I saw Richard this morning."

"You did?" She seemed genuinely surprised.

"Yeah, I did. He told me to leave it alone too. Said you saw it his way. That really true?" He could see that it wasn't. Hell, a blind man could see it, could hear that she was parroting things told to her. He let it hang there in the air for a bit, then said quietly to her, "All you have to do, Liz, is tell me that you want me to continue, and I will. I know you want to find Tracy . . . see that she's brought home safely. I'll keep my movements as on the down-low as possible, I swear. If Richard talks to you about it, you just tell him you *did* tell me to back off, and that I wouldn't listen, or lied about what I would do."

She had listened the entire time with her gaze trained on the dark liquid in her coffee cup. Tears appeared in her eyes. It was easy for him to see she was really torn the fuck up over the entire thing. He knew it wasn't easy to know what to do in life during normal circumstances, but under the shit that was going down now? This was probably a nightmare for her. A long, waking nightmare.

He took a sip of his coffee. "Liz? What's really going on? I can see there's more to it. I get that Richard would want to protect his privacy,

127

but really, why is he putting up walls at a time your daughter is missing? Walls that you obviously don't want up."

Then the tears really started coming and she put her cup down and covered her eyes, sobbing quietly. After a moment, she said in hoarse voice, "I don't know. He wants to handle it. Told me that he would handle it. I didn't know he'd go to see you."

"So he is going to leave it with the cops?"

A nod. "He has to, now. A policeman has been coming around. His name is Wong. He told Richard that the two girls Tracy went off with have arrest records. One might be involved in a very large drug ring. Now the police want to talk to Tracy, to see what she knows. They're looking for her as a possible witness, not a missing person."

"Well, it happens that way sometimes." He wondered about Wong visiting Goldman at home. It sounded very strange. Most cops call, only putting in appearances when they have questions to ask or very good, very bad, or very important news to give. On the other hand, this *was* the new mayor.

"Well," he finally said to her, "what do you want me to do, Liz? If you really want me to follow your husband's advice and back off, just say so. If not, all you have to do is nod, and I'll keep at it."

Liz sat there for a long time, saying nothing. Nobody moved. He could feel Chris's tension from across the table. She seemed tighter than a bowstring as she waited to see how Liz would respond.

In the end, all Liz did was give him a barely perceptible nod. She took one last sip of her coffee and got up. Swayed a little on her feet. Whether from the liquor and no sleep or from the emotional trauma, he couldn't tell. Luckily, Chris came to the rescue.

"Liz," Chris urged, "let me drive you home. I'll catch a cab back."

"I'm fine, Chris," she said as she went to the front door.

"No, really," Chris insisted. "I'd feel better knowing you got home okay."

Liz gave her a faint smile, and she waited as Chris grabbed a coat from the hall closet and shrugged into it. She grabbed her keys off the side table, along with her phone. "I'll be back within the hour," she said to Mallen. "Look after Anna, okay? She's in her room."

"You got it," he smiled back at her. Couldn't help but be excited at the opportunity.

———

Anna's door was slightly ajar. He went to it, guessing she didn't even know he was there. She would've come down if she'd heard him. He pushed it open a little and gazed inside. There she was on her bed, working on some sort of drawing with a bunch of crayons spread out all around her. She was so into it she didn't notice him at all. *Maybe she'll grow up to be an artist.* He'd like that, actually. As long as she followed her bliss, he'd be happy. He just stood there and watched his nine-year-old daughter work, thinking back over all the time he'd wasted not being there to watch her grow. He so wanted to be back here, the feeling smothered him. A part of him told him to go fuck himself, that he was crazy to even think it. Again the other part of him, maybe the more sadistic part, whispered to him to go ahead, envision it. He hated both sides. The tug-of-war was like a rubber band pulled too tight. But even as he stood there, he just couldn't tear his eyes away from that beautiful face with its intense gaze. She was probably already a perfectionist. Something she got from Chris, for sure.

He stepped into the room. "Hey, A."

At that she looked up and leapt off the bed with a squeal of excitement and surprise. Anna ran up to him, throwing her arms around his waist. "Daddy!" She said as she hugged him tightly.

"Sorry I disturbed your drawing. Mommy had to go out. I was just checking to see if you were okay."

"Like . . . like the 'old times,' right?"

He softly laughed at that. "Yeah, A. Like that. Mommy had to take a friend of hers home. She'll be right back."

"How long will you be here? For breakfast?" He could see that she hoped so.

"Well, that was the plan."

"Are you coming back?"

"Well," he said, "I'm sure I can come back next week. I'm—"

"To live?" Now there was a deep-rooted hope in her eyes as she looked up at him.

That broadsided him. Took him a moment to say, "Well, no, honey. It's not like that. Not that simple. I wish it were, but it's not. And you know it's not your mommy's fault, right? It's mine."

"I know," she said, bringing out that precocious side that seemed way brighter than he would ever be. "It was how you got in trouble with stuff. You had a problem."

He almost had to laugh at how simply it could be stated. A matter of fact, and there you go. *Bam.* Well, at least she'd said *had.* "That's true, A. I got into trouble with something bad. You remember I was a policeman, right?"

"Uh huh," came the reply. With a smile. Even now, at her age, policemen still carried respect. Wondered now how early that deteriorated. Maybe by thirteen? Hell, eleven?

"Well, I was a policeman who pretended he was a criminal, right? That was my job. To make the other criminals think I was one of them. You get that?"

"Yes. You were undercover."

He did laugh then. He'd underestimated her, and then some. He had a lot to learn about being a good father. "Right, A. Yeah… I was undercover. Well, that world … it … it, well, I just lost who I was, I guess. Made Mommy feel really bad, and I wasn't a very good daddy or husband then, in those days. Now though, I'm working to be a *very* good daddy and … friend to Mommy. We all make mistakes sometimes, honey. It's when we can see that we made a mistake, and understand that we … well, acted badly, that we start to try to make it good again, right? It's sorta like this: You draw with your crayons all over the wall in the living room, because it's what you think is fun and okay to do. When you're doing it, you're not thinking it might be wrong, because it's fun. But then you find out it *was* bad, and Mommy is angry with what you did. Don't you want to clean up the walls then? Make her happy again? Make her … well, okay with giving you your crayons back? Right?"

And as he watched Anna's face, he could see her working it all through that truly wonderful mind she was born with, and he found himself holding his breath.

"Yes," she finally said, with finality. "I don't want Mommy angry."

"Neither do I, kiddo. Neither do I. Think of me like working to have Mommy give me the crayons back. And those crayons are you, and you, and you!" He grabbed her then, and rubbed his beard stubble on her face and she laughed and laughed. He then held her out at arm's length and she gave him that look that only a child can give their father: like he was the strongest, safest human being in the world. And he saw that and pledged once again that he would never let her down. Not ever. "Now, you go back to working on your drawing, kiddo, and I'll call you down to breakfast when it's ready." He led her back to her bed and stroked her hair for a moment. He kissed her on the forehead and went to the door.

"Daddy?"

"Yeah, baby?"

"So, all that you told me? You mean you don't do drugs anymore?"

Yeah, he had a lot to learn about kids. "That's right, A. I don't do drugs anymore."

"And you won't?"

"No. No, I won't."

———

Chris came home about forty minutes later. He'd been sitting in the kitchen, having coffee. When he was looking for sugar for the coffee, he found half a bottle of whiskey in the cupboard. On the top shelf. The find sort of unsettled him, as the bottle was half gone. He knew that Chris never liked whiskey, at all. If she ever drank anything other than white wine, it was vodka. Well, maybe she'd given a party, right? He hoped that's what it was. However, it stayed in his mind.

She walked into the kitchen, seemed grateful he'd made more coffee. Got herself a cup. He waited until she sat, knowing that she never liked answering questions until she was settled.

"How'd it go?" he asked.

She rested her elbows on the table, taking a sip of her coffee. "She's not in a good place. Most of the ride she was silent. Stared out the window. Wiped at her eyes a couple times. I tried to get her to engage. Told her that Tracy would need her when you or the police

132

found her. Told her that Tracy's leaving was on Tracy's shoulders, not hers."

"You missed your calling," he said, "you shoulda been a psychologist, not an architect."

"Well, both professions have to pay attention to the details, right?"

"Right."

She glanced at the ceiling. "She give you any trouble?"

"None at all. I went up to check on her. She's up there drawing her heart out. We talked for a few minutes, then I told her I'd call her down for breakfast."

"She was probably so happy to see you."

"Sure seemed that way," he replied.

Chris sat there for a moment, and it felt to him that she wanted to say something but couldn't quite bring herself to say it. She took another sip of her coffee instead, then got up. "I'll get to work on that breakfast."

"Anything I can do to help?"

A smile. "God, you *have* changed, Mark." The phone rang then. He took a sip of his coffee as she got up and went into the other room, ignoring the fact there was a kitchen extension. The whiskey in the cupboard. A phone call she didn't want to take in front of him. Yeah … he got it. *Well, what the fuck do you expect, asshole? She's a wonderful, attractive, single woman.*

He sat and studied the dark liquid in his cup. Part of him thought he should just get up and go. Part of him wanted to know who the guy was.

She came back into the room a couple minutes later.

"You sure you're still up for making breakfast?" He said it with the best smile he could work up at that point.

"Sure," she said. "Hey, let me tell you about Anna's latest school project." She seemed relieved about the subject matter. Like she was glad he didn't ask about the phone call. Hell, how could he?

"School project?" he replied. "What of?"

"She made a bunch of sock puppets and performed *Romeo and Juliet* for her class."

"With just sock puppets?"

"That's your daughter: a master at acting."

He laughed, saying, "She's something else." Then he added, quietly, "You're doing a great job, Chris. Amazing, really."

She seemed genuinely grateful he'd said that. "Thank you, Mark. I appreciate that."

———

The breakfast of French toast, scrambled eggs, and bacon was great, and Anna seemed to be in heaven as she looked from her mother to her father, sitting there at the same table. She pretty much cornered the market on the talking. She talked to him about her school, about her teacher and her schoolmates. She got up at one point and went upstairs to come back with her now-finished drawing. It was of all sorts of fish swimming not in the water, but up in a light-blue sky with a huge sun hanging in the middle of it all. He loved it, and then to his surprise, she gave it to him. She seemed very proud of what she'd done and sat back down, very prim and proper, and asked for more jam. Chris had watched this entire episode, a small smile playing about her lips. After breakfast was over, he insisted on doing the dishes. As he did them though, his mind kept returning to the whiskey bottle and the phone call. He couldn't make those things go away, no matter how much he tried. He needed to get out of there.

Needed to get back to work. That would keep his mind occupied, off the fact that Chris obviously had a boyfriend, a boyfriend he had no right to be bugged about, but was.

He kissed Anna goodbye and promised he'd be back very soon. He hugged Chris briefly by the front door, and feeling her against him didn't help matters. His resolve to not do something stupid, like ask her about the phone call, was eroding quickly, so he beat it out of there and only relaxed when he was back in Gregor's truck, the engine kicking over.

TWENTY-ONE

MALLEN WAS ONLY THREE blocks away, heading down California Street for the Golden Gate, when he noticed a car in his rearview mirror. A dark BMW. It was hard to tell if it was *the* dark BMW. But if it was that car, then it was the same two guys inside. How had they tracked him?

And then it hit him: they'd either tracked him from his place without him tripping to it, which was fuckin' bad enough, or ...

Or they'd been waiting for him to show up at Chris's. To find that address would've taken some digging, and some police file kind of digging. The house was even registered in Chris's maiden name. They'd gone to a lot of trouble to avoid any blowback from his undercover work. How had these guys gotten that address?

He didn't make for the bridge. He needed time to deal with this. He made a few turns just to be sure he wasn't being paranoid. He wasn't. Made an illegal U-turn in the middle of the block. Pulled out his phone, and dialed Chris's number.

She picked up after only a few rings.

"It's me," he said. "Long time, no talk, right?"

"What's wrong?" she said.

"Look, I don't want to worry you, okay, but I won't be able to come around for a while."

"What? Why?"

"It's a helluva long story, and I'd tell you if I had the time. I'm being tailed. It might have to do with Tracy, or it might have to do with this other thing."

"What other thing?"

"The other thing I mentioned regarding my friend and him trying to locate his sister. She's disappeared too. Whoever they are, I might've picked them up before I got to your place. Or, they were there waiting. Got it?"

"Got it." And he knew she totally did. They used to go over their book of "What if?" scenarios together: what she would do if he dropped out of sight, what he would do if he'd ever been found out and she ended up being used as a bargaining chip. It always left them quiet and morose, as it reminded them of how dangerous their lives were because he'd decided to work undercover when the opportunity arose.

"Be a little more aware of the people around you when you're out," he said, "and have someone with Anna when she goes to and from school until you hear back from me that this thing is settled."

"You're scaring me."

"I don't mean to, trust me. Look, just be aware of your surroundings. You know, like back in the old days, that's all." He gave her Oberon's cell number. "Call him immediately if you can't reach me, okay?" He was heading west on California and made the right on Park Presidio. He wondered if the car would follow him back over

137

the bridge. If they didn't, then there would probably be someone else waiting for him, maybe back at his place; if they did, then maybe there were fewer of them than he thought. *A fleeing soldier counts every enemy twice*, went the old quote.

"Like I said," he continued, "if you see anything out of the ordinary, don't just dismiss it."

"I remember the drill," she replied, a bit defensively. Maybe it was dredging up all the old feelings she used to have about his job.

"I knew you would. Okay, be safe. I'll call in a couple days. Give Anna my love," he said and hung up. He gunned it out of the tunnel and through the toll plaza. He kept watch on his rearview mirror. Yeah, the car had taken the Merchant Road exit, right before the toll plaza. He took a deep breath and relaxed then. Rolled down his window and breathed in the sea air. He was okay until he got back to his place. And now he'd know to be more careful. Hoped it wasn't too late for that.

———

He pulled Mr. Gregor's Land Cruiser to the curb about half a block before the parking lot outside the pier. There had been no tail on this side of the bridge, so he figured maybe they'd be parked somewhere near the lot, waiting to see him come home. That would make sense. They'd be waiting for him, knowing that at some point he'd be back to his home. He walked calmly to the little-used second entrance to the parking lot. When he got to the lot, he made for a small grove of nearby cypress trees that shielded the lot from the street. There was a blanket of clouds overhead and that helped to keep the light down a bit.

The parking lot was fairly full. By now he knew the cars that belonged to most of his neighbors on the pier. It was an old habit, to do that about the cars. Most of them he saw either belonged to neighbors or didn't look like cars akin to the BMW that'd been tailing him. The visitor parking would be too open for them to be sitting there, but he looked it over anyway. No, all but one of the slots were empty, and the old pickup there was nothing that set off any alarms in his head. He looked out at the street, to the five metered parking spots there.

Yep, there it was: a black car with smoked windows. Not a BMW, but a Ford Crown Victoria. That shouted *cop* at him, as did the thing about finding Chris's home address. Couldn't tell if anyone was inside. He needed that plate number, and bad. His mind then kicked into stealth mode and he kept to cover as he stalked forward, using the parked cars as his hedgerow. Made it quietly to the street, four car lengths behind the Ford. Snuck along slowly, one movement for one breath. Now he was three car lengths behind, and one sidewalk width from the street. He crouched down into a duck squat, down onto his haunches. Moved to the street, into the blind spot right behind the Ford. The side windows were useless for anyone inside now. Now he just had to worry about the rearview. Kept his movements to molasses-in-winter speed as he crept forward. When he could just make out the license plate, he pulled out his pen and the folded-up piece of paper Chris had given him back when he'd first talked with Liz.

Old habits, the good kind, were definitely making a move back into his life. And that was a blessing, especially at moments like this. Took down the plate number: NC17B69. Checked it again, just to be sure. He'd have to ask his favorite police detective, Oberon Kane, to run it.

Then the passenger door opened, and Mallen hunched into a gargoyle-like position, freezing instantly. A man in a suit got out of the car. "Shut the fuck up," he said to the driver. "I'll be right fucking back, okay? I know he should be here by now. It's all the fucking coffee's fault." The man closed the door. Walked in the direction of the parking lot, probably going to piss between a couple of cars.

Mallen crept after the man, again using the cars as cover. As he crept along, he pulled out his gun, ready to use the butt of the handle to smash the fucker's head. Kept the man in his sights as he angled closer. He was now one car length away from him. All he had to be careful of was not being heard by his target or seen by the compatriot sitting his ass in the Ford. The man then stopped between a couple cars and unzipped his fly. Put his feet apart in the classic "guy pissing outdoors" stance. Mallen crept forward, not thinking he'd have long. Got behind the man, moving silently on the thick soles of his old Doc Martens.

He was an arm's length away when the man seemed to sense someone behind him. He began to turn, and Mallen brought the gun's butt down hard against the man's temple with everything he had. The man staggered back and started to fall, already out on his feet. Mallen caught him just in time and laid him gently to the ground. Checked for a pulse. Well, least he wouldn't have a murder rap on his hands. Quickly he frisked the man. Found a Glock in a shoulder holster. Took it. *Everybody's walking around with guns these days.* Found the man's wallet, and took that too. He'd look at it later. Crept back to the Ford. He figured he had less than three minutes before the man inside the car would begin to wonder about his buddy. From where he was, he could see the driver inside, smoking, the red cherry from the cig glowing hot for a moment as he took a drag.

Mallen squatted down and inched his way around the back of the car. Crept quietly along the left side of the car, knowing he was in sight of the side mirror. When he was even with the rear door, he leapt forward, bringing the gun down hard on the glass. The window shattered and then he had the gun muzzle pressed right at the driver's temple as the man straightened up, lap and front seat covered in glass.

"Hello and okay," Mallen said quietly. "Now we're gonna play a little game, and it's called You Take Out Your Gun Slowly."

He was an older guy, gray haired. Good suit. Mallen had to admit that this guy was polished. Never once looked at the gun, and the shock of the attack seemed to already have worn off. "Alright," the man answered, "what do I get if I play correctly?"

"A Get Out Alive card."

"Okay."

"Pull the gun, slowly. Hand it butt first to me." The man did so, and Mallen quickly pocketed it. He stepped back, keeping his gun low and as out of sight as he could. This street didn't get a lot of traffic, but a you couldn't be sure when a car would come by just as one man held a gun on another. "Now get out of the car."

The man did as he was told. He wasn't large, but he did seem to be in command of his emotions. If anything he was pissed, not scared. "Open the trunk," Mallen told him. He followed the man to the back of the car and kept a distance as the man opened the trunk. *Who knows,* he thought, *they might have a fuckin' shotgun back there. Anything.*

As soon as the trunk was open, Mallen instructed the man to put his hands on the trunk lid. He gave the man a fast frisk. Came up with another wallet, a cell, and the car keys. "Who you workin' for?" Mallen asked.

The man looked at him. Smiled. "If you don't know, I ain't saying, Mallen."

Mallen put the barrel of the gun under the man's chin. Forced his head back as he pulled the hammer. "Now it's only a few micro ounces, or an accident's worth, of pressure that's keeping you from getting your head blown all over your car, asshole. Who do you work for, and why are you following me?"

The man shook his head. Smiled. "You got nothing that will work on making me talk. Trust me on that one. However bad-ass you think you are, you ain't shit compared to my employers. You're dead, and you don't even know it yet. Your family too. Your friends. Everyone you ever knew is on the table, in play."

Mallen studied the man's eyes for a moment. He could see that this man was telling the truth about not being afraid of him. That he would rather die than have to answer to whomever he worked for. The thought scared Mallen down to the bottoms of his shoes too. He nodded. "Okay, asshole, I hear ya. Come on." He pushed the man over to where his partner still lay. The man looked at Mallen then down at his fallen comrade, like he hadn't believed Mallen could be that capable. "You're gonna drag your buddy here back to the car and put him in the fucking trunk."

"Or what?" came the reply, filled with defiance.

"Or"—Mallen stepped forward and pointed the gun at the man's knee—"I'll make sure you never walk again, man. Or be able to father children. You dig me? Now pick your fucking friend up and drag him over to the trunk. Put him in and you climb in after him. Maybe you're too scared of your employer to rat him out, but I bet he's just going to love hearing about how one burnout got the better of two such awesome enforcers, right?"

The man's smile drained from his face. Didn't look happy at all, now. But he did what Mallen said and dragged his partner back over to the car. The other man groaned in pain as he was hoisted up and into the Crown Vic's trunk.

"Get in," Mallen said.

"It's fuckin' tight in there, Mallen."

"I don't give a shit if you have to spoon your buddy here, just fucking get inside."

With a glare, the man did as requested and Mallen slammed the trunk lid down. He quickly got behind the wheel of the car and turned over the ignition. But before he put it in drive, he checked the glove box. Inside he found some recent employment papers for a private security firm called Darkstar Security. The name of the new employee was Brett Wallace. Well, no need to run the plate now at least. He wondered which wallet would belong to Wallace as he shoved the papers in his coat pocket and jammed the car into drive.

He drove calmly, not speeding. Drove as far as Sausalito proper and left the car in front of Lappert's Ice Cream, on Bridgeway. He went over the car one time, wiping off any of his prints. Checked under the front seats but found nothing. Kept the wallets and guns, locked the keys inside the car, and walked away back in the direction of his house. It wasn't that far and he needed the time to think. Leaving the car amid all the tourists and mommies with their kids seemed the best thing to do. When those guys got out, they'd be right in the middle of a crowd of onlookers. Let 'em explain that one. Would be even better if the fuckin' car got a parking ticket first. Or towed, even. It wasn't the bay sea air that made him feel alive at that moment; no, it was the feeling he'd just scored one small jab back at whoever was out there. They'd be pissed, both at him and at themselves for underestimating him. He smiled at that. Just like old times.

He walked as far as Marinship Park and went to the water. He pulled out the first wallet. Took the $120 in cash and looked at the driver's license. The other man, the driver, was named Phillip I. Grove. He was fifty years old. He had a Costco card, and was also an employee of Darkstar Security, judging by the business card in the wallet. There were some credit cards, and a condom.

"Well, keep goin', pops," Mallen mumbled as he tossed the condom into a nearby trash can. There were folded-up pieces of paper, mostly phone numbers. Strange they wouldn't be in the cell's phonebook. He kept those and tossed the wallet into the trash. Pulled out the other wallet. This one was Wallace's, and he guessed that his new employer might just fire him for failing so badly on a job. But who hired them in the first place? And why? Were they hired to watch Mallen lead them to someone else? He took Wallace's $76 and sent the wallet after the other one. Walked back toward his house, booting up one of the phones. If he was lucky, it wouldn't get locked or whatever by its owner for at least a couple hours, maybe a bit longer. Grove and Wallace would have to get out of the car by crawling through the escape in the backseat. Then they'd have to find a way to get a call to somebody, and then that someone or one of the men would have to get on a computer to lock their phones.

He pulled out Grove's phone. No go, it was password protected. Tossed it in a nearby mailbox. Pulled out Wallace's. *Ah, here we go,* he thought. No password. Maybe the new boy wasn't as hip to the company as his more-experienced partner. He'd for sure seen a lot of that, back when he was running dark dog in the drug gangs. Went to the phone list.

And wouldn't you know, the guy had only called two numbers on this phone. Neither had a name, only the number. He went to the outgoing list. Same two numbers. Maybe newbie wasn't so stupid, after all. He jotted down both number, just in case. Went through the rest of the phone. Wallace had a Facebook account, but he'd set the log in to not autofill. The guy was careful, after all. Went to the photos. There were a *lot* of photos, most of a woman and her toddler. The woman was young, mid-twenties. Toddler, a boy, usually on her knee. They'd gone to the park a lot. Then there were photos of the interior of a house, probably Wallace's. A few photos of him, mugging for the camera as he fixed a drain, dug up a dead tree in a back yard.

Just a regular guy.

Mallen checked the IMs and emails. Maybe there was something there, he told himself as he scrolled around. Found only a handful of emails, dating back only to two weeks ago. They were to *Dark HQ*. Mostly cryptic, military crap. He'd never make heads or tails of it. There was one, however, that seemed straightforward, and sweat broke out on the back of his neck when he read it. It was from *Dark HQ*, and read:

Strays to be put down. Kennel ready to go.

That was followed by another one:

Bitches hosed out. Rooms clean. Ready.

That kind of jingoistic bullshit always set his alarms off. Ran his imagination into the red. The burnt umber red. His mind filled with images of a vast, shadowy conspiracy. That, coupled with the use of a private security firm?

Shit.

He did not know what exactly to do next. It took him a moment to realize that he was stunned. Actually stunned. He'd tumbled into something that could blow up to Hell and back again. Worse than he'd ever imagined.

Shoved the phone back into his pocket and walked away from the water, back through the small park, feeling that everyone must know exactly where he was at that very moment.

He'd have to talk to Oberon. And that would be a problem, he knew. Obie would not be happy with about 90 percent of what he'd been up to lately. Hell, who *would* be?

TWENTY-TWO

WHEN MALLEN GOT BACK to the parking lot outside his place, he returned Mr. Gregor's truck to its usual space. He then went quickly down the dock to his home. Went upstairs to the file cabinet in his office and stashed one of the Glocks, along with Wallace's phone. The other gun went in the kitchen, behind some boxes of crackers. He still had Gato's pistol and some spare shells, and he kept both in his coat pocket. He then grabbed his own phone from his inner coat pocket. Dialed Oberon's number. The detective answered on the fourth ring.

"Kane."

"Obie, you in the middle of something?"

"Always. What is it?"

"Well, it's sort of involved."

A sigh. "It always is when it's you, Mark."

"Bad day?"

"Bad decade. I drew another red ball. And it's worse than usual."

"Yeah? How so?" His cop head kicked in again. Once there was a case, he was all antennae.

"Two young girls, early twenties. Maybe prostitutes, but I'm not sure. No one is, yet. Beaten to death, almost beyond recognition. Also signs of heavy sexual abuse and torture."

His heart skipped a beat then. "Either of them a white girl or Latina?" he managed to get out.

"No, why?"

"No identification?"

"Not unless you count the tattoos that are sleeved up and down the arms of the smaller one. And just why would you be asking me that?"

"The other one. African-American, right? Red hair, short, in braids, maybe?"

A pause. Longer than the usual Oberon one. "By the old ballpark. Just south, at the water. You can't miss the party. Get here now, please." And with that, Oberon hung up.

Mallen quickly rinsed his face with ice-cold water. Brushed his teeth and shrugged into his coat. Scribbled a quick note to Mr. Gregor that he'd still need the truck for a bit longer, and sorry but he'd pay for the rental on the first. He left then, depositing the note in Gregor's screen door, between frame and screen.

He scanned the parking lot before he walked out through the gate. It was something he was going to do every time he either left or returned to his place now. There were no cars that he didn't recognize. He wondered if Grove and Wallace had managed to escape yet, and how long it would take for two new guys to be put on his tail.

He crossed the parking lot quickly to Gregor's truck and got behind the wheel. He was out of the parking lot and on 101 south heading for the city in record time. As he drove, he wondered what to do if the two dead bodies down by Candlestick actually turned out to be the two girls Tracy had been running with. If it was them, then it sure as shit looked like people were tying up loose ends. Where the hell was Tracy? Had she also been a loose end? Was she already dead, somewhere in the area but unfound? Were these the "strays to be put down"? And when would the fucking answers come, he wondered savagely as he pushed more speed out of the truck.

It was like Oberon had said: It wasn't hard to miss the party. There were a lot of cop cars, both black and whites and unmarked. Large crowd, held back by the yellow crime scene tape and uniformed sentries. He parked as close as he could. Got out and made his way to the yellow tape. Once there he texted Oberon then waited. About five minutes later, he saw the detective emerge from a crowd of forensics people and cops. Came over to where Mallen was. He'd never seen Oberon look so tired.

"Why is it every time I have a bad case, you show up?" Oberon said to him.

All he could offer in response was a shrug, along with: "I promise to make it up to you in the next life."

"I would greatly appreciate it if you didn't wait until then. I most definitely would," came the reply.

"The bodies," Mallen said. "The African-American girl have a huge, knitted shoulder bag?"

Oberon sighed, lifted the tape, and passed underneath. The detective guided Mallen to a quiet, dark area where they could speak alone. "Well?" Oberon said, "What is it about my newest case that you know and I don't?"

Mallen pulled out his cigarettes. Lit one. The recovering junkie's curse. Blew the smoke out. "Try looking under their street names. Jinky and Minta. Minta might actually be her first name, don't know."

"And why would I do that?" Oberon responded as he pulled out his notebook and wrote the names down.

"You know about new Mayor Goldman's family troubles?"

Oberon studied him for a moment, almost in disbelief. He finally said, "His missing daughter. Yeah, I've heard. But this isn't her."

"I know that. And thank fuck it's not."

"But why would you even entertain the thought that this could have something to do with Tracy Goldman? What are you onto?"

"Well, it's more than I thought it would be, and that's a fact, Obie." He then told Oberon about how it had all started. About how Liz had asked, almost begged, for his help. About how he'd been trying to track down Tracy or the two girls she'd gone off with: Jinky or Minta. Related how Richard Goldman warned him off the case, and about the underlying threat Goldman had laid on him. He ended up by saying, "Well, if that *is* Jinky and Minta over there, then it's worse than I thought, Obie. And I thought it was pretty fucking bad anyways. And, well ... there's more."

"Yes? More? And what would that be? A nuclear war is about to start? Aliens have landed at the White House?"

"Guys from Darkstar Security are watching Chris and Anna, and I'm not sure if it's on their own time, or not." He described to Oberon how he'd been tailed from Chris's house to Sausalito. And what he'd done afterward.

In answer to everything he'd just been told, Oberon shook his head. Seemed even more tired now. "Mark ... you're destined to just kill me, son. Kill me dead." Rubbed his face with his hands. "Okay, you've reported it. By the way, Darkstar is huge, Mark. One of the largest private security firms in the country. Local offices in most major cities. They contributed to Goldman's run for mayor too. I don't like coincidences of that sort, and you know that." Oberon stood there a long time, staring at the ground and thinking. He shook his head a couple times, as if he were having some sort of interior battle. Mallen stood by and waited, knowing that if Obie went a certain way on this, it would put them at cross purposes and that would be a very bad thing. Very fuckin' bad.

"Mark," Oberon finally said, "you are asking a lot of me, son. You've committed a lot of crimes. You know that. I appreciate the names of my two bodies over there, however ..."

"I know. Just give me a couple more days to let me shake the trees a little longer. If nothing comes of it, then we'll figure out how to dump it in the lap of the Fourth Estate, or somewhere, with hopefully something more than just an ex-junkie ex-cop's wild and paranoid thoughts. I have nothing concrete right now, man. Only some pieces to a puzzle that I *think* I can see the connections to. I need more pieces. I'm going to go out and get those. I promise you, I won't burn the world down."

A faint smile creased Oberon's face. "Oh. You promise?"

"Well, I'll try not to."

———

As soon as he'd left Oberon and gotten back to Mr. Gregor's truck, he just sat there and leaned his head back on the seat. Closed his eyes, an action that felt like he'd last done an eon ago. Took a deep breath, then another. *Shit, being a junkie was hella easier than this crap.* Took one more deep breath, opened his eyes and started up the truck. *Hell, you're only one man,* his inner voice said. He told his inner voice to go fuck itself. His family was probably now in trouble. A lot of other people were also in trouble. People were dying. He had to do everything he possibly could to try and save them, even if it meant running all over town, 24/7 until this thing was over. No way he could've done this on the horse. But then, he wouldn't be doing this at all if he was on the horse.

He pulled out his phone and dialed up Gato.

To his surprise, Gato's mother answered. His heart quickened as he imagined her standing in an emergency room, her son fighting for his life. She laughed at the tone in Mallen's voice when he asked if everything was okay. She'd only answered because that *hijo perezoso* of hers had left his phone on the coffee table when he finally went to sleep, and the ringer was turned up to full volume. He told her he was on his way over, and could she make sure Gato knew that? She said she would, and wished him a *buen día* before hanging up.

Mallen spent the drive over wondering about Tracy, and if she was alive. He had to find out somehow but had no idea just how to go about that right now. Wondered then about his "other case," and what Teddy might do if he were as pissed as Gato had said he was. Would he come out into the open? Do something that was so obviously wanted of him? If so, then he *had* be there when the pimp put his head above the bush line.

———

Gato was still sleeping when he got to the house. His mother smiled as she went to wake her son, but not before winking at him once and blushing as she left.

When she returned from Gato's room, she said quietly to him, "Have you any news on my Lupe? My son won't say."

He shook his head. "No ma'am, I'm afraid not. But I do think we might be turning a corner on it very soon."

"I thank you for trying," she said.

"Thank me when we've found her."

Gato entered then, all ready for the street. "We need to go, bro," he said.

"What's up?"

He obviously didn't want to speak in front of his mother. "We need to go."

"Okay," Mallen replied. They went quickly down the stairs. Gato was silent as they came out of the building. He seemed preoccupied with something.

"What's up?" Mallen asked his friend.

"One of my boys called me. About an hour ago. Got a line on that shitbag Carpy. Says he saw him at a needle house over on Quint."

"Your guys are thorough."

They turned left after exiting the building. Went around the nearby corner. Stopped in front of an old, closed-off business that looked like it had been a mechanic's at one time. Mallen wondered if he was finally going to learn where Gato got all his vehicles from. His question was answered when Gato unlocked the wide door with a key that hung from a large key ring he pulled from a pants pocket.

"You own this?" Mallen said.

A nod. "My *padre* did. Left it to my *madre.*"

"Hey man, what's wrong?"

"My boy that called? He wasn't just being thorough; he was *at* the needle house."

"Ah." Pictured a man who'd been good, walking the clear path only to fall in a small flash of weakness. To an addict in recovery, the fear of starting up again was a constant companion. Like some dark nightmare creature sitting on their shoulder, always ready to whisper to them that the time was now and that it was only once so why be afraid, right?

You've been clean for some time now. You can handle it.

Go ahead. It'll be okay …

"Sorry to hear that, G," Mallen said, pushing away in his head what a visual of a man succumbing back to the needle would look like. "How long had he been clean?"

"A year," Gato said as he went over to the Falcon. There were three other cars there, each one a collector's dream. A black 1969 Malibu was parked next to a red 1967 Impala, completely tricked out. Across from those two lovelies waited a souped-up, Root-Beer metal flake '68 Mercury Cougar. The room was a fortune in classic cars. Mallen couldn't believe it. It was like he'd walked into one of his early pubescent dreams.

Gato got behind the wheel of the Falcon. Mallen rode shotgun. His friend reached under the seat and pulled out a Beretta Tomcat with an extra clip. Stuck it in his waistband. Mallen really had to wonder where his friend got his arsenal, but he knew better than to ask. It would be considered bad manners, and anyway, he trusted by now that his friend knew what he was doing.

The engine turned over with a roar, and they pulled into the street. Mallen jumped out and locked the garage door. Hopped back inside. After they'd driven a couple blocks, Gato said, "My friend can't do any more work for us."

"Figured as much. Anything we can do for him? I got some connections. Well, a couple chips left. Could call 'em in, get him into a good rehab program, maybe."

"Again, your good heart does you credit, *vato*," Gato replied. "I'm going to put him on the sidelines with some homies that'll help him get straight again."

———

The shooting gallery was an old, broken-down storefront that looked as strung out as the people who frequented it. Mallen had recognized where they were going about four blocks away. He used to have a connection there, a back-up should Dreamo ever let him down. Dreamo never had, so Mallen had never stepped inside the grunged, dilapidated structure.

Gato drove around the block a couple times, checking out the lay of the land, as usual, then parked at the corner just up from the building. He got out. Asked Mallen to wait. Went to the end of the block. Checked out the scene, then turned to the Falcon and nodded his head. Mallen got out and went over to him.

"Back is the way in, from what he told me," Gato said as Mallen walked up. They went around to the rear alley. Mallen realized he was getting more and more leery of entering the building the closer he got. Would he ever live in a life that didn't have shooting galleries? Probably not, came the answer.

They went quietly down the dirty, trash-strewn alley. Found the back of the store. Sure enough, the way in was only nominally covered by a large sheet of warped plywood stuck to the wall by one huge nail in the upper corner. Gato pushed the board up, exposing the dark, empty window frame. Beyond it was blackness. Blackness like bad dreams. Mallen paused before climbing through the window.

"What is it?" Gato said, then looked at the entry. "Oh, man, I get it. Don't want to see that world again, right?"

"No, no … I'm good. I'm good," he replied. Took a deep breath then blew it out quickly. "Strong as iron. Let's just fuckin' go and get the little prick." He crawled through the window before Gato could say another word.

The acrid smell of stale crack smoke hit him like a tsunami wave. An undercurrent of cooked heroin instantly hung on him. Almost like it knew this was the first time he'd smelled that smell since he'd quit. As he moved farther into the building, the space between his shoulder blades went tight. A strange giddiness filled him. Felt like the only way to get rid of it would be to yell at the top of his lungs.

Suddenly he felt Gato's hand on his shoulder. "Like you said, bro," his friend whispered to him, "let's do this, and get back out into the light."

He nodded and the two men crept forward, trying to step lightly on the thin carpet of broken glass and trash. They could make out the dark husks of people sitting in the corners, little flickers of fire flashing between them in the darkness. A cough echoed. A rodent skittered over old, dry newspaper. A woman giggled. All the sign-posts of the world he'd recently left were there.

They didn't find Carpy in the first two large rooms. Probably had been stockrooms once upon a time. Carpet remnants were strewn all over the concrete floor, long ago soiled beyond recognition. The main room was the only one left.

Long and wide. The far wall looked boarded over with many sheets of manically tagged plywood. He noticed a few people lying in the shadows, staring at nothing. A couple men in a nearby corner watched them pass, like they were only waiting for an opening to attack and rob them.

Gato motioned for them to split up, each taking a side of the large space. Gato then moved off into the gloom. He wasn't hard to track due to his stark white T-shirt.

Mallen moved slowly down along the wall, checking each face as he went. He was almost at the end when he saw Carpy huddled next to a large column, a woman with him. She was rail thin, dressed in a short skirt and tank top despite the colder weather. They were huddled over something between them. He could make out their soft whispers, but not the words.

He didn't want to risk anything by alerting Gato, so he decided to do this on his own. Changed his angle. Walked so that he would pass behind Carpy and his lady friend.

He was still a good six feet away when Carpy looked up, right at him. Instantly recognized him. Sprung to his feet with a speed that surprised. *Jesus, did the guy switch to meth?* A short-bladed knife appeared in the addict's hand as the woman he was with looked from one to the other, a perplexed expression on her face. Like she wasn't sure if what she was seeing was real or not.

"Hi Carp," he said, keeping his hands where Carpy could see them. "How's Teddy?"

"Fuck you, man. You drew down fire on my sister."

"I know. But I didn't mean for that to happen, man. If I'd known there were guys following me, I would've done it different." As he spoke, he noticed a flash of white behind Carpy and the woman. It was Gato, moving in. All he had to do now was to keep Carpy busy.

"You still involved her, asshole," Carpy replied, edging closer. Couldn't believe the guy was edging closer and not away. Somebody must've gotten to him. Strengthened him up or scared the fuck out of him. The woman was huddled against the column, knees up tight. She'd figured out this was real, all right.

Mallen could spy Gato at the edge of his vision, moving in slowly like a cat in on a bird. Only a couple more seconds...

And then the woman noticed Gato. She screamed a throat blaster that tore Mallen's ear drums. Carpy spun toward Gato, and that was the opportunity Mallen needed. He lunged at Carpy's blind side. The junkie realized his mistake, but just a split-bit too late. Spun back around, the knife blade flashing in a deadly arc. Mallen tried to dodge out of the way. Couldn't make it in time. His hand exploded in pain as he forgot *the* most important rule in knife fighting: don't automatically reach for it. He was still rusty, had been stupid, and paid the price. The slash of pain across his right palm sent shards of anguish straight to his brain. He lost his footing on the moldy carpet, just like a rookie. Went down, his bloodied hand screaming in agony as he unconsciously put it out to catch himself from the fall. There was a yell from Carpy as Gato drove his knee deep into Carpy's back, sending him forward to topple to the ground. The woman bolted for the exit. So did a couple other addicts in the room. The rest just sat there, continuing to get high, enjoying the show.

Mallen was on Carpy before the man knew what hit him. With his left hand, he grabbed Carpy by the hair, screaming. Drove his knee into Carpy's stomach, and the man went down flat on the ground. Gave him another kick for good measure. Grabbed him back up by his shirt, the buttons ripping off, scattering over the filthy ground.

"Carpy," he said, his voice even and low, "I'm only going to say this one time. Once, got it? What the fuck does Teddy have that would bring all this down on him? That's the only thing I want to hear from you, got me?"

Carpy nodded frantically. Clutched at Mallen's coat as he spoke. "Look, Teddy's gone off the reservation. Scoping Ali was the final straw. That's family, right? Girl family. His little sister, man. Fuckin' Teddy used to push her around in this homemade cart thing we all worked on this one summer back when we were kids, you know? Back when we had stars in our eyes."

"And? Where the fuck can I find him? I know he needs help. I know he says he doesn't want it, but he's wrong. We can help him."

"Man," Carpy said, strangely quiet at that moment, "my brother don't need any help. He's a man on a mission. A mission, and *he's* got the leverage."

Mallen then remembered Ali's words to him. Words about video. About movies. He played a hunch: "What movies does your brother have?"

That made Carpy pause. He tried to scratch at a barely healed cut on his face, but Mallen slapped the hand away, leaving his blood on Carpy's face. "I'm getting fucking tired of asking fucking questions, man. You hear me? What movies does Teddy have that would bring the world down on him like this?"

A glance from Carpy told him there was something he didn't want to say, not right there in the room. Not right then. He dragged

Carpy out. Gato brought up the rear, making sure no one else in the room tried anything. The effort wasn't needed though; as soon as the other addicts realized the show was over, they went back to shooting their dope or smoking their crack.

Carpy blinked in the light as Mallen pushed him head first through the window frame. He then grabbed Carpy, pushing him against the wall of the needle house. Shoved his gun under the addict's chin. Gato stood close by, glancing up and down the alley.

"Look," Mallen said to Carpy, "I don't want to hurt Teddy, okay? Live and let live, right? But I need information about him. Answer my fucking question. And we better be real clear on one point: I'm going to oh-so-fuck-up your world if you don't tell me what I want to know."

Sweat ran down Carpy's face. Mallen pulled the hammer back on his gun. "Okay, okay!" Carpy finally said, beaten. "You heard Teddy talk about her. He cared about her. It was right before he took her off the streets. He was already falling for her, you know?"

"I asked about movies. Not Lupe. What's the connection?"

"She comes into Teddy's pad one night, says she's had enough. Tells about the movie thing. Some expensive john had shown her something that was totally fucked up. She threatens to leave it all behind, Teddy included."

Gato grumbled something Mallen couldn't catch.

"Okay, so she said that. What then?" Mallen asked.

"He didn't want to let her go. Told her everything would be okay. That he'd get enough money to get them both out of it all so they could start over. But you know, that Lupe, that was one strong bitch." Caught himself too late. Glanced over at Gato, who took a threatening step forward. Carpy pushed himself into the wall, like he wished he could tear right through it. "She didn't believe him. Figured he just couldn't do it, not with what she'd seen. How bad it was. I knew…knew she'd leave, and I told Teddy that after she walked out of the room. He just laughed. Next day, she was gone."

"Fucker killed my sister, man!" Gato said, but Mallen quieted him with a look. Turned back to Carpy.

"So she was gone the next day?"

"Yeah. I swear. I don't know that Teddy did anything! I was high most of the next day. Never saw her again."

"The movies. What about them? What are they? The city fathers, taking it up the ass from a strap-on? Child porn? What? What did Lupe see that made her leave her family behind without a word? What was it that made Teddy run like he's done?"

Carpy was wracked by a sudden, violent cough. Snorted out some blood onto his already-soaked shirt. Sighed, like he finally, at the last, realized how far he'd fallen. Looked up at Mallen then, eye to eye. "Snuff."

"You're fuckin' kidding me," Mallen said. "Snuff films? Didn't those go out back in the eighties?" Women killed on film? Nowadays? In the age of instant upload and amateur porn run rampant? Crazy.

"No man, not kidding. Not just snuff of any guy doing any woman. The guys that are doing it? It's *those guys* who want the movies back. Bad."

"The guys who are doing it? You mean the guys making the movies?"

A nod. "Those are the same guys who are *in* the movies, man. And they're big business guys too. Big fucks in city politics are in those movies. And they're fucking killing these women and getting off on filming it. Like hunters and trophy shit. It's fucking sick, man. And not flash drive, CD, upload my life onto the Internet, either. It's old-school video, man. Sick."

Mallen took a step back. Let Carpy's words sink in. Could it be true? This age had bred all sorts of darkness. People did horrible things and got away with it by going to rehab. Ended up with a fucking reality show. Could it be? Snuff? Really?

He exchanged looks with Gato. Could see that the ramification of what Carpy had said had hit his friend too.

"How did Teddy get his hands on the movies?" he asked Carpy.

"One of his girls. She's gone now," he ended quietly. "Died a few days ago. In some bathtub. She was the one that hipped Teddy to the whole setup. She saw one of them, the films, and I think she wanted in on whatever she could get. I think they were using Teddy to find the girls, but I don't know, man, I just don't know. He's my brother...I don't...I don't know."

"How'd the girl manage that? See one of 'em?"

"Her john. He was a freak. A real freak. Like Lupe's last one. Teddy told me about him, but would only say he lived at City Hall. Anyway, the girl came to Teddy after this one date with Freaky. Told him she'd watched one. That he'd made her watch it, even though he said he wasn't into it. Told Teddy she didn't want to see Freaky anymore. Spilled to Teddy about what she saw, and heard. And where this had gone down too. Told him that it was like some big underground network of guys. Teddy started diggin'. What he found, or how he did it, I don't know. You think he'd trust a junkie, even if he was his brother?" Carpy paused, then said, "That's what started it."

Then it hit Mallen. He'd been too wrapped up in listening to what Carpy was laying down to at first realize...

Bathtub. She'd died in some bathtub ...

"What did this girl look like? How'd she die?"

"Some hardcore dudes that work for these guys took her to this house and killed her. Beat her all to hell. Left her dead in a bathtub."

Gato spat on the ground. Turned away, shaking his head. "*Madre de dios,*" he said as he crossed himself.

Carpy looked like he realized he was getting to them. "Look, you got what you needed, yeah? Can I go back inside now?"

Mallen pushed him back into the wall. "No, we're not done yet, Carp. Names. I want names. Who the fuck is making those films? If you won't tell me that, then you give me your brother's present location, and I'll get 'em from him."

"I can't do that. You crazy? I can't rat on Teddy, not again."

"Then give me names."

"I don't know any, man," Carpy whined. "I don't!"

"Bullshit, motherfucker," Gato said. "You watched the films. You know you did."

"No!"

Gato smacked him across the face. "You did," Gato said quietly. "Now, you tell us what faces you saw, or I will kill you right here and now, motherfucker."

Mallen could see the fight taking place inside of the addict. Talk, or live to shoot another day? Would it be names, or his brother? The side the junkie was scared of more would be the answer.

Carpy looked down at the ground. Whispered, "Teddy's set a meeting with them. They think he's scared. He knows they're gonna try for him, but he's gonna be loaded. He's gonna have some surprises for those guys."

"Where, Carp? When? I want to help him. He shouldn't do this alone," Mallen said.

"He won't be alone, man. He's gonna have like six guys with him, guns coming out their asses. The plan is, the owners come in, get whacked. I'm tellin' you, I think he's gone crazy."

"Where?"

Carpy wiped at his face. Looked at the ground. "Pier nineteen. Eleven tonight."

It would be dicey, but they could figure it out. "Okay. Thanks for the info." He glanced over at Gato. Nodded.

Carpy never knew what hit him. Gato's fist, which held a black-jack, blasted Carpy across the temple. The junkie went down like a sack of wet manure.

"Tie him up," Mallen said. "Take him to your posse. Keep him on ice until after we see Teddy. Don't need him running around like a chicken without a head, telling anyone else what he told us, or alerting T-Mac."

TWENTY-THREE

THEY'D SPENT THE RIDE back to Gato's hood scoping to see if they were being tailed. Kept an eye out for any black BMWs or Town Cars. There'd been a couple, but they weren't tailing the Falcon. Maybe the lack of a tail meant the other side was getting ready for its meet with Teddy.

Gato pulled up right next to Mr. Gregor's Land Cruiser outside his building. Mallen turned to his friend. "Those guys will keep Carpy on ice, no sweat?" They'd left Carpy with a couple of Gato's buddies that Gato went to church with every Sunday. One looked like he could play defensive back for the Niners; the other looked like he could eat the first for lunch.

"No worries, *vato*," Gato assured him. "He'll be safe and sound, except for the cold-turkey aspect his life's about to take on." It wasn't lost on Mallen that his friend seemed to take an immense pleasure in that fact.

"Okay. Let's meet back here at eight. Then we go to the pier."

"Should I bring more troops?"

"No, man," he replied. "Just us two. This is the deal: We go there and shoot photos, not people. Pics of the fuckers Teddy meets with could be of great value, either now or down the road. Our other objective is to act as Teddy's guardian angels. If it looks like he's gonna get killed, we step in. We need him alive, and I'm thinking about Lupe here, too, yeah? If she hears he's dead, she might come out of hiding, or run deeper into the woods. We don't want either scenario."

"So we need some weaponry and a good camera?"

"Yeah. Is that workable?"

Gato thought for a moment. "It is. No sweat." He smiled as he started up the Falcon. Mallen got out and opened the door to the Land Cruiser. "See you at eight, *vato*," Gato said, and with that he gunned the engine and roared away down the street.

———

Mallen didn't go home. He was too anxious. Too edgy. He stayed in the city, feeling he needed the anonymity. Drove over to Polk Street and parked a couple blocks north of California. Hit a drug store and patched up his hand. Wasn't that bad, but it sure stung when he applied the antiseptic. Who knew where Carpy's knife had been. Then he went and ate at Victor's. The grapevines and old wine bottles hanging from the ceiling leant him a strange sense of safety. A bottle of Chianti and plate of thick pasta with hearty pesto later, he felt ready for the coming maneuvers. Spent the rest of his time strolling up and down Polk, looking in store windows, checking to see if he was being followed. Couldn't help it: A part of him wished again he'd stayed a junkie. Life was sure the fuck more simple, and that was a fact. Shoot, cop some more H, shoot again. Rinse and repeat. Easy.

At the cigarette shop on the corner of California and Polk, he bought another pack of cigarettes, along with a small-bladed knife that whipped open when you pushed a side button. The cheap, black plastic grip was cut to fit the hand well enough. The blade was single edged, would probably stay sharp enough for one or two incidents. Was just under the limit of what a guy could carry without having to have it displayed on a belt, and it came with a clip. Did nicely hooked on the inside of his left boot.

The sun had gone down a couple hours ago. The temp was now down into the high forties. That fact would make the waiting harder. Stakeouts in the cold were miserable, but it was sure as hell easier to stay awake. Then it was time to go. He slid behind the wheel of the truck and drove down to Gato's. His friend met him around the corner, outside his father's old garage, as per their agreement. Gato opened the garage door and Mallen pulled inside. Put the keys in the glove box; he wouldn't need them. Thankfully his friend had decided on all black for his clothing. No white t-shirts tonight.

On the hood of the parked Falcon was a camera case alongside a dark, beat-up leather brief. Gato opened the briefcase to show him the guns. There were two pistols inside. Both after-market automatics, both .45s. There was also a sawed-off, double-barreled shotgun with a pistol grip. Just like something out of a Dirty Harry movie. Good amount of ammo for everybody. Mallen checked each one. None of them had serial numbers, and all of them were in fine working order. The .45s would have better stopping power than the .38 of Gato's he'd been carrying. He switched guns, putting Gato's smaller pistol in the case.

"Well, I said we're there to shoot pictures, not people," Mallen said as he picked up the shotgun and inspected it. "But yeah ... better to be prepared. Let's hope it doesn't come to this, though."

"'*Planee para el mejor, prepárese para el peor,* my *padre* always said," Gato replied as he opened the camera case, pulling out a night vision lens.

"What's that mean? Some old Spanish proverb or something?"

"No, *vato*. It means to plan for the best, prepare for the worst."

Mallen laughed. Felt good to laugh. It released the tension in his chest. "We should go," he said. "I want a good vantage point, from a higher elevation if we can."

There was a click as Gato assembled the camera. It was a nice and sweet automatic 35-millimeter with a zoom lens. "This should work just fine."

"Good. Since I have trouble programming a microwave, you're on camera duty. I want faces, license plates, and the transaction when it goes down, okay?

"You got it, *hombre*."

———

Traffic wasn't too bad as they made their way over to the waterfront. Maybe the weather worked on everybody the same, keeping them home. They did a couple drive-bys of the pier. Made Mallen think back to the night he took a dive from one of these piers and into the bay in order to save himself from being overdosed by Jas and Griffin, guys he'd once run with back in his undercover days. They hadn't appreciated his eventual outing as a narc. Well, he'd lived to tell the tale. That's how it goes, sometimes.

Mallen scanned the dark, dilapidated building spanning the length of the pier. Getting over the fence would be the easy part. "Park nearby. Somewhere out of the way but easy to get to, yeah?" he said.

Gato complied. Found them a spot near the next pier, in the shadow of a closed-up restaurant. Theirs wasn't the only car in evidence on the street, so it wouldn't stand out. They exited without a word. Mallen's coat pockets were heavy with the weight of the gun and ammo. After deliberating the entire way over, he decided to leave the shotgun in the trunk. It was a close-quarters weapon, and if luck were with them, they'd never get that close. Gato had put on a black leather jacket. Carried the camera slung across his chest, hiding it under the garment.

The chain-link fence that ran across the front of the pier sagged in spots from people climbing over. Hopefully, there would be no one inside fucking around or shooting drugs. They crept over silently. Walked along the warehouse, careful of the open, black holes in the cement pier. Mallen knew that if a guy went through one of those, it was twenty feet down into the frigid San Francisco Bay. He shuddered as he passed one of the holes.

"Bro," Gato said as they stalked along the south wall of the pier, "what if Carpy was lying? What if nothing happens tonight?"

"That's a possibility, sure. It could also be a setup and we'll get shot. Carpy could've rolled over for the guys behind the snuff ring before we ever got to him. Hell, he'd do anything if you offered up enough H. What I'm hangin' my hat on, though, is that I really *do* believe he cares for his family. Especially Ali."

The building seemed fairly sound. There was a soft slap below as water hit the corroding pilings that kept the pier up. The high windows were all broken out, the building's large loading doors locked tight. Glass crunched under their boots as they checked the rest of the structure. At the back was a set of stairs leading up to a rusty metal door. There was a broken light fixture above it, covered in bird shit. They crept up. On their right was a great view of the bay, the Bay Bridge all lit up. *Woulda been a great place to shoot dope,* Mallen thought with a soft laugh. Checked the metal door. Wouldn't budge. He'd planned for something like this and brought out the tire iron he'd taken from the Falcon's trunk. Put the end between the door and the jamb, right where the handle was. Leaned all his weight on the bar, grunting with the effort. There was a loud, snapping sound as the lock gave. He almost lost his grip on the bar, catching it just before it hit the metal stairs. The door opened with a loud squeak of salt-watered hinges.

As expected, the building was one very long, open warehouse. Mallen judged it to be well over 300 yards. Faint light from outside gave just enough for them to see by as they crept along the gangway that hugged the wall, one story up. He prayed it wouldn't collapse under their weight, the bolts holding it up having long ago rusted. It squeaked loudly as they made their way along. They'd have to be careful, *very* careful, when the meeting started.

"Where should we set?" Gato whispered.

He spied around as they moved forward. Where would the meeting take place? He had the sudden, anxious feeling that it might not even take place inside. But, if these guys were as bad and powerful as Carpy had said, they wouldn't take chances meeting outdoors. He and Gato would also have to be in a position to maybe save Teddy's life. He gazed upward. There was the answer: a small catwalk that ran the perimeter of the place, just under the roof. He could even make out a door that hopefully led to an outside staircase. They quickly hunted around until they found a ladder that would take them up another level. There turned out to be several such ladders, at regular intervals. Mallen guessed the catwalk had been used by men needing to scan huge mountains of crates and cargo coming in from all parts of the world.

The walk was of heavy crisscrossed wire, held stable by corrugated metal supports. Felt solid enough under their feet, but they'd again have to be very careful about noise. They decided to keep close to one of the ladders almost dead center in the building. This would help shave seconds off in case they had to drop in fast and get Teddy out of there. From where they were, they had a perfect view of the entire floor. The camera would do the rest.

Mallen checked the door he'd seen from below. An old fire door. There should be a ladder or stairs behind it. He broke the lock. Beyond was a metal ladder, chopped off ten feet or so above the ground to prevent vandals getting in. It would have to do for an escape route if the shit hit the fan.

They then hunkered down to wait, huddling against the wall as they tried to keep away from the cold bay air that blew in through all the broken windows. Mallen wanted to risk a cigarette, but thought better of it. Gato seemed nervous, checking and re-checking the clip in his gun.

As Mallen sat there, all the old feelings of being on stakeout flooded back. Before he'd gone under deep cover, he'd been on only a handful of stakeouts. Some had turned out well, some had turned up nothing. Being on a stakeout was one of the hardest duties he ever pulled. Couldn't believe there were guys out there who got a charge from it, who actually sought out the assignment.

"What do we do if it goes clusterfuck, *vato*?" his friend said quietly as he again checked the lens setting on the camera.

"Like I said, we need Teddy alive. He's our only real link to your sister, right? If it goes bad, shoot at the guys shooting at Teddy. If we're too late and Teddy takes one, then we grab our photos and get out. If there's a chance of saving Teddy, we take it, okay?"

Gato nodded. "Got it."

———

It felt like it could've been two days, but a check of Gato's watch showed only two hours had passed. The traffic outside had grown quieter over that time. Mallen was just shifting a bit to stretch his hamstrings when they heard a vehicle drive down the pier outside and stop. There was the sharp sound of a lock being forced, followed by the groan of rusty wheels as one of the large loading gates below rolled open. A black van drove in, the door instantly rolling shut behind it by a man dressed all in black.

The van prowled to the middle of the warehouse and stopped. Seven men got out and quietly took up positions around the van. Mallen nodded to Gato, who began to get faces photographed.

"You know any of those guys?" he whispered to Gato.

"No, but I've seen a few of them around the hood. Here's Teddy."

Mallen watched as Teddy stepped out of the van. Wore dark clothes under a long black coat. Carried a metal briefcase in his hand. Spoke a few words to two of his men, who then nodded and took up positions at either end of the van. Mallen zeroed in on the metal case, wondering if it was the item Teddy had taken from his shack hideout a few days ago.

"Would you call Teddy a hothead?" he asked Gato.

"Not more than anyone else."

"So, he's got more of a plan than to just shoot it out with whoever arrives, right?"

"Fuckin' hope so, bro. Hope so."

Two more minutes passed. Gato had by that time gotten photos of all of Teddy's men. Mallen felt something was wrong. Some of those guys might be from the hood, but at least four of them seemed like professionals to him. It was the way they moved. The way they kept their attention on their surroundings. It would be hard to take those guys unawares. Teddy was a pimp; why would he be able to recruit professionals, if that's what they actually were?

Other vehicles were heard approaching outside. Maybe two, could be three or more. Mallen quietly shifted into a position that would allow him to move into action quickly. The door slid open again. Three black Lincoln Navigators rolled through. Parked twenty feet away from the van, hoods pointed right at it. There was the soft click of the shutter as Gato took photos of the license plates. The air was thick with tension. Automatically, Mallen pulled out the .45. Flipped up the safety. Never took his eyes off of what was going on down below.

The doors of two of the Navigators opened in sync, and eight men got out. Gato snapped away. Mallen couldn't be sure, but he could swear that one of the men had been in the department when he was still there. Another man turned to glance around the warehouse. Mallen recognized him. Last he'd heard, that man had been head of security for one of the financial heavyweights in the city.

The tension in the air ratcheted up as Teddy walked toward the group of men, case still in hand. The door to the van had been left open. Hands were in coat pockets. Everyone kept everyone else in their field of vision. Six of the eight men who had just arrived hung back as two came forward, one being the guy he remembered as working for the rich dude. The two parties stopped about eight feet from each other. Words were exchanged. Teddy shook his head. Pointed at the men, saying something that had the effect of some sort of ultimatum. Mallen shifted the .45 in his hand. The most dangerous time would be once Teddy handed over the briefcase. Gato continued to snap images.

One of the men said something to Teddy, who spread his hands out, like saying, "this is all I have, man." Teddy thought for a moment. Stepped forward a yard, putting the case down on the ground. Spit on it. Turned and went to the van. One of the six men who'd hung back now went and picked up the case. Brought it back to the second Navigator, the two negotiators going back to the other vehicle. Maybe it was all going to come off without a hitch, after all.

"We follow Teddy, right?" Gato whispered as he paused his picture taking. Mallen nodded, keeping his eyes on the men below.

That was when it all went to hell.

As Teddy went to get into the van, one of the men he'd arrived with earlier, one that Gato had recognized, whipped out his gun and shot Teddy in the back. Teddy fell to the ground and the world moved into the red. In the shock and awe, the traitor managed to bolt to where the Navigators were parked.

"Fuck," Mallen shouted. "Get to Teddy!" He began shooting at the men around the Navigators. They were taken by surprise. He calmed down and focused on the traitor. Pulled the trigger and was happy to see a chunk of the man's head explode in a thick red mist. Guess he still knew how to shoot, after all.

He'd just gotten to his feet to move down the nearby ladder when the warehouse was rocked by a huge explosion. The concussion threw him backward against the railing and he was momentarily blinded. When his vision returned, he saw the second of the three Navigators engulfed in flames. The third one had caught fire as well, the windows blown out. It appeared Teddy had given them a little something special in that case. The first Navigator screeched around. Roared out of the warehouse and away into the night. Whoever those guys of Teddy's were, they ended up not being very good, as they were all dead. Mallen and Gato bolted down the stairs to get to Teddy. Mallen knew they only had seconds before sirens would be heard.

"Check the other guys, see if any are alive," he yelled as he went and knelt by Teddy. Teddy was barely breathing, but he wasn't dead. His eyes looked up at the ceiling. Maybe searching for a god that wasn't there. The bullet had hit him square in the back.

"Teddy, can you hear me?" Mallen asked. The pimp's eyes focused on him then. He nodded.

"Where's Gato's sister? You know, don't you? You were lying, man. Because you love her. You were trying to protect her, right?"

Teddy's eyes moved to Gato as he came up. "Lupe," he said, and coughed up some blood. "L.A."

"Los Angeles?" Gato said. "You sure, man?"

He smiled grimly. "Dying man's confession. Went ... L.A. Didn't want .. to be a part ... of this. I loved her, man." Coughed up some blood before continuing. "Loved her ... wanted to get money ... for us to get away ..."

"About these guys," Mallen said to him. "Do you have any more ammo on the guys that did this to you? Where's the stash? You didn't blow it up. I know you didn't."

For an answer, Teddy moved his eyes to the van. It was the last thing he did before dying. Mallen leapt into the van, desperate to find whatever Teddy was talking about.

Inside was a dingy-looking shoebox. This was what they'd seen the outline of back in the tiny shed south of City College, for sure. Grabbed it up and was rewarded by the banging together of things that definitely sounded like something other than a pair of high tops. Pulled the cover off. Inside were VCR tapes. A lot of 'em.

"Mallen! We best be leaving, bro!" Gato yelled nervously.

"Go! I'm there!" he replied. Leaped out of the van. Glanced over at the Navigator sitting there. The doors were still open, the occupants having escaped with the other men. He stopped dead then. Couldn't believe what he saw.

A woman's hand. Just peeking over the bottom edge of the rear door window. Mallen threw the box at Gato as he ran to the SUV. There was somebody left behind, and if they were still here, then they might be in need of a very quick evac. Whatever way it would fall out, he couldn't just risk leaving them to die. Gato was moving toward a side door, yelling at him again, urging him to hurry the fuck up. Mallen got to the SUV. The hand belonged to a young girl. Blonde hair. Between eighteen and twenty. She'd been horribly beaten on, and he noted needle-like marks on her neck. Wore nothing but torn jeans and dirty T-shirt filled with holes. Felt for a pulse. There was one. An interview would have to wait. Mallen grabbed her up and out of the van. Hauled her up with all his ability over his shoulder. Sirens were getting close, fast.

"Go!" he yelled at Gato. But his friend still waited until Mallen caught up with him and they got out of a side door and onto the pier. Mallen could swear he heard emergency services entering through the huge doors on the opposite side just as they left. They'd only just gotten out.

Gato eyed the body over Mallen's shoulder. Then at the shoebox in his own hand. He seemed at a loss for words. The two men made it through the shadows back to the fence and this time, Gato pulled up the bottom of the bent, rusted fence with all his might, grunting with the effort. Mallen rolled the girl through the opening. She never woke up as Mallen crawled after her and then Gato climbed over the fence. They made it back to the Falcon and jumped inside. Mallen got in back with the girl. Gato started up the car and did a U-turn, driving away at a normal speed, checking the rearview for any signs of cops.

Mallen checked the girl's pulse again. It was there. Not strong, not weak. Looked again at the bruising and the needle marks. He squeezed her hand, to see if she'd come around. Tapped her on the cheek. Her eyelids fluttered.

"Hey," he said. "You're safe. We got you away from the people that did this to you. You understand me? You're safe now."

A faint nod. She tried to speak.

"Gato," Mallen said. "You got any water up there?" Gato nodded and handed over a half-full bottle of water. Mallen poured a little down her throat. Splashed some on her forehead.

"What's your name?" he asked, then said, "G, we need a hospital. We gotta take this girl to General, okay? I go in with her to emergency, you stay with the car."

Gato nodded. "Okay, *vato.*"

She coughed, and that seemed to take all her strength. Then her eyes opened again. She said something, but he couldn't catch it, so leaned closer, putting his ear to her mouth. "Tracy," she said. "Goldman. Tracy."

He couldn't believe it, believe how the world turned. "You're Tracy Goldman? The mayor's daughter?" What he got back was a faint nod. *Jesus fucking Christ.* His entire world just took yet another upending. There were answers here, but he needed time and some space to think it all through. Wondered if the hospital would be safe for her after all, if the men that did this found out she'd gotten out of there. He sighed. There really wasn't a choice; she needed medical attention he couldn't provide. But now it'd gotten even more complicated. He'd have to beat it out of the hospital before giving his name or getting at all tied up with it. Word would get out. Liz would be notified. He'd have to be a ghost ... the unknown Good Samaritan.

"You rest," he told her quietly. "We're almost at the hospital." She closed her eyes then, in an almost grateful manner.

Mallen reached over the seat and grabbed up the shoebox with VCR tapes inside. Fanned through them. There white labels were blank except for a series of numbers. That was it. Teddy's code for something? The owner's? Whatever the numbers meant, the answer was gone now, and it was up to him to figure out the puzzle.

"Gato?" he said as they drove along the waterfront, "Once we secure Tracy safely at the hospital, we need to find a VCR somewhere, fast. Those guys will realize this shit is still out there. We gotta assume somebody on their side saw us, just like we saw them."

Gato nodded, and for the first time since he'd met the man, Mallen could see that his friend was scared.

TWENTY-FOUR

Gato pulled into a parking spot near the emergency entrance. Kept the motor running. He'd been quiet the entire way over. Just stared out the windshield as he drove. Mallen got out, pulling Tracy from the car and putting her arm around his neck. He managed to hold her up as they went inside. The admitting nurse looked at the both of them, and he could tell by her expression that they probably looked like a couple of homeless needle fiends to her.

"I found this girl in an alley," he said. "She's alive, but man … you can see how she's been treated, yeah? She needs help, quick."

The nurse only nodded. Called for a couple other nurses. A gurney appeared almost as if by magic, and they took Tracy away. It was only then that Mallen breathed a sigh of relief. He turned and began to walk out.

"Wait," said the nurse behind him. "We need her name, and yours."

He turned back. "I think she said it was Tracy. Tracy Goldman. Not sure though. Mine's Dash. Dash Hammett." Didn't wait for her to write it down. Knew they got shit like this all the damn time. Junkies dropping off other junkies. Hopefully they'd treat her right once they realized who she was. And they would realize it. He pulled out his phone and called Chris. She answered immediately.

"You okay?" she asked before he could say a word.

"Yeah, but I gotta keep this short. Tell Liz that Tracy is at SF General. In emergency."

"What? You found her? How?"

"It's more like she found me, in a way. Look, I'll tell you more later. Just get that to Liz. And tell her that . . . tell her that Tracy has been treated very badly. She's going to need a lot of help to get back to the girl she was, if she ever can. Okay?"

"Okay, Mark. I understand." There was a pause, then she said, "Good job, copper."

"Thanks, but really I can't take credit for it. Kiss Anna for me, and I'll call when I can. You're being careful, right?"

"Yes," she reported. "No strange cars or anything."

"Good. See ya." He hung up as he reached the Falcon. Got in the front and Gato drove off into the night.

They went back to the garage. Gato told him to wait and he disappeared through the back door. Was back in five minutes with an old VCR under his arm.

"I didn't think you'd have one here, man," Mallen said.

"It's my *madre*'s. I gotta have it back by the time she wakes up in the morning," Gato replied as he led him to what had been the garage office. There, in the corner, next to a mini-fridge and a dusty microwave was an old, small TV. Gato hooked the VCR up to it, and turned on both electronics. Handed the VCR remote to Mallen.

Mallen rifled through the box, shuddering when he realized the "dirt" smudges were actually blood. Picked three tapes at random. Written on the first tape was a numerical code: 04260966.

"We have to decode these numbers. All the tapes have 'em."

Gato checked the other tapes. "It's either eight or nine numbers, bro. How we going to do that?"

"Workin' on it," he replied as he put a tape into the VCR.

"Why tapes, *vato*? That's all 1980s an' shit."

Mallen thought about that. "Well, you know … it might actually be safer these days. Harder to copy this fucker than it would be to copy digital, yeah? How easy is it to upload and copy a movie you made with your phone, right? A few clicks is all. Maybe old-school is now safe school?"

Gato shrugged, not convinced. "Well, hit the play button, man. Let's go."

It was the sound that was the worst.

It was like whoever had filmed it wanted to capture every whimper, every breath. Every grunt. Capture every drop of blood. The film opened with a pan shot of a room. Not a dirty, dark room, like what he would've expected. Looked like some normal, anonymous motel room. And that fact scared the shit out of him. Because if it *was* a sorta movie set, then these guys were monied. The camera showed an array of shiny, medical-looking implements on a low dresser. Each instrument was lovingly filmed. The final shot was of a wooden chair and some leather straps laying on the floor, like they'd been tossed there and forgotten. And they were stained dark in places. Sweat or blood; either answer was ugly. Evil and ugly.

Then the girl was brought in. She was young. Asian. Dressed like a hooker, all glitz and sadness. Thai, probably. That was confirmed when she spoke, quickly and with mounting fear. Heavy Thai accent, speaking English. Two men, looking very much like a couple comic-book thugs dressed all in black and wearing balaclavas, tied her up with the straps and then gagged her. The men's clothes were plain. Not expensive or flashy, just black hoodies and military-style pants and boots. He wondered where this was taking place. Had to be here, on these shores. Not overseas. Something about her clothes, the way she wore them. He'd seen enough hookers to know this one was American. She was Thai, but probably shopped at Ross.

They stripped her. She cried. Begged. But the two large men in balaclavas didn't rape her. Instead just left her there, gagged and strapped.

Then another man entered. Wearing, in a sick twist, a Joker mask. Wasn't wearing clothes, but a dark robe. A white guy. Walked slowly around the girl, who kept struggling and whimpering.

Then the man picked up the forceps. Gato turned away, mumbling out a quiet prayer.

Mallen watched as much as he could. Forced himself to, hoping for some clue. Why would they go to so much trouble to get the tapes back if there wasn't something that could tag the owners back to these images?

What he was seeking came toward the end, about twenty horrible minutes later. He wiped at his face, not really registering his tears. He was too numb by that point. What was left of the girl was still alive, as evidenced by the pumps of blood. Then the man, nude at this point except for the mask, pulled out of her and howled like an animal. The cry was cut short, and then he posed next to her body, aimed straight at the camera. Like a hunter posing next to a kill.

Mallen hit the pause button then. There was no way to recognize the man's face because of the mask. Gray hair on the arms and chest. Definitely older, maybe late fifties. Didn't work out much, either. He wasn't sure, but Mallen could swear the man was missing his left pinky. Put all together, it would be enough to pin the fucker to the wall that was for sure. He hit the eject button. The screen went black.

The tape came out with a soft whirring noise. The two men stood silent. Gato had turned back to the screen at the end, evidently forcing himself to do so. He was pale. Shaken.

"Mallen," Gato finally said, "I think I know that guy."

"What? How?"

"The missing pinky. I know him. I *know* I know him." He was sounding more and more sure.

"Well, fuckin' how, man?"

"*Déjame pensar!*" Gato turned away, closing his eyes. After a moment, he looked back at him, his expression stony. "Man... that guy? I *knew* I knew him. Shit..."

"What?" Mallen said. Gato was making him really nervous. "Who is he?"

"Remember what I said about Lupe getting arrested that first time? About a hard-assed judge?" Gato nodded toward the TV. "He's the judge that sent Lupe to jail the first time."

"Jesus... Gato, look... lots of guys have missing pinkies. Lots of fat fucks running around in the world..."

Gato grabbed the remote and shoved the tape back in. Rewound it. Played it frame by frame, during a scene that was a closeup of the man pulling the woman's hair as she was forced to blow him. "That,"

Gato said with finality as he pressed the pause button. "Look at that, man."

Mallen studied the screen. Then he saw it. Part of a tattoo. Just a sliver of one, on the back of the man's left hand. Some sort of word, maybe. And maybe something green, like a vine.

"I can even tell you what the tat says, bro. I remember it, because I hated that fucker. He was way too hardcore with Lupe. It was only her first time. I got close to him, one time out in the hallway. I was angry. Wanted to plead her case with my hands, you know? I stopped, but not before I saw that tat. Two roses, entwined. The word *love* in a fancy script, over them. It was faded, like he got it back when he was a young asshole. I'm positive, man. Fuckin' one hundred percent."

"A judge," Mallen said to himself. *A fuckin' conspiracy, all right.* He sat down in an old sagging office chair. Took a deep breath, realizing this was how Alice must've felt falling down the rabbit hole. Well, now there *really* was no turning back. Not like he'd ever done it anyway, given the opportunity. Rifled through the box. Pulled out another tape. This one had nine numbers on it. Shoved it into the VCR. Hesitated for a moment before he hit the play button. The movie was the same basic setup, though the room was different. Still grabbed him as a movie set, though. The woman this time was a young blonde who spoke a language that reminded him of Russian. He popped out the tape. Checked another. This one had 11290866 written on it. Shoved it into the VCR. Same setup, even using the room from the first tape. This one was another Thai woman. He ejected the tape, looked long at the number. After a moment, he dug through until he found all the tapes whose code ended in 66. There were three. He then checked them. On those three, all the woman had been Thai.

"I think I know the code, at least," he said.

Gato had spent this time staring out the window into the night. Mallen knew his friend enough to know that he was wrestling with something. "Yeah, *vato*? What?"

"The first six numbers are the date." He held up one of the tapes. "Ten, eighteen, eleven? October eighteenth, two thousand eleven."

"Dude, don't play around. What are the last two?"

"International calling codes. Look, all the ones with Thai women have sixty-six. I bet that's the calling code for Thailand."

"Okay. So what? What does that get us?"

"I don't know, man. Maybe these guys are able to get women from all over the world and bring them here. That one woman? The blonde? She could be here illegally. I'm thinkin' she is. This might be part of a human trafficking ring."

Gato shook his head. "This is crazy. What are we gonna do?"

"I don't know." What could they do against something like this? "First thing we do is stash this shit somewhere safe. It's the only bargaining chip we have." He put the tapes back in the box. "I'm not going home tonight. I'm going to camp out in North Beach instead. I don't go there a lot. You pack and find somewhere safe to crash. Somewhere you've never crashed before."

"I can't do that," Gato said quietly.

"What do you mean?" he replied, but he thought he knew what was coming.

"I have to go after Lupe. Teddy said she went to L.A., and that makes sense. She's got friends down there. Way-back friends, from when we were little. She would've been scared to shit by all this, just like Carpy told us. I'm *positivo* that's the reason she skipped town. I have to go after her. What if she knows something, and they find that out? I don't want to leave you like this, man, but ..."

"But nothing," he said. "I owe you ten times over, brother. You do what you have to do, and I'll back your play. Don't fucking worry about leavin', okay? I'll be fine. But you, my brother, better fucking keep me posted, all right? I don't need *you* disappearing."

They walked around the corner to Gato's place, and Gato immediately began packing. His mother looked from one to the other. She got it that something was up.

"*¿Qué es?*" Esperanza asked Mallen.

He knew enough Spanish to know that she asked what was happening. "We might have a line on Lupe. Gato is going to go and check it out down in Los Angeles."

"She might be down there?" came the hopeful question.

"Yes, it's possible. He'll find out. You know he will."

———

Gato was packed in under ten minutes. Ate a few bites from the refrigerator even though his mother wanted to do more for him. He called and woke up a neighbor who'd known them both since before his father had died and asked her to look after his mother for a couple days. Just check on her, make sure she was doing okay. Mallen heard the neighbor readily agree to look after "little Esper," as she called Gato's mother.

Gato thanked her profusely, promising all sorts of support in return. Hung up and kissed his mother on the forehead, then left. Mallen put a reassuring hand on her shoulder for a moment, then followed.

Gato was going to drive through what was left of the night. Mallen kept the box of tapes, the camera, and the two .45s. Gato drove him back to the garage, where the Land Cruiser was still parked, Gato told him to wait. He went quickly to the trunk of the Falcon as Mallen stowed the gear in the truck. Gato came back and handed him the shotgun and a box of shells.

"You sure you're not gonna need it?" Mallen said as he took the items.

Gato only smiled. "Go with God, *vato*. Keep your eyes peeled, and don't go all *Boondock Saints* without telling me first."

"Same back at you. Call often, alright?" he said as he got in the truck and started it up. Put it in gear. Gato waved and got inside the Falcon and Mallen sat there, watching his friend drive away. Wondered when he'd see him again, and if he ever would. *We're in the shit, and who knows anything anymore,* he thought as he gunned the engine and headed for North Beach.

It was almost three in the morning, with very little movement on the streets. If someone were tailing him, he'd know. As he drove, he began to ponder where the hell to stash the box. Wondered also when and if Tracy would be able to tell him something. He bet she would know pieces to the puzzle that would fuckin' help him out. He thought then about stashing the box at the bus station, but that seemed the most obvious choice. What if they saw him put it in there? He chuckled; he was getting very paranoid. *But then again, maybe not,* said the voice inside him. A lot of careers and lives would be ruined over these tapes. He knew what his ultimate goal was: to bring these guys crashing down. That's what was known in the police world as an FFS, or Fucking For Sure.

As he drove, he toyed briefly with the idea of turning them over to the DA, but he couldn't trust even that right now. Oberon? Obie was the only guy besides Gato he could trust a hundred percent, but involving him might also be endangering the man's life. He wasn't willing to do that. No, he had to get names first, more evidence on the men in the movies. Maybe he could use the photos they'd taken of the meeting? Maybe the judge himself could be leveraged? He'd forgotten to get the name!

Quickly dialed Gato's number as he made the left from Mission Street, heading onto Van Ness. Gato answered straight away, obviously already on the freeway.

"What was the name of the judge?" he said.

"I'll never forget that fucker's name," Gato replied. "Reynolds. Judge Toland Reynolds. Total *pendejo*."

"Reynolds. Thanks."

"What are you thinkin'?"

"Don't know, yet. But I will. Drive safe."

Mallen didn't drive to North Beach after all. The idea hit him a couple blocks south of Geary. There was a mailbox rental place out at the beach. Nondescript, near the Safeway. That would be perfect. Got off of Van Ness at Turk. Quickly headed west. The place wouldn't open for about four hours or so. He found a quiet place to park at the top of 48th Avenue. Nothing there but residential shit. Climbed in the back of the truck and got as comfortable as possible. Had the shotgun at hand, and that made him feel better. It was so cold out. The only companion he had was the steady beat of the ocean waves as they hit the beach only a few blocks away. As he fell asleep, he reflected that if he had to die tonight, at least he'd die with the sound of the ocean in his ears. There were worse ways to go, and that was a fact.

———

He woke the next morning to stiffness he'd never known. He'd curled up against the nighttime cold and now unbending was agony. Guess he was getting older. He stashed the shotgun out of sight, thankful that nobody had reported him sleeping in his vehicle. Checked the clock on his phone. Just after eight a.m. Got out of the truck and stretched his legs. Then got behind the wheel and drove quickly over to the mailbox rental store.

The few vehicles in the lot were a couple trucks and a van parked at the far west side. People camping, he figured. There were a few cars there too, probably people who worked at the stores, there early to open up. He parked and went inside. There was a young guy behind the counter with big hair and metal band insignias tatted on his forearms. Looked hungover and pissed off, probably at having to be up so early.

"I'm thinking of renting one of your large-size post office boxes," Mallen said. "But I'm going out of the country for at least a month and I might get a package in the interim. I don't want it returned if I don't claim it for thirty-plus days. How long do you keep stuff around?"

"Pretty long," the guy said with a shrug. "Is it a big thing you're expecting?"

"No. I'm pretty sure it would fit in a mailbox."

He shrugged. "As long as you continue to pay your rent and let us know you'll be around, we'll keep it for up to three months or so. One guy that rents from us had a huge box here for six months before he came to get it. It can be a problem during the holidays, though. You know, all the packages take up space, and then we sorta need for you to come and fly it out of here."

"Fair enough," he replied as he pulled out his wallet. Got a box, paying two months in advance, just in case. He then drove to the nearest post office he knew of, on 22nd Avenue in the Sunset. Went inside and found some packing tape on a metal roll that had been nailed to the counter. He then pulled out two of the VCR tapes before taping the box shut: the one of the judge and another one, randomly chosen.

For security against what the future might bring, he said to himself. His old man had always preached that you never gave it all away; keep back a little for a rainy day. Or a rainy week. Ol' "Monster" Mallen had never given anything away. Never.

He put a label on the box, addressed it, and mailed it to his brand-new mailing address. Sent off the two he'd kept back to Bill at the Cornerstone, scribbling on the back of the padded envelope a note to Bill not to open it until called for, and to trust him.

TWENTY-FIVE

MALLEN PULLED INTO THE parking garage near SF General. He'd called, trying to find out how Tracy was doing, but had gotten the usual guarded, hospital-privacy bullshit. As he'd driven over, he fought his tired brain for a plan. In the end, he felt the best thing to do was to just play as it lays.

The reception desk was busy, the lobby filled with patients waiting for rides or for admission. This was General, so the clientele was the greater part of the city's population: in need of both medical help and the insurance to pay for it. He walked to the reception desk, the woman behind it looking up at him, already with that questioning gaze in her eyes that asked, "Why are you here and what is your name?" He gave her his best smile laced with worry.

"Can you help me? I was told my little sister was brought in here last night. Well, early this morning, actually," he said, working the flustered, caring brother thing for all it was worth.

She turned to her computer screen. "Name?"

"Goldman. Tracy Goldman."

"And you're her brother?"

"Yeah. Robert. Robert Goldman. Is she still here?"

Keys were tapped, the screen was studied. "Yes, she's still here. She's been moved upstairs."

A sigh of relief escaped his mouth. He almost fell over with relief. Ran his hand over his face, relieved to have found "his sister."

"Can I see her? Only just to let her know I was here?"

The woman consulted the clock on the nearby wall. "Visiting hours don't begin for about two hours."

"Oh. Are you sure? I really just want to hold her hand for a moment."

"I'm sorry," came the reply.

"Well, can you tell me what room she's in, so when I come back I'll know where to go?"

She gave him a look, like trying to decide if he was legit or not. Glanced at her screen. "Room six-nineteen."

He'd never given such a great smile. "Thank you," he said. "I'll need to come here and get a name badge first, right?"

"Hospital policy. We need to write the name and room of the person you're here to see on it."

"Got it, thanks." Mallen knew he couldn't wait and come back later. Time was not something he felt he had a lot of right about now. He left the waiting area and went back outside. Moved to the door where the paramedics brought in the patients who come off the ambulances. Bent down to tie his shoe. An ambulance pulled up almost instantly. All he had to do was follow the paramedics and the gurney inside the doors, wringing his hands and looking like a concerned relative of the man on the gurney, who looked like he'd sustained some sort of gunshot wound.

It was easy to get lost in the confusion, and Mallen made his way to the doors that led out of the area. Went immediately to the nearest bank of elevators. Pushed the up button. He was nervous, but there were just too many people moving in and out of the ward for anyone to notice him. Hell, he was sure the woman behind the reception desk had already forgotten about him. He was just one more strung-out-looking guy looking for a relative. How many of them did she see every day?

The elevator car arrived and he entered. As it went up to the sixth floor, he got ready for what might come next: not being able to enter Tracy's room. It would all depend on how fast the connection had been made to Tracy's last name. Or, he figured, how busy the hospital staff were.

The elevator doors opened with a hiss and he got out and walked down the hall like he knew what the fuck he was doing. That often got you past a lot of guards, under a lot of different situations. Wish he could've found a name badge to use. As it turned out, he was in luck: there was no one outside of 619. He checked the names on the room board outside the door. There was Tracy's name. He pushed through the door and went inside.

She was in the bed by the window. The nearer bed was empty, but recently so, judging by the rumpled sheets and blankets and the half-empty water jug. Tracy lay there, hooked up to an IV. She looked only a little better than when he'd pulled her out of the SUV back in the warehouse. Someone had cleaned off her make-up, and in the hospital gown, she looked younger than the nineteen-year-old he knew her to be. Her eyes were closed, and she looked asleep. As he got closer, he could see that her vitals were stable and pretty strong. That was good news. He moved closer to the bed, and that was when her eyelids fluttered and then opened. She didn't recognize him. Went for the nurse call button, and he put up a hand.

"Wait, Tracy. I'm a friend. I was the guy who found you last night and took you out of the warehouse."

"Warehouse?"

"Right. On the waterfront. You were in a black SUV. There was an explosion, then a fire."

"Right ... I was in the backseat, I think."

"Yes, that's right. I'm Mallen. Mark Mallen. I know your mother."

It was a moment before she said, "Why do you know my mother? How do you know her?"

"She ever mention the name Chris Mallen? Or maybe Chris Shaw?"

"Yeah," she said. "My mother talked about someone she went to college with. Some friend. Chris. Chris ... Mallen."

"Right," he said. "I'm Chris's ... I'm a friend of Chris's. Her ex-husband. I used to be a cop."

"What happened? Why did you stop being a cop?"

For an answer he rolled up his sleeves. Figured real honesty would resonate more right now than any other road. Showed her the scars on the crook of his right arm. The scars that were almost gone, but were still with him. Sometimes it seemed that they would never fade. And once more he thought that he would be okay with that. That he would *need* it to be that way. The scars seemed to have an impact. Tracy looked at him differently now. Like he wasn't one of "them." Instead, he was someone who she might be able to talk to.

"How're you feeling?" he asked.

"I hurt."

"I bet. Tracy...I..." Then it was difficult to continue. How to bring it up? How to talk about it? "I...saw—"

"You saw?" Tears came to her eyes.

He caught it. Knew then. "No," he said, quietly. "I saw the... the other women. You mean they made a video of you?"

Brief nod. She began to cry. Really cry. Like she was trying to cry out more than just her anguish—the anguish of everyone she'd ever met or heard about. He wasn't sure what to do. Went and pulled a couple tissues from the nearby box. Handed them to her.

"Tracy, do you know if your parents know you're here?"

She wiped at her eyes. Shrugged. "I've been pretty out of it, so I don't really know. I think my mother was here. I can't be sure."

That could change things for him. Richard Goldman, or Liz, might tell him it was all over and thank you, but goodbye. He had to get some information. There were too many things going on, too many people in danger.

"Tracy," he began. "Yeah, I've seen the videos. I saw the deal go down with Teddy Mac, and how it all went south. Why were you there? Were you part of the deal? Do you know?"

"No," she replied as she folded and unfolded the tissue in her hands. "I think...I think they were going to turn me over to the man they were meeting. When they had finished... filming me, one of the men told me to tell my father about it. That 'he'd know what to do'. I was drugged right after that. I don't remember anything else."

He thought about it. Teddy would've let her go once they'd given her to him. Probably would've had someone do what Mallen ended up doing: bring her here. She would've gotten back to her family and then she'd be able to tell her father all about it. It was one hell of a warning to Mayor Goldman.

Tracy started to cry again. Like she was caught in a nightmare she couldn't get out of. He wondered if she would ever be able to get to a place where she could deal with what had happened. He knew he had no conception of how badly she'd been abused, but using the videos as a benchmark, it must've been off the charts. *One more reason to bring it all crashing down on the bastards behind it*, he thought. *One more reason to hate them.* He wished he knew how much time he had before he'd be interrupted. Glanced at the door, then said to her, "It was Jinky that got you hooked up with it all, wasn't it?"

A nod. "Minta introduced me to Jinky. I thought they liked me, you know? Thought I was cool. I'd never been cool before. Just Richard Goldman's daughter."

"Did you ever see any of the men?"

"No, they wore masks." A huge shudder wracked her body then. She put her face in her hands.

"Are you positive about what they wanted you to tell your father?"

"Yes. I'm sure that's what he told me." Her eyes went distant then, going back to that time. Tears came to her eyes.

A nurse entered then, along with another woman dressed in street clothes, holding a laptop and some papers. Probably a rape counselor. The nurse spoke to Mallen. "We've brought someone to speak with her. I'm sorry, but you'll have to wait outside."

"Sure thing," he said as he moved for the door.

"Mallen?" Tracy said. He turned to face her. "Thank you for rescuing me."

Smiled at her. "My pleasure, Tracy. I'll be just outside, okay?"

"Okay."

He went out into the hallway. *So* wanted a cigarette. Figured he needed to call Gato and see how he was doing, but got voicemail.

That was okay, he reasoned. It was natural. Hell, he'd probably just got there and was maybe catching some shut eye. Left a message for Gato to call him. Hung up just in time to turn and find himself face to face with Mayor Richard Goldman, Liz, and a couple of men in suits. Mallen recognized the two men immediately as being Darkstar operatives. It was the suits, the way they wore them. He'd seen enough of them by now to know them on sight.

"Mallen," Goldman said to him, looking and sounding nervous. On edge. "I thought we understood each other."

"Yeah, well ... *understanding* is a relative term, most times."

Goldman and Liz went to Tracy's hospital room door, but Mallen stopped them. "She's in there with a rape counselor."

Goldman went white as a sheet. Liz forced back tears. "A ... rape counselor?" Goldman said, sounding like he'd eaten a mouthful of sand.

Mallen only nodded. "I spoke with her, Mr. Mayor. She had some interesting things to say to me."

The two Darkstar employees came a little closer. And really, if Mallen needed anything more to go on, it was that simple move that said it all and confirmed a helluva lot. One of the operatives— a tall, thin man with a whisper of a moustache and John Lennon glasses—moved up closer. "The girl's parents are here now, junkie. You can go."

"Ex-junkie, asshole." Then to Goldman he said quietly, "You don't want to know what she told me?"

"I need to see my daughter," Liz urged Goldman. He nodded to her, and she went inside. Mallen couldn't keep her out. She *was* Tracy's mother. He had no real jurisdiction on this, nothing more than what he could fabricate on his own.

Goldman waited until she was gone. He'd gone even more ashen. Suddenly looked beaten. "What...what did she tell you?" he said just above a whisper. The Darkstar men continued to stand there. One of them said, "Mr. Mayor? Remember what my supervisor discussed with you earlier?"

"I do," came the beaten-sounding reply.

For a response, the man only nodded. Then the two men went and stood out of earshot.

Goldman then said, almost like a man getting a sentence pronounced on him, "What did she tell you?"

"You sound like you already know. What *do* you know, Mr. Mayor?"

Goldman glanced over at the two Darkstar men. Said quietly, "What I know, Mallen, is way beyond your abilities. I don't care whether you're clean now or not. I've looked at your record; it's impressive. However, it doesn't measure up to what's happening, or what's happened. For the safety of my family, please just drop it and go away."

"I can't do that. You see...I have the films."

Goldman looked like he'd just been stabbed in the gut with a fencepost. "You...you've seen them?"

"Yeah. I have. What sort of sick shit are you mixed up in? I could blow it all up for you, Mr. Mayor. All I need to do is run to the nearest newspaper. Fuck man, the nearest blogger."

"You can't do that! These men would kill my wife and daughter." Goldman's voice was low but desperate.

"We can call in the FBI. Get you and your family safe."

"It's impossible, don't you see? These men? This organization? They're everywhere. We'd never really be sure. All I can do is what I am doing to ensure the safety of my family." Then he added, "What … what did Tracy tell you?"

"That the man who raped and abused her told her that you would know what to do. They were going to let her go, so their message would get back to you. There was an explosion, but she made it out of there. And now their message has been delivered, Mr. Mayor."

So, it was blackmail. They had a hook into Goldman. That hook would get them a free pass in the city. To make as many films here as they wanted to. Kill as many women as they wanted to. But, as Mallen stood there, he realized that kidnapping Tracy wouldn't be enough. Not if they were using her as a message by letting her go. No, there had to be more. And then he got it.

"You were in the films, weren't you?" Mallen said.

Goldman shook his head. Turned away. "Not… not in those. In another. One where I had sex with a woman who was tied up. She struggled. I fought back. I…I…held her down while she struggled."

"You raped her?" He took a step toward the mayor. The Darkstar men began to edge their way over. "You raped a girl on film for kicks, and they used that against you. That's it, isn't it?"

Goldman's shoulders sagged. "Yes. It was the only time I did that. They… made me feel like I belonged to this group, and—"

And that was when the Darkstar guys came back into the picture. "Mr. Mayor. You should go be with your daughter."

Goldman nodded. Looked once more at Mallen, like a small child told by his parents to go and clean his room. Mallen wondered how much more Goldman knew. He made a move to follow Goldman into Tracy's room, but the security men stopped him with their hands on his shoulders. He tried to shrug them off, then felt the stab of a gun pressed into his back.

"Careful now," the man with the glasses told Mallen. "We're just going to go over to the elevator and take you out of here. If we have to do it with you on a gurney, we will, Mallen. Your call." He had no choice but to comply. He looked back one last time at Tracy's door. Wondered how it would all fall out as he was pushed down the hall to the elevator. The doors opened, and the three men went inside. One in front of Mallen, one behind. The Darkstar operative behind continued to jam the gun into his back.

The elevator hit the lobby, and Mallen allowed himself to be walked outside. No business starting something in the lobby, he figured. Once outside, they walked him toward the parking garage. It was a dark, cloudy day. Perfect for the mood that was overwhelming him. He had to try something, anything, to let these guys know he wasn't an easy mark. He stumbled for a moment, like he'd caught his shoe, then rammed his elbow around into the face of the man behind him. The man went down, dropping his gun and Mallen went for it, but not before he felt the pain of a gun barrel jammed into the back of his head.

"Either way you want it, you junkie loser fuck, I'll give it to you. I could shoot you here and walk tomorrow morning. But if you want to live, stay away from Goldman, got it?"

Mallen nodded, put his hands where they could be seen. Stood upright. The security man helped his partner to his feet. Both men looked daggers at him. One then moved behind him as the other came forward. The man he'd clubbed—the one who'd moved be-hind him—was the one he knew would make a move. They moved him to the parking structure. The corner. Then it wasn't long in coming. He heard a foot scuff on the concrete and he ducked out of the way of a fist he imagined was coming. He used his momentum to throw himself into the man in front of him, the one with the gun trained on him. They both went down to the ground, the gun skittering away and underneath a nearby Honda.

But that was Mallen's only victory. He was immediately seized by the second man and pulled to his feet. Then it was all a hail of fists and feet and he was down on his hands and knees, and then blackness. The only thing he felt he could take solace in was the fact that they must be under orders to not kill him, and if they weren't going to kill him, then he was going to keep coming and coming after them. That was the last thing he remembered before he was beaten into darkness.

———

He woke up to the vision of a front door. It took him a moment to realize that it belonged to him. He'd been left on the porch of his floating home. Glanced up at the sky. Looked like early afternoon. Groaned as he got to his feet.

"You certainly are one of the more interesting tenants, Mallen," said Mr. Gregor as he walked up, a beer in his hand. He held the beer out to Mallen, who took it gratefully.

"Reads like interesting, maybe," Mallen replied as he took a long pull. "You the one that put me here?"

"No, I just found you there. Not but a few minutes ago. Heard a car pull up, along with my truck. Then feet scuffing along the dock. Looked out. There you were, between two guys that looked like poster children for government agents. You would've passed for drunk, except for the blood," he added with an admiring smile.

"You have my thanks. I owe ya." Mallen toasted with the beer.

"You don't owe me shit, Mallen. Just find the men that did this to you and give 'em back better than you got."

He thought about that. There wasn't much he could do regarding Tracy. Her parents would have the final say on who she spoke to, even if she was over eighteen. The mayor had told him to back the fuck off, as had Liz.

The two men who beat him, though … Well, that was different. "You didn't happen to get a license plate did you?"

A weathered smile creased Gregor's thin lips. He pulled out a slip of paper. "7R06232, belonging to a black Cadillac Escalade, looking almost brand-new. Smoked windows too."

That sounded like a cookie cutter version of the ones at the pier. And that figured. He needed more on Darkstar, and that was a fact. Got slowly to his feet, his upper back and shoulders on fire. Felt like someone had taken a sledge to his neck. Drained the beer as he went inside the house. Mr. Gregor followed him in. Mallen took off his coat and tossed it onto the kitchen counter. Ran his head under the sink faucet. Took a nearby dishtowel and dried his hair as best he could. Then he went over to the kitchen cabinet and got out the Glock he'd put in there earlier. Checked the clip and put it in his coat pocket.

Gregor let out a low whistle when he saw the gun. "If the police ask, I did not see that loaded firearm, okay? I want to help ya, but … well, that's something else."

Mallen smiled back at him. "Don't worry. I'm on the side of the angels in this, as I think you've guessed. Trust me, I'll never ask you to do something you're not comfortable doing." He went and changed into a new shirt then laced up his boots and shrugged grimacing into his coat. The weight of the Glock was a welcome thing.

"Thanks for the help. I appreciate it," he said as he went to the door, Gregor following.

"What are neighbors for, right?" As they walked out onto the dock, Gregor said, "I'm guessin' you'll be needin' my truck just a bit longer, right?"

"It's lookin' that way."

"Then have at it. Just be sure you win the next round, Mallen, okay?"

TWENTY-SIX

AFTER GREGOR LEFT, MALLEN pulled out his phone and called Chris. Wanted to give an update on Tracy. She answered quickly, and her voice had that strident quality that it got when she was stressed about something he'd done. "Bad time?" he said.

"Depends on what you're asking."

"Tracy Goldman is still in the hospital. She'd been through the ringer and back again, but I talked with her earlier this morning, and I think she'll be all right. I mean, physically all right."

"Liz told me about it when I spoke to her a little while ago." There was no relief there.

"I also spoke with Mayor Goldman."

"I heard about that too. He told you to leave it in their hands now."

"You could put it that way, yeah."

"They took her home."

"What?" He thought of Tracy with her father. The man who, by his own admission, was in one of the videos and was being blackmailed by the very men who'd hurt his daughter. He then thought of the two Darkstar jackoffs who'd beat on him. He could bet those men went home with the Goldmans to keep tabs on them. Keep Goldman in line. *Jesus*, he thought, *what kind of power do these guys have that they can just take a girl out of the hospital?*

"Liz told me they put Tracy in her bedroom, set it up like a sick room. Brought in a home health nurse to care for her."

"How did Liz sound?"

"Distraught. Tired. What's going on, Mark?"

"I really don't think I should tell you right now, Chris. The Goldmans are into something deep. Something deep and ugly. I have to help them. I'm doing it for Liz and Tracy ... that I *can* tell you."

"Not for Richard?"

"No, not him. He's the reason it's dark and ugly."

"Mark. If you think you can help Liz, then please help her. She's one of my oldest friends and she never was any good at controlling her life. If she needs help, please do what you can, okay?"

"I will, trust me." A thought then occurred to him. "Did Liz say if Mr. Mayor was home with her and Tracy?"

"He's not. He's at City Hall for a big budget meeting."

"Thanks," he said.

"Remember that Anna's looking forward to seeing you next weekend. Stay alive so you can be there."

"I will. See ya," he said and hung up the call. So Liz was alone with Tracy, except for a couple of those Darkstar guys. He bet that Liz *wanted* to talk to him, if she thought she could do so safely. He could tell she was really on his side. Hell, she'd given him the go ahead to keep pushing. And he'd keep doing that, no matter what.

As he walked to Gregor's truck, he put his hand around the butt of the Glock in his coat pocket. These guys would have to pay for what they did to him. He was tired of being beaten on.

———

The Goldman home was at the very top of 25th Avenue, overlooking the Presidio and the Pacific Ocean. A renovated Mediterranean villa, complete with gate and thick walls on the street side. He parked back at the beginning of the block. Quietly walked towards the house. He glanced through the gate. Saw that the driveway was populated by the same black SUV with smoked windows that Mr. Gregor had described to him. He checked the plate number. Yeah, it was the same one. There was also a yellow, late-model Mercedes parked nearby. That was probably Liz's.

He thought hard about how to enter. He needed a plan, and fast. Couldn't just go the fuck up and knock, not with those goons there. Couldn't break in either. Obviously, the goons would need to be put on the sidelines. He smiled at that. It had been a long time since an option like that was actually an option. Had it really only been a few months ago that he'd been writhing in a drunk tank, sweating out the remains of his heroin addiction?

After a moment figuring out what he was going to do, he moved to the thick wall, as far away from the lights as possible. Quiet like a whisper, he pulled himself atop the wall. There was no dog, and he took that as a happy sign. Dropped into the back yard. Scanned for security cameras. There were none, though he noticed some crates piled by the back door. The sides of the crates read Darkstar Security. So, better security was coming, compliments of the black-mailers themselves. How fucking generous of them. He sidled over to the back door and peered through the gap in the small curtained window there. One of the Darkstar assholes sat at the kitchen table, reading a magazine, coffee near at hand. Liz and Tracy would be upstairs in a bedroom. He hoped goon number two was in the front of the house, in case someone came that way. That would make sense.

Mallen grabbed up some pebbles and dirt. Crept back to the door then flattened against the wall, just to the right of the door handle. Crouched down and sluiced the gravel and rocks over the back porch, but in a concentrated manner. Cut it off sharp, like someone trying to cut off the sound of being discovered. He heard a chair move inside. The creak of a board. Saw a shadow appear on the back porch, then heard more than saw the back door opening. Of course the guy would check. He would have to ere on the side of caution.

The shadow appeared in starker relief now that it was no longer diffused by the back door window. The man appeared as he stepped forward, gun already in hand. Mallen sprung up, pressing the Glock's muzzle to the man's temple. Time froze. He could almost see the *aw shit* above the man's head like some cartoon balloon.

"Easy, pal," Mallen said to the man as he took his sidearm. "I'm here to play it safe. You're cool. We're good."

"Like hell."

"Now don't be that way," he said as he frisked the man quickly. Came away with a set of cuffs and two spare clips. "Turn around," he said.

The man did so. Mallen cuffed him, then walked him back off the porch. Quietly pulled him away from the house lights. It was steadily getting darker and soon it was possible that the exterior lights would be on motion sensors. He had to get inside, and quickly. Mallen could tell by the way the man walked and the sag of his shoulders that he thought he was going to be executed. Mallen let him think so.

When they were in a pool of blackness made by the wall and some Japanese maples, Mallen stopped the man as he hoisted up the Glock, butt-first. "Just need you out of the picture for a while, pal," he said, then slammed the man at the base of the neck. He went down like a lead weight. Mallen took the man's tie off and gagged him with it. Left him there and went back to the porch. Crept into the house. It was quiet and still. Padded to the door that led out of the kitchen and peered into the next room. The dining room. Huge, dark wood table there. Country-style sideboards. He could see into the living room. Standing there, looking out the large picture window, was the other Darkstar man. Had his back to Mallen.

Mallen decided to let that man be. There was too much ground between the two of them for any hope of getting close enough to take him out. And he didn't have time to wait for the guy to go use the bathroom or decide he needed a glass of water.

He crept back into the kitchen and went up the back stairs, silent as night. Got to the upper floor. Found himself in a hallway. Most of the doors were closed, but the one on his right, two down, was open. He thought he heard a woman's voice coming from that room. Soft and consoling. He figured it would probably be Liz. Mallen put his gun back in his pocket. Smoothed down his hair. Prayed that she would feel more kindly toward him than the Darkstar boys did. He peered inside the room. It really did resemble a hospital room, complete with IV and heart rate monitor. He didn't see the nurse that Chris had mentioned. Maybe she was nearby in one of the other rooms, taking a break. Tracy was in the bed. Looked like she was sleeping. Liz sat on the edge, gazing at her daughter. Liz had a couple crumpled Kleenex in her hand. Her other hand was on Tracy's leg, and she was murmuring soothing words to her. The picture of a worried mother.

Malen walked into the room, softly shutting the door behind him. Put his index finger up to his mouth as Liz rose off the bed. He wasn't sure, but he could swear Liz looked relieved to see him.

"Liz," he said to her quietly, "there's a man in your living room, guarding the front of the house. His buddy is out in the back yard, sleeping peacefully. Sorry to enter with so much drama, but well … I'm sure you can understand, yeah? Things have gotten away from us a bit. Did your husband tell you that we talked some more back at the hospital?"

"Yes, he did."

Malen wondered just how much the good mayor had told her. "You were the one that called me into this. You gotta know that I just can't go away. I was a cop before I was a junkie, and a man before I was both. I can help you and Tracy, and I intend to."

Liz sat back down on the bed then. Nodded. Looked again at her daughter. "I can't believe what they did to her. Animals. Sick, filthy animals."

"Exactly. Do you know anything about this?"

"Just that it all started when Richard began his run for the mayor's office. He told me he was getting a lot of donations from this Darkstar place. Also from some out-of-state companies. He thinks now that they were just funneling money for Darkstar. He was also getting a lot of support from people in the justice system."

He thought back to the tape he'd watched with Gato. "Judge Toland Reynolds, right? I bet he really helped guide Richard through the minefield that a mayor's race can be."

"That's right," she said. "What do *you* know, Mallen? Is my husband in more trouble than he's letting on?"

"Yeah, I think he is."

"What sort of trouble is it? Can you tell me?"

"Not now, Liz. I will, trust me, but not until this is over." Now was about exposing these maniacs and destroying their whole sick organization.

"Okay. I'm trusting you that you'll keep your word, Mallen."

"I will. I promise." He then went to the bed. Looked down at Tracy. "Darkstar get her out of the hospital?"

"Yes."

"Has she been conscious at all? Talk to you at all?"

"No. After the counselor left, a nurse at the hospital gave her something so she'd sleep. She's been out since." She came and sat at the foot of the bed. "Like you said to Chris: it's going to be a long road back for her."

Longer than any of us think. "And you're sure it was Judge Reynolds that helped your husband?"

"Yes."

"Okay, thanks. I'll be in touch. Don't lose faith, Liz."

He left the room and crept back down the hallway, then down the stairs. The Darkstar man wasn't on the couch. Shit. He wondered if the guy was in the kitchen, but quickly heard a nearby toilet flush. Of course there would be a downstairs bathroom. Mallen couldn't help himself. Thought back to the beating he'd taken from these guys. He moved quickly over to where the sound had come from. Found the door he was looking for. Heard the water running in the sink. He stood right there, right in front of the door, left hand balled into a fist. After a couple seconds the door opened, and Mallen put everything he had behind a punch that went straight for the man's face. He heard cartilage crack as the man fell backward, his nose broken. There was a large thud as the man's head bounced off the tile. Out like a light. Hot damn. Mallen rubbed his knuckles. Felt like he'd paid off the debt he owed those two bozos, if only a little. Turned off the bathroom light and closed the door. Exited quickly. Before he left the grounds, he went and checked on the man he'd left in the woods. Still out but with a steady pulse.

Made his truck and jumped inside. He'd parked on a hill, so all he had to do was release the parking brake, put it in neutral, and let the vehicle roll backward down the hill, using the brakes for guidance. *Thank fuck for manual brakes*, he thought. Made the intersection and only then started the engine. He put the car in gear and sped off into the night. He figured it would be a good idea to stay away from home. For maybe a long while. Wondered where he could stay. Then it came to him.

Yeah, he thought, *that could work, at least for a night.*

TWENTY-SEVEN

EARLIER THAT AFTERNOON, GATO did another cruise of the south Los Angeles hood. He'd been driving around these streets for what felt like twenty-four hours straight since he'd arrived to hunt for Lupe, though it had only been six or so. He'd contacted a few people he knew, made some inquiries. Time and time again, he was met with the same answer: No one had seen her, no one had heard about her even being in town. That worried him. Did that *pendejo* Teddy Mac actually have the balls to lie to him and Mallen? He was beginning to believe that she either never came down here or was way underground. He knew his sister. She had a strong will. *Ella era una mujer fuerte.* And if anything, she wasn't dumb.

His hands tightened on the steering wheel. If Teddy had played him and Mallen for fools, he'd dig that fucker's body up, piss all over it, then toss it to the dogs. He was about to call Mallen and update him on his lack of progress when his phone rang. Gato smiled as he pulled the cell out of his pocket. Figured it would be Mallen with some more of his private detective shit. Turned out it wasn't. It was one of his old buddies from down here, from his L.A. days. Reyes.

"Yo, Reyes," he said into the phone.

"Gato," came the voice. "I think I got something, bro."

"Yeah? What? What do you think you have?"

"I have a line on Lupe, man. At least, I think I do."

"Okay, well what the fuck is it, man?"

"You pay, right?"

"Yeah, I pay. Said I would, didn't I? Of course I'll pay." *Idiota.*

"Then meet me at Mar Vista Lanes, bro. I'll take you to the man who can take you to Lupe."

"I'll be there in about thirty," Gato replied.

"You'll find me in the parking lot, bro. Coolness."

He had to stop at a red light and was glad that he did. Something about the call … he didn't like it. All of a sudden it felt too easy. Yeah, he'd met Reyes over ten years ago. And they'd even kept up a little. Reyes had looked him up in the past, just to say hello. Both of them had been in jail about the same time too. That can sort of make guys into street brothers. That was why he'd called on Reyes when he got into L.A. But now he was wondering: Was it just money that Reyes was after? Maybe the bro had hit on hard times. Fuck man, lots of people had. If it was that, then Gato would help him. Maybe he just didn't want to ask for the dollars over the phone. Yeah, he could understand Reyes feeling that way.

———

At this time of day on a weekday, the bowling alley wasn't very busy. Only a few cars in the cracked asphalt lot. There was Reyes though, standing near an old, pretty beat-up Dodge Dart. The car looked like it had once been cherry, but that was probably years ago. Reyes's hair was way longer than Gato remembered, and it now seemed like a nest for some demonic bird. The guy hadn't shaved in days, either. Shirt looked dirty. Gato wondered if Reyes was using again. He knew if that was the fucking case, then whatever came out of this wouldn't be a real lead to Lupe.

Gato pulled up and threw open the passenger side door. Reyes leaned in to look at him. Smiled. "Gato, you look good, man."

"Thanks, Reyes. You look like it's been rough. You okay?"

"Yeah, yeah... been fine. Just out of work is all."

Gato wasn't buying it. Reyes looked strung out. He knew that look like a farmer can tell a sick calf. "So, where do we go? You really have a line on Lupe? Don't take this wrong, but you don't look like you could have a line on shit right now." Reyes forced a laugh. Gato could see he'd put the man off, and there was always the outside chance he really was trying to help. "Sorry, Reyes," Gato said. "It's just been a long ass day, you know? I'm just worried about *mi hermana*."

Reyes got in the car, slamming the door behind him. Smiled again. "Well, that's why I'm here, bro. To help you, man. I know where she's been staying."

"And where's that?"

"Over in Willowbrook, this side of Compton. She's been holed up with some girlfriends off One-Twentieth."

Gato put the car in gear. Decided on asking a question that would seem innocent and honest. "Why she been holed up at all, man? You know why?"

"No man, I don't. All I heard was that she ran from the north because of something heavy. She's been trying to lose herself in this huge pile of shit called a city."

The apartment building seemed exactly like every other apartment building in the hood. It was tagged all to hell, had tape keeping the cracked windows together, and weeds that had long ago choked out the crab grass. At the front was a dented and rusty fence with a missing gate and a broken intercom system. Gato started to have a very bad feeling about it all. He reached under his seat and pulled out his Colt 9.

"Hey man," Reyes said, "we're good, man. No need for the paranoia."

"Bro, if you'd seen the shit I've seen the last few days? You wouldn't go anywhere without a loaded baby. The world is a bad fucking place these days." Opened his car door. "Lead on, *vato*."

Reyes hesitated, which tightened Gato's nerves even more. Reyes got out and led him up the walk and through the open gateway. They were now in the shadowy, ill-kept inner courtyard. As he walked behind Reyes, Gato's radar went into high gear. *What the fuck is going on?* Would Reyes end up saying to him, "Oh, man … she's already gone!" and then ask for payment? Was all this just a fucking act so he could get some drug money? Gato tucked his shirt behind the butt of the Colt so he could pull it out fast, if necessary.

Reyes walked him past all the first-floor apartments, and started to lead him toward the back gate. *Fuck this shit*, he thought. This was going nowhere fast, and he'd had enough. He lunged forward, catching Reyes around the neck with an arm. Put a chokehold on Reyes. Pulled him back away from the rear gate.

"Reyes," he said softly, in a friendly voice, "you make me nervous man. Walking past all those apartments. Where is my sister? Is she even here? I no longer think so."

Reyes began to sweat. Shake his head. "No, man! She's here! Just in a small place in the back, is all! Come on, man … I wouldn't lie to you."

"Except for enough money, right?"

And before Reyes could answer, Gato heard the rush of soft-soled shoes coming up behind him. He tried to spin around, to use Reyes as a shield, but he was too late. Something crashed down on the side of his head and he let go of Reyes, who then pushed him to the ground. There was the feeling of a blow to his stomach. Felt his gun yanked from his waistband. Had the impression it was Reyes that did that. Man, he'd really blown it. Now Mallen would be all on his own against all of this. And his friend wasn't even so strong that he could stay clean forever. Not yet.

There was another hit, this time against his head, and his world went dark.

———

Gato woke to pain in his head like a thousand people jumping on his brain. He rolled onto his back, only then realizing he was on the ground and still on the property where Reyes had led him. Because that's what had happened: he'd been led right into the trap. But why would these guys want his sister so bad?

But then again, what if it wasn't about his sister?

That train of thought didn't even get to leave the station before he heard someone walk up and his side erupted in agony from a kick. Through his blurred vision he made out three figures: one was

Reyes, standing off to the side and looking like he wanted to be any-where else; the other two guys were dressed just like how he imag-ined the fuckin' CIA would look if they tried to blend in, in South L.A. Meaning they looked like white boys dressed like white rapper wannabes. Shirts untucked to look "cool," and baggy pants almost perfectly baggy. Like they'd never worn them before. Both were me-dium build, short blondish hair. Almost interchangeable. Not CIA, though. The CIA would've fit in better. These guys were something else. And for some reason, that scared him.

"Where's the tapes you stole?" said the first one.

The tapes? Not his sister? They didn't even care about her leav-ing Teddy Mac. And that also scared him.

"Tapes?" he said. He tried to sit up but was pushed back down. "I don't know no tapes, man. I'm down here tracking down *mi hermana*."

"Well," said the man to his partner, "we have to assume then that this asshole left the tapes with his crazy old mother, don't we?" He looked down at Gato, and said, "You just stay here, and we'll go check." Silence reigned then. Gato went cold all over, because he could feel these fuckers were not bluffing. If they bothered to track him down over five hundred miles away, and could do that success-fully, they'd kill his *madre* without the blink of an eye.

He was fucked and knew it, just like he knew he'd never see an-other sunrise if he played this wrong. He tried to force himself to his feet, but one of the men put a shoe on his chest. He grabbed it and twisted, pushing upward. The man fell backward, landing hard as Gato leapt up. A gun was produced by the other man, and Reyes looked uncomfortable then. The guy was sweating like the pig he was.

Gato froze, hands outward. "Okay, *vato*, okay. But man, you mentioned killing my sainted *madre*. What you want me to do? Draw you a fuckin' map, bro?"

The man almost smiled. "The tapes. We know you and that ex-cop junkie fuckhead have them. You got them from the blow-up at the warehouse. You didn't send them to the cops, or we'd know. You didn't send them to the press, or we'd know. So, you still have them. Why? Are you just stupid, or angling to muscle in on what Teddy wanted?"

Gato shrugged. "Teddy was just a fuckin' dirtbag pimp, man. If he was stupid enough to handle it all the way he did, then why not someone else come in and angle for something better, right?" Was that Reyes, slowly moving to his right, moving behind the man? The second man had gotten back to his feet and was looking like he wanted to break Gato into little pieces. Produced a straight knife from behind his waist. Yeah, that guy would want to hurt him. Gato figured at that point that he had to keep them talking as long as possible.

"So, where are the tapes?"

Gato shook his head. "Not until a deal is on the table." Knew it was weak, but it was all he could think up on the fly.

The man with the knife shook his head. "Spic, you'll never live to see *any* money, or another morning. If you tell me what we want to know, then maybe I'll be nice and kill you fast. Don't you get what's going on here? This isn't some gang, street-type bullshit. This is beyond your understanding, you little piece of shit. And—"

And that was when Reyes pulled a gun on them all. In fact, it was Gato's gun. Reyes stood back, saying, "You two just stop what you're doing, right now. We didn't talk about this. All you said was find him and bring him here. You said he'd have something you could lift off him, man! I didn't sign up for the rest of this!"

Both men froze, shocked. Then the white guy with the gun made a bad mistake. He turned, bringing his gun around to point at Reyes. Maybe he thought Reyes wouldn't shoot. Whatever it was, that was all Gato needed. He jumped at the chance, grabbing the man's wrist with one hand as he chopped at that wrist with the other. The gun came loose as the other man leaned in to stab him, but then the air was blasted apart from the gun in Reyes's hand. The man with the knife fell backward, blood exploding from his stomach. Not easy to miss at less than five feet. Gato punched the other man in the ear to keep him from going for the gun that had fallen to the ground. Gato then scooped the gun up and viciously slapped the man across the face with it. The man fell to one knee with a groan and Gato slapped him a couple more times, using the gun as a bludgeon. The man fell to the concrete, dazed and confused.

Gato looked over at Reyes. Reyes just stood there, gazing down at the man he'd shot dead. His face was blank. Gato swooped in and took his gun back. Grabbed Reyes by the shirt and dragged him away, back the way they'd originally come. "Come on, *pendejo!* We need to make tracks!" He shoved and pulled Reyes back through the apartment complex. Checked through the fence. No sounds of sirens, or of anyone else. He walked Reyes calmly to his car and put him in the passenger seat. Got behind the wheel and drove away fast, but not fast enough to draw attention. Or so he hoped.

A mile later, lost among the traffic maze of Los Angeles, Gato said, "Thank you for saving my life, *pendejo.*"

Reyes had stared straight ahead the entire time. Shook his head. "I didn't think they'd fuck you up like that. If they'd do that to you, man, no doubt I was next."

"So you did it for your own ass?" Gato asked.

"Yeah, man. I guess I did."

"Good enough," Gato replied with a shrug. He then pulled out his phone and dialed Mallen's number. A recording came on, saying the phone he'd dialed was out of range. He didn't like what that might mean. Dialed his house. His mother answered, and relief flooded him.

"*Mamá*," he said, "I don't have time to explain, but have any men come to the house looking for me or Mallen?"

"No, Eduardo. Why do you ask me that? Are you in trouble?"

"When one fights on the side of the angels, *Mamacita*, one can usually be in trouble. Me and Mallen? Well ... we are."

"Have you found my Lupe?"

"No, I'm sorry, *Mamá*." He glanced over at Reyes. "I thought I had a lead, but it turned out to only lead to some trouble. That's why I called you. These people that are trouble might try to hurt you to get to me. I need you to go and stay with your brother." He cringed then, knowing the firestorm to come.

And he unfortunately wasn't disappointed. She let go with a string of Spanish swear words that would make any gang member in east L.A. blush. He knew she didn't want to leave her home. Why would she? And of course she wouldn't be able to understand the reasons why she had to do what he asked. He held up at a light, put his hand over the receiver and said to Reyes, "Get the fuck out. Consider us even. You gave me back my life, and now I give you back yours."

"Gato—"

"Shut the fuck up, *pendejo,* and get the fuck out of my car. Don't ever let me find your name associated with *any* business of mine, or I'll forget this conversation."

Reyes looked for a moment like he wanted to say more. Almost like he needed to say more. The light changed. A horn behind them sounded. Reyes leapt out and slammed the door as Gato gunned the engine. He focused back on his mother, who had finally calmed down and was asking why didn't he answer her.

"Sorry, *Mamá,* I was stuck in traffic. I'm clear now."

"I don't like your uncle. You know that."

"I do know that. But it's a matter of your life. He'll understand. You know he will." It was true. Uncle Peche had been through the ringer: gangs, drugs, prison, being shot numerous times. All before he'd hit thirty. He'd finally gotten clean and found solace not in the Lord, but in music. He now played a mean blues piano. Was living well, with a small family that cared for and loved him. His mother would be safe there. Peche would know how to handle his little sister.

After a moment, she said to him, "Okay, Eduardo. I call Peche."

"No, *Mamá.* I'll call him. You just wait there and he'll come and get you. He will probably call first. But you just wait there and you don't open the door for anyone, okay? No one except Peche."

"Okay, okay. But you better find Lupe though. *La necesitamos.*"

"I know, *Mamá,* I know. Either me or Peche will call you back. Check the caller ID before answering. Got that? You check."

"Okay, okay! You act like I'm some crazy old lady."

"No, I don't. Just my crazy old *Mamacita.*" He was happy to hear a chuckle on the other end of the phone. He ended the call and dialed his uncle's number. The call was brief; his uncle had never lost that ability to hit the ground running when the shit hit the fan.

Peche listened quietly as Gato explained as much as he could, saying that what he'd found himself in while trying to find Lupe was bad. Told how this had landed him and his mother in the shit. It was silent on the other end of the phone for only a few seconds after he'd finished; then his uncle told him he would run over to their house and pick up his sister. She'd be safe with him, he assured Gato. Also told Gato he was happy to hear that he was staying clean, if not staying out of trouble. Gato thanked him and hung up.

His head throbbed and his vision was blurring by this point. He needed some down time before he headed back north. He knew he would need all his energy if he were to find Mallen. He tried the number again, if only on a whim, and again got a recording saying the number was out of range. He swore as he cut the call and tossed the phone onto the seat beside him. He wanted to be away, driving through the night, on the road to finding his friend. But he knew he couldn't do it without some rest first. He decided to drive north, get out of L.A. proper, and find a rest stop. If traffic was generous, he figured he could manage another hour or so before he'd be too gone to drive.

Why didn't Mallen answer?

TWENTY-EIGHT

MALLEN STARED AT THE ceiling above him, wishing for sleep. The ceiling belonged to the back room of the Cornerstone. This decrepit little waystation for booze and bags of prized pretzels was the only place he could come up with that felt like no one would be able to find him. He lay on the floor, on a couple blankets, smoking and thinking about what had been going down, and what his next move should be. He needed to figure out a way to make the most of the chip he had: the tapes. The more he learned about the people behind this and how high up it went, including judges and CEOs and who the fuck else, the less inclined he was to even try and go back to pick up the tapes. His enemies seemed to be everyfuckingwhere.

Young women were dying. Brutally murdered, on film. He had Gato's assurance that the man in one of the videos they'd watched had a tattoo that belonged to a local judge. Judge Toland Reynolds. The same judge who helped Mayor Goldman get elected, and probably helped him into the blackmail net. Yes, the world could be a fuckin' dark place. Sure, it'd been dark before, and would be dark again. That was just part of it all. But sometimes? Well, sometimes the darkness stretched over the line. Into a space that was reserved only for the Hitlers, Mansons, and Pol Pots of the world.

A plan of action began to take shape deep down in his heart. It was desperate, but it was maybe the only way to force the entire thing to its conclusion. He was weighing the pros and cons of his new plan when Bill walked in. Mallen thought he was just there to restock the bar, but then the man said, "Justin wants to see you."

"Dreamo? He say why?"

Bill nodded. "And I made sure it had nothing to do with sending you back on the horse, got me?"

Mallen put out his cigarette in a nearby ashtray made from a cut-open beer can. "I hear ya, B. And thanks for looking out for me."

Bill looked at him then, right in the eyes. Then relaxed with a smile. "For my next trick, I'll bring Hendrix back from the dead."

Mallen got up. Left the storeroom. Went down the hall past the walls covered with layers and layers of graffiti and carved initials. Pushed open the door to the men's room.

It hadn't changed much. Jesus, what the fuck had he been expecting, anyway? Flowers? The walls painted? "Dreamo?" he said quietly.

And just like it had always been, back when he'd been scoring horse, the answering voice came from the stall. The voice like an oracle: dusty and forgotten, filled with the words he wanted to hear. "Mal, been awhile, man. Come ahead, ex-customer."

Mallen moved to the stall, quietly pushing on the stall door. There was Dreamo, sagging Mohawk and wrinkled clothing. A couple candles burned on the tank behind him. Mallen had to smile. It was indeed like seeing an oracle or shaman.

Dreamo stared at him for a moment. At his eyes. "No," he said with an almost hiss, "you haven't fallen back into the shit yet. I think I might be happy to know that. Maybe. Dunno. Was surprised to find you living in the back, Mallen."

He pulled out his cigarettes. Lit one. "Only temp, Dream."

"Only temp," Dreamo echoed. "Maybe you'd be safer here than other places."

It took Mallen a moment to find his voice. "You hear something?"

A nod.

"What did you hear?"

"Lots of guys out looking for an ex-cop, ex-needlenose."

"They say why?"

And here Dreamo looked squarely at him. "You know why, Mal, right? Hey, man … I'm just telling you what I heard, is all."

Mallen took another drag from his cigarette. Glad now that he hadn't gone home. He'd have to stay gone and deep underground for a while. Would they strike out at Chris and Anna to get to him? That would be crazy though, right? But then he'd be an idiot to think otherwise. "Yeah, and thanks for telling me. I appreciate it." Took another drag, and blew the smoke out slowly, then said, "Judge Toland Reynolds. Hear anything about that fuck?"

Dreamo let out a silent whistle. It was as sagging a whistle as the Mohawk he pushed out of his eyes. "Too much, man. Why?"

"Because."

And here Dreamo actually laughed. He'd never really heard Dreamo laugh a real laugh before. This was a hearty, throaty, cough-filled laugh that Mallen thought might kill the dealer if it went on much longer. After a moment, Dreamo got a hold of himself enough to say, "Right. Because." Added a faint, "Sorry, Mal. That shit is too deep for me to swim in."

"He that bad-ass?"

Another nod. "Yeah," Dreamo answered, "I've been hearing some really weird shit, of late. Some of my customers, they've lost women. Whispers along the vine said it was like some Jack the Ripper dude. You ever hear of him?"

"Just by reputation."

Another cackle from Dreamo. "Mal, you kill me, man. You really fuckin' do."

"I ran across a couple of their ... herders," Mallen told him. "Both dead, down by the ballpark. It wasn't pretty."

"And when is death ever pretty, Mal?"

"I had toyed with the idea of calling in reinforcements. Badge-like."

Another shake of the sagging Mohawk. "Big mistake, ex-customer of mine."

Mallen stood there a moment before answering. "Seriously?"

"Oh yeah. How you think this shit keeps getting quieted?" He stared at Mallen then. "You were sharper when you were using the sharps, man."

Mallen took another drag. "Maybe. Maybe fuckin' so. Thanks for the talk, Dream. Appreciate it."

Dreamo only laughed in response. A laugh that turned into the sound of a stalling-out old engine. "I didn't help you at all, Mal. Hell, your troubles only beginnin' if you're involved in this sort of shit."

TWENTY-NINE

CHRIS PULLED UP TO Anna's school twenty minutes early for the half-Friday release. She wished that she had never given up cigarettes and cursed Mark silently. She was torn, right down the middle: half was extremely happy with how he seemed to be turning his life around, and the other half wished that she'd cut all ties with him so she didn't have to deal with the fallout from that turnaround. It reminded her too much of when he'd been a policeman. *That's what you get for getting enamored with a Don Quixote type, Christine.*

Men. Men and their war-think. Always at war. Again, she wished she had a cigarette. Glanced at her watch. Fifteen minutes to go. Started to watch the gate where Anna would exit. Maybe she should get out of the car and just be there, waiting. Cursed Mallen again for bringing paranoia and fear back into her life. She got out of the car and walked over to the gate.

Fifteen minutes later the children began to file out, either running to meet their parents, or the older ones walking out to meet the yellow bus that sat at the nearby curb. Anna was almost ready to ride that bus on her own. Chris knew that her daughter was very excited to be old enough to ride with the bigger kids. She hoped that whatever Mark was into would be over soon, so Anna could do what she wanted.

Anna saw her and came over. She was trying to act cool: it was just her mother, no big deal. Chris hung back, let Anna act the older, cooler girl. When Anna got there, they hugged quickly and Chris led her back to the car. She put Anna in the back seat and Anna buckled herself in. Chris got behind the wheel. "How was school?" she asked.

"Okay," came the noncommittal answer.

"Did you give your science presentation to the class?" It'd been a history of snakes. Anna's presentation had included drawings of snakes and even clay figures in dioramas. There was one clay figure of a boa constrictor after it had eaten its prey; it was a long snake with a bulge in the middle. Anna had been absurdly proud of it.

"Yeah, I did," she said.

"And?"

"And what, Mommy?"

"Well, did they like it? Did your teacher like it?"

A moment, then Anna said, "I got an 'A.'" Like it was nothing at all. Just another grade.

"Well," Chris said as she glanced in her rearview, "we'll have to ..."

There was a black BMW back there. *No reason in the world there shouldn't be, Chris, lots of people own black BMWs.* She made a left on the next street. The BMW did also. Okay, that was one. She then made a right. Increased her speed. Let her get a ticket if there was a cop around. She'd appreciate that. The BMW kept on going.

Jesus. Chris. Don't get so paranoid. She drove north, crossing Geary. Anna hadn't said another word the entire way home. She'd pulled a book out of her bag and begun to read. It was only ten minutes later they pulled onto their street and turned into the driveway. Chris hit the garage door opener and the door crept open. She pulled inside. The light hadn't come on like it usually did. She'd have to remember to buy a new bulb.

Anna undid her seatbelt and opened the door at the same time Chris got out. That was when she heard the rush of a body through space. The displacement. She turned to the sound, just like Mark had trained her, her knee coming up like it was shot from a cannon. Felt contact all the way up her leg. She barely registered the fact that the man was dressed all in black and had a hockey mask over his face. He grunted as his balls were slammed by her knee and he went down, clutching his sack. Dropped a white cotton pad.

"Run, Anna!" she yelled at her daughter and Anna took off out of the garage, barely escaping a second man who appeared out of nowhere and tried to catch her with a bear hug.

Chris saw a gun in the man's waistband she'd just eunuched. Went for it but was grabbed from behind. Then there was another set of hands. Then there was something over her mouth and nose. Some sort of cloth, and then everything turned to black.

———

Mallen had slept late. Way later than he'd meant to. Couldn't believe the time it was when he checked his phone. He left the back room and made his way to the bar. Washed up in the sink where the glasses were washed. Knew better than to entertain the idea of washing up in the bathroom that was Dreamo's office. He'd thought about it, just a little, but then realized he didn't want, didn't need, to see Dreamo again. Dunked his head under the tap and rinsed out his mouth with mineral water. Made some coffee and drank it down, eating some of the Chex Mix that Bill kept for weekend nights. His phone rang and he grabbed it up. With relief he saw that it was Gato's number. "Fuck man," he said, "where you been?"

"Wasting time, bro," Gato said. It was easy to hear the sad tone in his voice.

"No luck?"

"No."

"You still down there?"

"Only an hour away from home. Had to stop for sleep and some first aid." Gato told him about what had happened in L.A. "Mallen," he finished, "I'm out of options. These guys…I…I don't know, man. Feels like taking on the government or some shit."

"I know what you mean." There was a tone in his ear, from the phone. It was the first time another call had come in while he was talking to someone, and at first he didn't know what the hell was going on. "Wait a minute, man," he said to Gato. "I think I actually have another fuckin' call." He pressed the talk button, thinking that was the thing to do. "Hello?"

"Daddy?" It took just a second to realize it was his daughter.

"Hey A. What's up? I didn't know you had this number."

"Mommy put it in my phone. Daddy…Mommy…Mommy's been…" She started to cry. That was all he needed.

"Where are you, honey? Where? Do you know? Are you alone?"

There was a moment where he heard the phone passed from one hand to another. He knew that sound. His heart raced. It was bad. Very bad, and he knew it.

"Mr. Mallen?" came a voice that he thought he could remember, but it was a faint memory. An older woman's voice.

"Yes? Who is this?"

"It's Mrs. Netter. I live across the street from Chris and Anna."

Right. She was the "go to" lady that Chris had instilled in Anna. He remembered now setting it up with Mrs. Netter. She was very kind, and supportive. Understood about his work. Seemed like she got it—that he really did love his daughter. "Mrs. Netter," he answered, "thank you for looking after Anna, but what's going on? Where is Chris? What's going on?"

"I'm not sure. Anna showed up at my door, crying. Said something about Chris being gone. Told me that some men showed up and ... and had taken her away? I was just about to call the police."

His heart constricted. He was already up and leaving the bar. "Hang on, okay, Mrs. Netter? I'll be right back." Clicked off that call and said to Gato, "G? Something bad has happened to Chris, okay? Very bad."

"What, *vato?* What's happened?"

"I think she's been kidnapped. Just burn rubber to get back here if you can. I'll be at Chris's. Might be across the street. Honk when you get there." He clicked off, going back to Mrs. Netter. "Mrs. Netter?" He was moving fast down the street, heading for the garage where the truck was parked. "How long ago did Anna show up? Did she show up right after it happened?"

"I think so. It's been about fifteen minutes now, maybe twenty or so. You don't want me to call the police?"

Shit. That was a long time. His mind raced on what to do, how to do it ...

"Just take care of Anna, okay? I know some cops and will call them myself. It'll be okay, trust me. Can you put Anna on for me?" There was only one cop he could trust right now, and that was Oberon. Calling the regulars was off the table, no matter how much he would've loved to call 911, the air force, the marines, and the army.

"Okay," said Mrs. Netter. He heard the phone handed back to his daughter.

"Anna?"

"Yes, Daddy?" She really sounded upset, but he could tell she was also trying to hold it steady. Just like her mother would. Great kid.

"Honey, I'll be there in fifteen minutes, okay? I'm on my way to you. Right now. You do not leave Mrs. Netter's house, okay? I repeat: you do not leave Mrs. Netter's house. I'll be right there, baby. Okay? Now let me talk to Mrs. Netter again."

There was a small "okay" on the other end. Mrs. Netter got back on the line. "What should I do?" she said.

"Nothing. Just lock the door. Don't leave her alone, okay? I'm on my way there."

"What's going on?" she asked, and she had every right to ask that.

"I'm not sure, Mrs. Netter. But thank you for being there for my little girl. I'll be right over." And with that he ended the call and kicked it into high gear, running faster than he could ever remember running in order to get back to the truck. He threw the parking tag and money at the attendant. Practically yanked the guy from the truck as he leapt inside and tore off.

The fuckers had indeed done an end-around. They'd fucking gone after his family. He had the tapes, and now they had Chris. As he drove, he tried to calm down but found it hard. Visions of Chris in the hands of men who made snuff tapes, raped and beat women to death, made him see red. Sent his heart into his throat. He ran a couple red lights, was lucky not to get pulled over. Tried to recapture his breath. Pulled out his phone. Dialed Oberon.

The detective answered on the fourth ring. "Kane," he said.

"Obie. It's Mallen."

There was the sigh, the one that always seemed to precede Oberon's answers when Mallen called. "Yes? What is it now? You found my suspect in a massage parlor run by an ex-mafia who—"

"Obie. It's not like that. They got Chris, man. Chris!"

"Who has her? This have to do with our other meeting?"

"Like you wouldn't believe. I need your help, man. And in a serious way."

A slight pause, then, "Where are you?"

"On my way to Chris's now. Haven't called anyone else into it."

"And why is that?"

"Not safe, Obie. Not safe. We need to treat it that way."

"Okay. I'm on my way."

———

By the time Mallen got there, Oberon was already on the scene. He stood in the driveway to Mallen's old house, hands on hips, staring at the open garage door. Mallen quickly exited the truck and went over to him.

"I don't like what I see here, Mark," the cop told him. Pointed at the white cloth that had been left on the floor by the front of the car. "I will bet that has chloroform on it. You can see some blood over by the driver's side door too."

"I have to see Anna," Mallen replied. Blood and chloroform on a rag only made his body fill with adrenaline. He needed more information. A lot more information.

"I'm right in believing that you have what these men want? The men who have abducted Chris?"

"Yeah."

"We really should call in reinforcements, Mark. There are good men on the force. I know them. We could make up a good group—"

"I know!" Mallen replied, with more heat than he'd intended. "Look, they'll contact me, right? That's why they took her. They'll call. There's nothing we can do except try to track them down before that happens. We don't need a bunch of guys you can trust fucking it all up. And how long would it take to get that group together, yeah? No, we gotta do this my way, okay?"

Oberon stood there for a while, looking down at the ground. Thinking it all over. "Okay," he finally said. "I do have to say that I think you're right, though it flies in the face of everything I've ever been taught regarding being a policeman."

"Thanks, Obie," Mallen replied, putting his hand on the man's shoulder for a moment. He wanted this man to think of him as a friend. That meant a lot to him. He didn't want Oberon to think for a moment that Mallen was using him in some way. Not at all. "I gotta go see Anna. Make sure she's okay."

"Go ahead. I'll start looking around more in the garage. Maybe something will turn up," Oberon said, then moved into the garage.

Mallen crossed the street to Mrs. Netter's. The door opened before he got to the top of the stairs and Anna came running out, her eyes wet and red. She ran to her father and threw her arms around his waist. Mallen picked her up and held her tightly. Mrs. Netter stood there in the doorway, a worried expression on her face. "Thank you for looking after my daughter, Mrs. Netter," he said as he petted Anna's head. "I will never forget it, trust me."

"What are neighbors for?" she said with a smile.

He stroked Anna's head. "Hey, A," he said quietly. "It'll be okay, I promise."

She held onto him like he was the last sane thing in the world. Pulled back enough to look at him. "Mommy will be back?"

"Oh yeah, she will. She will."

"When?"

"Well, that I don't know, honey. You and me? We need to be strong for Mommy, so when she comes back, we're ready to love her like she needs us to, okay?"

A nod from Anna and he held her tightly again for a moment. "It's going to be okay, honey. I swear to you, it will be okay." He then put her down on the ground. Crouched down so he could look right at her. "Did you see anything, honey? Anything at all? Can you tell me what happened? I need to know what you saw."

The girl looked down at the ground. Like she was thinking. Wiped at her eyes. "There were men. When we got out of the car."

"How many?"

A shake of her head. "I heard Mommy yell for me to run. One of the men tried to get me. I ran. Ran over here."

"Did you see what car they put Mommy in? Please, baby: think. Did you see the car?"

She nodded. "It was black. A black SUV."

That only confirmed what he already new. "Anna, you sure you don't remember anything about the men that took Mommy? I know it happened fast, and you were scared. Very scared. I just need to ask again, okay? Was there anything you can remember about the men?"

Tears came to her eyes as she stared down at the ground. Mallen knew he couldn't ask anything else of her. He would just have to wait for their phone call or text. He was sure it wouldn't be long in coming. He needed to get Chris back safely and then kill any of the men who had touched her. And those men would die, and die very hard.

"Daddy?" Anna said suddenly, looking up at him. "I think I saw the license plate. I think I did."

"What? You did?"

She nodded. Seemed more sure. "I did. I was over here, and looked back. I saw an I and a four and a K and…" she had to think more, her forehead wrinkling, "a Z!" she finished up. Proud.

"That's great, A!" They would be able to track that car. A black SUV, with those letters and number? Fuck yeah they could trace it. "Are you sure?"

"Yes," she said with a definite air. "You taught me how to always remember license plate numbers, remember?"

That was right. He'd made a game of it, making up words for the letters, just like they did on the police radios. She'd been good at it, too, as evidenced by what she'd just done for them now. He hugged her tightly, then held her out at arms length, grinning at her. He couldn't be more proud of her now for anything. "Anna, what you did was awesome, okay? You really did a big help here. I'm going to go now and talk with Oberon. Then I have to go and start looking for Mommy." He looked up at Mrs. Netter. "Can she stay the night? I know it's all last-minute. I swear that I'll figure something out tomorrow, but right now I need to be figuring out where Chris is. I'm really sorry for the imposition."

"Oh stop now. Don't worry about it. Anna is always welcome here," Mrs. Netter said with a smile as she looked at Mallen's daughter. "And I figured there would be some excitement at some point, living across from a policeman. Never figured it would be years in the coming, but that's okay."

"Thank you," he replied. Hugged Anna again, whispering, "I'll be back as soon as I can. I promise. You get some sleep, A, okay?"

"Okay, Daddy." She hugged him back and he left her on the porch as he went quickly down the stairs and over to the garage. Oberon stood up from where he'd been crouching, looking at the bloodstain. Pointed to a scratch on the driver's side door of Chris's car.

"Looks like Chris put up a good fight," Oberon said as he pointed at the scratch on the car. "That's from the heel of a woman's shoe, I'm sure. And this blood pattern? I think it's from the captor, not the captive. Maybe we'll find someone with recent scratches on their hands or forearms."

"Obie," Mallen said, "I have a partial plate and a vehicle make."

Oberon had his battered notebook out in an instant. Mallen told him what Anna had said. "We should be able to find that vehicle with this," the detective told Mallen. "There can't be too many black SUVs with these numbers in the system. We'll hope so, anyway."

Mallen nodded. Looked at the car. At the blood. At the rag soaked in chloroform. "Yeah ..." he said in a forced voice. Like he'd had his guts kicked out. "We'll hope so."

THIRTY

THE MOMENT CHRIS OPENED her eyes, she wished she hadn't. Her head pounded, and she felt sick to her stomach. Took a moment to realize she was laid out on a cot. The room was about the size of a monk's cell. No windows. The door looked like something that belonged to an old-fashioned meat freezer. *Anna.* That word blew through her mind, exploding her fear. Where was her daughter?

Goddamn you, Mark . . .

Whatever he was into, it had blown over into her and her daughter's life. Just like everything they'd ever feared, and it didn't even happen when he'd been an actual policeman. Took the man getting clean and involved with life again to bring all this down on her and Anna.

How long had she been out? Where was she? Was it in the city? A different city? What had happened to Anna? The faint memory of Anna running out of the garage. The faint memory of reaching for a gun. He daughter might be okay. She knew that Anna would call Mark. They'd revised the drill once he'd gotten cleaned up. She'd believed him, that he wanted to be a part of their lives. And she knew that if he was clean, he was more dependable than any other man she'd ever known. He would never stop until he achieved what he wanted, needed, or believed in.

Then she heard a key in the door lock, and the panic set in. Two men entered. Dressed in black, wearing ski masks. She would've laughed at the sight, like something out of a bad movie, had she not really been right here, right now. Chris drew a breath and focused on staying alive. For Anna. For herself.

"Where's my daughter?" she asked, defiant.

No answer. They only stood there for a moment. "Where's my goddamned daughter, you bastards!" They came over to her, calm as robots. She tried to fight, but they were strong. She screamed and fought like tiger, but they were just too strong. She yelled and struggled as they went for her pants. She crossed her legs, spit at them, tried to bite them. Her pants were ripped off of her and then her top. She screamed as they took her shoes, panties, and bra. They grabbed her torn clothes and left, locking the door behind them.

Chris huddled on the floor, in the corner. Her mind turned over at what had just happened. She couldn't believe it. Wouldn't. Had to. *Anna. Anna. Anna. Anna* … It was a chant in her head. *Have to say alive for her. Have to get away. Get out. Mark* …

———

They came for her again. She'd been counting to sixty, slowly, over and over. Trying to guess the passage of time. Mark had taught her that. It focused you. Kept you linked up to life, to *your* life. It was a lifeline, that counting. She'd counted to sixty, sixty-four times when they came back in the room. She got to her feet when she heard the key in the lock. Ran at them as they came in. Kicked one, aiming for his nuts. Missed but heard him grunt. He went to hit her but was kept back by the other man. They tackled her like she was a running back caught behind the line of scrimmage. She felt hands on her. Then she was handcuffed and a sack went over her head. She cried then as the feeling of futility got to her. She was dragged out of the cell, her arms screaming as her shoulders felt like both rotator cuffs were tearing. There was a thought, though, just a small one, way down deep inside her: The one man kept the other from hitting her. They didn't want to hit her. What did that mean?

They dragged her along the rough concrete floor, tearing up her feet and shins. The sound changed, as did the air. It was colder now but she was sweating, and that made her colder yet. Then she was forced onto a stiff-backed chair. She felt her feet bound to it, spreading her legs. Were they belts of some sort? The cuffs were practically ripped off her wrists and then her hands were bound behind her to the chair. She worked hard not to shake, but she couldn't help it. Then the bag was pulled off her head. She blinked in the face of the large arc lights pointed at her. She was blinded to just about everything behind them. It took her mind a moment to realize what it was she saw.

A man stood between the lights, pointing an old video camera at her. Filming her. She thought he was one of the men who had brought her here from the cell. Where was the other man? She heard some scuffling noise then, along with the sound of wheels over concrete. Then the other man appeared, silent like before. He pushed a chrome metal medical cart. The top of the cart had a white cloth over it.

"Where's my daughter? Where am I?" she said. There was no answer as the man wheeled the cart up next to her, and pulled off the cloth with a flourish. Her breath caught in her throat when she saw the medical instruments. She recognized the speculum right off. Sweat broke out anew all over her body. She struggled with everything she had as she tried to break the straps. No good. Tried to focus on Anna and her safety. "Where's my daughter?" she said, her voice a hoarse croak, unable to mask the fear anymore.

Then another figure appeared. A man wearing a rubber mask of a bull's head, dressed in a long, dark blue bathrobe. His hands were covered in black leather gloves.

Chris screamed as he came forward. The man in the mask walked around her. Slowly, as the other man kept filming. Then the man stood just to the right of her. Turned to the camera and, in some bizarre moment, actually waved at the camera. Then he turned lightning fast and struck her across the face with his open hand. The slap stunned her, bringing stinging tears to her eyes. But she was Mark Mallen's wife, and she knew that he'd gone through hell and back numerous times over. She could be that strong.

"Where's my daughter, you fucking bastard?" she asked as loud as she could. She heard a soft chuckle come from the mask. Then she was hit again. And again. Harder than last time. She tasted blood. The man walked over to the table, and she tried to be brave but fear flooded her. She shook as if she were in an ice freezer. The man in the mask picked up a scalpel. The mask turned to look at her, towering above her, as hideous as every nightmare she'd ever had rolled into one. He then traced a weird design on her stomach with the index finger of his left hand. He did it very lightly, trailing his finger down her stomach into her pubic hair and stopping right before touching her vagina. She couldn't tell what sort of design it was. He then looked at the camera as he trailed that finger back up over her stomach to her breasts. He cupped one as he looked at the camera. Then held the scalpel up to the other breast, resting it on her left nipple. She held as still as she could, knowing that if she moved, the scalpel would cut her. The man then let go of her breast and tweaked her right nipple until she cried out in pain. Again there was the soft laugh, barely heard over the pounding in her ears from the blood rushing through her. The adrenaline made her head feel light. The man traced his finger over her stomach again. She couldn't figure out anything anymore. She'd gone into survival mode: fight or flight.

And she couldn't do either.

Then the man began to trace the design again, ever so lightly, this time with the scalpel ...

———

Mallen waited inside the garage belonging to what had once been his and Chris's home. Oberon was on the phone, running what they had on the black SUV. Mallen couldn't focus on anything except Chris. The moment his mind came back to the reality of what she must be experiencing, he had a tightness in his chest that felt like it was crushing his ribs. He couldn't help but visualize in his mind's eye every dark thing he'd ever heard about when someone is kidnapped. And the videos. These thoughts were followed by a deep and cold anger. He would kill the men who'd taken her. He would make them pay. He was powerless to, however. He couldn't risk anything that would bring harm to Chris. He knew they would kill her if they had to. He'd seen enough of these people and this organization to know they would sacrifice anything and anyone to get those tapes back.

"Yes?" Oberon said after being on hold for over ten minutes. He wrote something down in his notebook. "Got it. Thanks, Tom. Appreciate the quickness." Oberon closed the call and turned to Mallen. "The vehicle is registered to one John Westbrook. He resides at Francisco Street and Grant. And"—he hesitated before he continued—"he's an employee of Darkstar Security."

Mallen turned and headed for his truck, but Oberon told him, "Wait here, Mark. You can't go. You know that."

"If you don't take me with you, Obie, I'll go on my own. And you know that, yeah?"

Oberon smiled then. "Yes, Mark. Only too true. Let's go then."

THIRTY-ONE

MALLEN RAN BACK ACROSS the street to see Anna one more time before they left. He hugged her, long and hard, and kissed her on the forehead. Told her one more time that he would be back as soon as he could. Gave Mrs. Netter Anna's house key. Told her to use it to get Anna a change of clothes or anything at all that she might want to make her feel safe.

As he was walking over to Oberon's car, he heard a now-familiar sound: Gato's Ford Falcon. He watched as it tore around the corner and came roaring up the street. Oberon was out of his vehicle instantly, his weapon drawn, but Mallen stopped him. "It's okay, Obie," he said, "he's a friendly."

The Falcon skidded to the curb and Gato leaped out. Mallen noticed right away the beating his friend had taken.

Gato ran over to him. "*Vato!*" he said. "What the fuck is going on, man? They took your *esposa?*" It was then he really noticed Oberon, and the fact that he was a cop.

"Gato," Mallen said, "this is Detective Oberon Kane. Good friend from my police days. He's the one other person I can trust right now, okay?"

Gato nodded, not entirely convinced. Oberon smiled as he put out his hand. "Mark hasn't always been a good judge of character in the past, but now that is all behind him. If he calls you a friend, then we're on the same team."

It took a moment, but Gato shook Oberon's hand. "I never thought I'd be shaking the hand of a cop, man," he said with a slight grin. "But as you say, if Mallen vouches for you, then yeah … we're all wearin' the same fucking colors, bro." He then turned to Mallen, saying, "So what the hell's gone down, man? I got here as soon as I could."

Mallen filled him in on what had happened, and what they thought had happened. Gato got more and more angry the more he heard "Shit!" he finally exploded, "I told you, man. We need to fuck their shit *up*, man! Now."

"Well, that would be one answer, yes," Oberon replied. "But we have a lead on the man who might've been driving the vehicle for the men who abducted her. We need to follow that up, first."

"Then let's do it, man. Why the fuck are we standing around?" Gato spun on his heel and was about to take off for his car when Mallen stopped him.

"Gato," he told him, "me and Obie are going to do this one, okay?"

His friend looked like he hadn't heard him right. Mallen said, "G, I need you to stay here and guard Anna, okay? I need you to guard my daughter, got it? Those guys? They might come back, right? They might know that she saw them. She'd be just one more bargaining chip to them, right? Right?"

For an answer, Gato only nodded. Obviously didn't like being sidelined.

"I need you to do this for me, okay, Gato? There's no one else I can trust. I'm trusting you with the safety of my daughter, man. You hear me on that?"

"I do, Mallen. I do. Don't worry, man. I'd lay down my life for your daughter, no sweat."

"I know you would. Let's hope it doesn't come to that. Who else would drive me the fuck all over town in such cool cars, yeah?" He grabbed Gato by the shoulder and squeezed it once, then went with Oberon over to the detective's car, leaving the Land Cruiser at the curb.

The last sight of Gato Mallen had was of the man taking up a position on the steps leading to Mrs. Netter's house. Mallen knew he couldn't find a better guard anywhere, and that he was blessed with very good friends.

———

The short drive over to Westbrook's house seemed to take forever. He'd wanted to go right to the Darkstar offices, but Oberon had overridden him. If the man had been involved in a kidnapping earlier today, he probably would not have gone to the office afterward. It was possible he wouldn't be home, either, but of the two it was the better bet.

They made a right onto Stockton from Bay, then a quick left onto Francisco. The address belonged to a modern cement building. Oberon parked in the nearest red zone and the two men walked across the street. Mallen counted only four mailboxes. Odds were these were condos and not apartments. There had been no black SUVs on the street, but the street-level floor of the building was a gated tenant garage. Mallen looked at the heavy lock system. Would be hard to get beyond that, for sure. Oberon led him back to the lobby door. There was Westbrook's name on one of the mailboxes. Number three. Top floor. Oberon looked up and down the street. Checking for pedestrians. Pulled out a lock pick kit from an inner pocket.

"Obie," Mallen said, "I would never have fucking thought it possible."

"Needs must when the devil drives, or so they say." Oberon had the lobby door open in under a minute, and both men went inside. They found the entry door to the garage and went through. In the garage was a Mini, a white Lexus SUV, and a Harley Davidson. Slot three was empty. Oberon turned on his heel and went back to the lobby. Mallen followed as they went up to the stairs to number three. Oberon knocked a cop's knock. They could hear movement inside, then the door opened. Before them stood a youngish man of medium height. Hair cut in a short business style. Clean shaven. Pale eyes. Stood there in a tank top and jogging shorts. Just another guy at home. The man took one look at Mallen; looking in those pale eyes, Mallen knew they had the right guy.

"John Westbrook?" Oberon asked.

Took the man a moment to bring a smile to his face. Then he said, "Yes. Does this have to do with my stolen truck?"

Oberon took out his badge and showed it to Westbrook. Mallen found it hard not to reach out and grab the man by his throat and shake him. Stolen. That was the weakest fucking excuse anyone could give.

"Your truck was stolen?" Oberon inquired. "Did you report it?"

"Yeah," Westbrook replied. He seemed all of sudden more confident about it all. "About ten minutes ago. I went down to go to the gym, and it was gone. I knew I shouldn't have parked it on the street, but well, I came home a little drunk and just grabbed the first parking spot I saw nearby."

"And why was that?"

Westbrook looked appropriately sheepish as he replied. "I didn't trust myself to navigate the parking garage."

"I see," Oberon replied as he brought out his notebook. Wrote something down in it.

"What's this all about, Officer? And how do you know my name?"

"We're just checking on all the high-end black SUVs we can. One was used in a robbery this morning." Oberon glanced at his notebook. "So you called in the missing vehicle ten minutes ago?"

"Give or take." And here he glanced at Mallen.

Oberon then asked, "You work for Darkstar Security, yes?"

"That's correct. That's another reason I didn't want to try getting it parked. It's a company car. My boss doesn't like his employees drinking all that much. He's a pretty straight arrow."

Mallen couldn't stand it. He butted in, "And who's your boss over there?"

"And who might you be?" Westbrook replied, eyeing Mallen with a cool eye now. He seemed confident that he had the situation under control.

"A consultant on the rise of street crimes in the city is all."

"We may need to speak to him, naturally," Oberon said.

"I see," came the reply, followed by a gaze at Oberon. "My supervisor is George Septemberson."

Oberon wrote that down. "Thank you, Mr. Westbrook. The department will let you know if we find your vehicle."

"I hope so. Mr. Septemberson doesn't take kindly to company vehicles going missing."

Oberon walked away, and Mallen had no choice but to follow. Outside on the street Mallen grabbed Oberon by the shoulder. "Obie, what the fuck are we doing? You know that sack of shit was lying. His car was stolen? Bullshit, and you know it!"

"Yes, I do know it," Oberon said, shaking off Mallen's hand. "But did it occur to you that he said he reported it missing only ten minutes ago, 'or so'? Let me prove my point." Oberon dialed the station and asked about a stolen vehicle report. Nodded, wrote something in his notebook. "Thanks," he said as he ended the call.

"Well?" Mallen said.

"The vehicle was reported missing about twenty minutes ago. That would be about ten minutes *after* I called in looking for it. Don't you see? There's someone inside the department who may have been told about that SUV, and to be on the lookout for any inquiries into it."

Mallen got it then. Looked up at the sky as he took a deep breath, like a diver before a dive. "Jesus . . . they really have it all covered." He leaned against the apartment building. "What are we going to do, Obie? They're one or more steps ahead of us."

"I don't know, son. I really don't. I would say we go and talk with this Septemberson. Maybe he can be pressured."

"You really think so?" Mallen replied. Thought about it all. There was only one thing he felt he could do. He had to play it hard. Sighed for effect. "You go on, Obie, if you want to talk to Septemberson. You can't show up with me on your heels. They obviously know my face. If Septemberson is in on it someway, we'd be broadcasting it all and maybe hurt Chris's chance to get out of this alive."

"And what will you be doing, Mark?" Oberon said, eyeing him.

"I'm going to go over to Vesuvio. Get a drink and think about my next move. Let's meet up back at Chris's in about an hour, if you can. Maybe I'll have an idea by then. Something that will get my little girl's mother back for her."

Oberon stood there for a moment, and Mallen knew he wasn't buying any of it. But would he throw down over it? Mallen had to wonder. It would depend on just how big Oberon thought the entire thing was. If the detective believed the operation to be huge, and he had no reason to think otherwise, he would know that Mallen could do more than he could because the law really no longer applied to him.

"Okay," Oberon finally said. "Call me in a couple. Good luck with your … thinking." And with that he walked back to his car.

Mallen waited until he saw Oberon's car turn the corner. He went back to the lobby door of Westbrook's building. Oberon hadn't noticed that when they left, Mallen had stuck a wad of paper from his pocket into the lock mechanism, keeping it from shutting the entire way. He pushed inside to the lobby. Took the stairs up to Westbrook's apartment. As he climbed, all his anger rose back to the surface and all he could see was Westbrook's face, all calm, practically smiling at them as he figured he was invulnerable to anything they could throw at him from a law standpoint.

Well, Mallen didn't work from a law standpoint anymore. His vision was red tinged, his muscles taut with anger at not being able to do anything straight away to save Chris. Well, his not being able to do anything was about to end.

Stopped at Westbrook's door. Put his ear to it. He could hear Westbrook talking. Probably calling his boss to tell him about being visited by the police and the guy who had the videos. Mallen pulled his gun. Knocked with his right hand. Used his cop knock. If Westbrook used the peephole, then so be it. Mallen knew Westbrook would be curious enough to answer. The man would bring a weapon. He'd also feel superior. Ninty-eight percent of people in the world thought he was still just a burned-out, recovering junkie.

He saw the flash of darkness at the peephole. Heard the lock click. Saw the knob turning. And he hit the door with all his body weight behind it. Just like the old days. The door caught Westbrook in the face and he staggered back, trying to catch his balance as Mallen bulled in. There was an automatic in Westbrook's right hand. Mallen smashed his own gun down on the man's wrist, and the gun dropped to the carpeted entryway. Mallen then whipped his gun upward like a club, catching Westbrook on the jaw. Followed with a right suckerpunch to the solar plexus. Westbrook fell to the ground, gasping for breath. Mallen shut the door quietly. Kicked Westbrook's gun down the hallway on his left. Grabbed Westbrook by his ankle and hauled him into the man's living room. It took all the muscle he'd regained, but he managed it with a lot of tugging and hauling. Westbrook was not a small guy. He dropped the man's leg when they got to the center of the room, then he spun on his heel and smashed Westbrook across the face a couple times with the gun barrel. There was blood now, from Westbrook's mouth. Mallen punched him in the nose. More blood. No matter how big they were, the sight of their own blood unnerved a guy just about 90 percent of the time. Westbrook was in that 90 percent. The guy still hadn't gotten over the shock of Mallen entering like he did. Finally found his breath. Wiped at his face, but Mallen kicked that hand away.

"You clean up when we're done."

"You're making a big mistake." It was definite.

"Am I?" He kicked Westbrook in the side. The man groaned and curled up. "Where's my wife, you fuckhole? Where is she?"

"I dunno," came the reply.

"Nope. Not gonna cut it." He bashed Westbrook in the face again with the barrel of the gun. More blood. "I know it was your vehicle. I know you were there. I could tell, see? Soon as I saw you. You get that, yeah? You think I'm just gonna go away now? Where is she?"

A shake of the head. Westbrook spit out some blood. "I don't know, man! Don't know what you're talking about."

Mallen stood there a moment. Gazed around the apartment, figuring out what to do next. Caught a glimpse through the kitchen door. That would do. He grabbed Westbrook by his gym shirt and dragged him struggling into the kitchen. Westbrook's condo had all the latest kitchen amenities. Would've been one of the selling points. There was a very chic new stove and oven. Not a gas one. Electric. He turned on the right front burner. Turned it on full. Westbrook saw this. Tried to break free, but Mallen caught him and pressed the muzzle of the gun to the man's temple, hard.

"Where is my wife?" he asked quietly.

It was almost a whine. "I don't know, man! I don't!"

"You just don't get it, yeah? I'm not putting your hand on it, or sitting you on this burner; I'm putting the side of your face down there like it's a cheap piece of meat. If you don't want to go through life with half your face looking like a nightmare, you'll tell me what the fuck you know about my wife's kidnapping, and let's start with the place she is."

Westbrook looked at him then. There was fear there that Mallen rarely saw. Hadn't seen in a long fucking time. "I don't know," Westbrook said in a strained voice. "I was told to work with a couple other guys for a snatch and grab. They gave me the address. I'd heard your name mentioned. Figured it out. There's been rumblings about you. About something you got involved in. I don't know what. I'm not paid to know, I'm paid to carry out my orders."

He needed to be sure. He grabbed up Westbrook, still pressing the barrel to the man's temple. Stood behind him. Removed the gun as he pressed the man downward, toward the burner that glowed a bright red. Blood from his face dripped down and sizzled as it hit the burner. "No!" Westbrook cried out. "I don't know! Reynolds knows! Reynolds!"

Mallen pulled the man back. Swung him around and jammed the gun right into the man's shattered nose. "Reynolds? Toland Reynolds?"

"Yes! Reynolds! He was the one that sent us there."

Mallen pressed harder. Westbrook's eyes turned red. Tears of pain there. "Not your boss? Why do you want me to believe that a fucking San Francisco judge would give an order like that? When you work for some fucking top-end security firm? What? You think I'm a dumbass, willing to believe anything? Fuck you." He bent Westbrook backward. He knew the man could feel the heat from the burner. Held the blood-slippery gun steady as he pressed Westbrook backward.

"No!" Westbrook gasped. "It was Reynolds! Reynolds, I tell you! He was the one that contacted us! He called me. Gave me the code to pick up your wife!"

"And take her where?"

"I don't know, man! I don't!" Westbrook had sweated through his clothes at this point. Mallen could smell the man's hair as it began to smoke from the intense heat.

Mallen pulled him up. Moved the gun under Westbrook's chin. It left a bloody smear there. "If you didn't know, then what did you do with her?"

"We dropped her down near the airport. There was another group waiting for us. It was the usual setup. A van was there. Where they take the women, we never know. We're just the snatch-and-grab team. I'm being honest with you, Mallen, I swear!"

And he found it was hard to doubt that. It would be Toland Reynolds next. The guy that Gato had told him about, what seemed like decades ago. Okay then. He removed the gun from Westbrook's neck and dragged him through the kitchen and into the bedroom. He needed this man out of the fuckin' way for as long as possible. His plan was to knock Westbrook out and tie him up, putting him in the closet, a closet that would hopefully be a walk-in and not a sliding door one so he could jam a chair up under the knob.

But as he was about to take the butt of his gun to the back of Westbrook's head, Westbrook finally found his stones and acted. His arm extended behind him, and he caught Mallen right behind the knee and yanked. Mallen's knee buckled and he fell backward. Tried to regain his footing, but Westbrook lashed out with his other hand and it landed right in Mallen's stomach, toppling him, dislodging the gun from his hand. Mallen's mind reacted instantly, on pure instinct. He didn't leap for the gun, but instead went for Westbrook with everything he had, grappling on the floor with the man. They clutched and clawed at each other in a silence cut only by their labor and hissing breath. Mallen knew he couldn't outlast a guy who obviously worked out, who obviously knew self-defense. Catching Westbrook unawares had been his only saving grace. Westbrook was beat up and his head had been knocked about, so he probably wasn't at full strength. But even with that, Mallen knew his own strength was no match for a guy like this. He felt his grip failing, and then Westbrook reached out for the gun that lay on the carpet nearby, right out of reach . . .

He did the only thing he could do. He had a hold of Westbrook's left arm and was pulling on it in a desperate attempt to drag Westbrook away from the gun. And then he remembered the knife. The knife he'd had in his boot since he'd bought it at that cigarette store on Polk the day that he and Gato had gone to the pier warehouse.

Mallen gambled with one of his hands. Gambled with his life. He released Westbrook's arm and went for his boot. Yanked up his pants leg in what seemed like slow motion. Grabbed the knife out of his boot just as Westbrook got his hand around the butt of Mallen's gun. Mallen heard the soft click as the blade flicked open and then he swung the small blade around blindly right as he heard the hammer go back on his gun . . . then he could feel the knife blade bite and saw he'd struck Westbrook right in the side of the neck. Blood instantly began to shoot out from the cut artery. The man had only moments before he was dead. The gun was already forgotten as Westbrook went for the knife in his neck. Mallen rolled away, grabbing up his gun. Westbrook's blood was everywhere and then his eyes closed and the blood pumping out of him became a soft gurgle.

It seemed forever that Mallen lay there, gasping for breath, chest laboring. He shook himself out of his daze, then shook the sweat out of his eyes. Checked Westbrook. The man had most definitely gone to the big gym in the sky. Got slowly to his feet, having to rest half the way up.

The hallway was a wreck. A bloody wreck. He wondered how long he had until a unit showed up. Someone would've heard the struggle, if anyone was home. Wondered what Obie would say when he heard about this. Really didn't care so much right now. He'd figure it out on the fly. There was no other way. Went into the bathroom and checked how he looked. Not bad, if having blood all over your face and the front of your coat passed for not bad. Washed it away from his face and hands. Tried to make his coat look presentable, given he was under the clock. Dried off with a nearby towel. Remembered to wipe the blood off the gun. Shoved that back in his coat pocket and went to the front door.

Opened it, but first checked the hallway to see if anyone had tripped to the fight. It seemed that no one had. He decided at the last moment to scope the kitchen for a back door. Found one and padded down the stairs to where the garbage cans were. Found a door that led to a concrete path back to the street. He walked down that street until he hit Columbus, then hailed a cab that would take him back to Chris's. To his daughter, Gato, and his truck. He knew what he would do after that. Knew exactly what he would do.

THIRTY-TWO

GATO WAS SITTING ON the stoop of Mrs. Netter's house when Mallen's cab came up the street and stopped at the curb. Mallen got out and came over to his friend, who reminded him of a dog guarding his territory. Gato came to meet him immediately.

"How's it been?" Mallen asked.

"A black Ford Crown Victoria with two men inside drove up the street. Slow like, right? I think they slowed down as they approached your pad, but sped up when I think... *think* they saw me and changed their fuckin' *la mente*."

"Okay. These guys don't waste any time, do they?"

"What's the next move, *vato*?"

"There's a man I have to see." He then told Gato about what Westbrook had told him about Reynolds, and how that jibed with what had happened with Lupe. "I'm feelin'," Mallen said at the end, "that Judge Toland Reynolds is dirty as shit and is very connected with what is going on. He might even be point man. I'm going to talk to him."

"You still need me on guard duty, *vato*?" Mallen could see that Gato was hoping Mallen would say no. He wanted to be back in the fray. It was written all over him.

"Yeah, man. You're the only one I can trust right now to watch over my little girl. I'll figure out some sort of shift change when I get back, okay? But think about it, yeah? Those guys in that black car? They might've been cops, sure. But cops *not* looking to solve crimes. Instead they might've been cops wanting to *commit* them. We know this runs very deep into local structures, man. I still need you here, looking after Anna."

Gato didn't like it. Smoothed out his hair. Cracked his knuckles. "*Vato*," he said, "you going in there alone is crazy wrong, man. *Está loco*. You need backup."

"You're only a phone call away, yeah? Oberon too." He then gave Gato Oberon's number, telling him to put it into his phone. "I know he's a cop," Mallen said when Gato seemed reluctant to enter the digits, "and it'll make you look like a snitch, but just use a different name, okay? Call him ... call him *the strategy*."

"*La estrategia*," Gato replied. "Okay," he said as he punched Oberon's number into his phone. It was obvious to Mallen that his friend did not like the way things were developing one fuckin' bit.

"It'll be alright," Mallen reassured him. "I'll call in reinforcements the second I think I can't handle it, okay?"

That resonated. Gato nodded. Put his hand on Mallen's shoulder, "*En esta vida, tenemos que cuidar de nuestros seres queridos.*"

"What does that mean?"

"It means, 'In this life, we have to care for our loved ones.'"

"Well," Mallen said with a faint smile, "I guess truer words were never spoken, yeah?" He then went to his truck, got in, and drove off.

On the way, Mallen called 411 for the number to Judge Reynolds's office. He jotted it down on a napkin he'd found in the glove box, along with a petrified bagel and an old withered garter. What secrets did Mr. Gregor have? Shook his head as he grabbed up the napkin, "We're all just a well of secrets, right?" he said under his breath.

Mallen had never liked coincidences, and the one of Lupe and Reynolds bugged him, ever since Gato had mentioned Reynolds being the judge in Lupe's case. Then there was the pinky. Had to be the same man. Gato wasn't stupid; he could be hot-headed, but he was smart. Sharp. Based in reality. Anyway, he was out of other options. Reynolds was a lead, and he had to run that string out, all the way to the end. Chris's life depended on it. Dialed the number just as he made the right onto Van Ness, heading south toward Civic Center. Pressed through all the options until he got the receptionist.

A woman's voice answered, "Judge Reynolds's office, how may I help you?"

"Judge Reynolds, please?" he said, putting on his business tone.

"Who's calling?"

"A business associate."

Only a brief silence. "I'm sorry, the judge is unavailable at the moment. Would you like to leave a message?"

The usual runaround. He'd heard it a thousand times while waiting to see DAs. "No thank you. I'll try back at a later time." Hung up. A voice in his head told him, *Fuck it, just play it hard*. He was slowly beginning to recognize that voice. It was his old cop voice. The one he'd followed all his years on the force.

Mallen found parking not far from City Hall, near the far corner of the plaza in front of the east face of the building. Considering the time of day, it was almost an act of God. Left his gun under the seat, knowing there was a metal detector in his near future. You couldn't get into such a building without going through one.

He passed bare trees and dry fountains on his way to the glass door entrance of the building. Went up the steps and into the lobby. Made his way through the detector and over to the directory. Reynolds's office was on the third floor. He moved up the marble steps, trying not to let his anger get the better of him as he thought about Chris being kidnapped.

The receptionist smiled pleasantly at him when he entered. A smile she probably used on everyone she was going to kick out of the office.

"I need to speak with Judge Reynolds, please," he said.

"Do you have an appointment?"

"No, I'm afraid I don't. However, I know he'll want to see me."

"Really?"

"Yes. Tell him that a man who was on the pier a few nights ago is now standing in his office."

She looked at him for a moment, like she couldn't be sure he was serious or not. He noted her left hand moving for the edge of the desk right near her. Probably getting in place for the alarm. "I'm afraid I'll need a name, sir. He hates it when I don't get people's names."

"Okay," he smiled, "the name's Mallen. Tell him it's very important." Figured there were only a few ways this was going to fall out. The judge wouldn't see him. The judge would make a call for backup, *then* he'd get a brief audience and be tailed on his way back to his truck. Or Judge Reynolds would see him first, then make that call. He might figure Mallen had come to bargain for his wife's life.

As he stood there, waiting, he thought back to something Gato had told him a while back about not going all *Boondock Saints*. His friend had probably been right. But here he now stood, following his instincts. Just like the old days.

Reynolds kept him waiting five minutes. *Just long enough for him to make a call and get instructions*, Mallen thought.

"Go on in," the receptionist told him.

The office looked out over Van Ness Avenue, which was clogged with the usual traffic. Judge Toland Reynolds was a medium-height man in his early sixties with very little gray hair left on his head. Mustache was trimmed and neat. The dark eyes were piercing, and very unfriendly at the moment. He was indeed missing part of the pinky on his left hand.

"Do I know you?" Reynolds asked in a well-modulated, firm voice. The voice of a man who was used to having order in his court. This was a man who expected people to jump when he barked.

"Only by reputation, maybe. But more to the point, Judge, is that I know you. Very well. You look ravishing in a Joker mask, missing pinky and all."

Reynolds glanced down at his hand. Laughed softly to himself. Like a man realizing he'd made a really fucking stupid blunder.

"You know I'm serious here, Judge. You know I got the tapes from Teddy, just like I know you guys have my wife. Now let's cut the bullshit."

Reynolds sat there, studying Mallen's face. Looked him in the eyes. After a moment, he sighed. "I warned them. Warned them that taking her wasn't the answer. I told them it would force your hand.

I checked your old police file. Told them what kind of cop you'd been and that you were no longer a junkie."

"I want my wife."

"We want our tapes."

"I don't have them on me, man. But I know where they are."

Reynolds shook his head. "I can't make that decision. Someone else will have to."

"Look, you sick bastard, I want my wife. You have her, and I want her back. If you don't give her back to me, alive, then I will set your entire world on fire. I won't stop until I have the fuckholes who orchestrated this shit, and then the ones above them. You read me on this, Judge? If I don't get my wife back, I won't stop until you're all either in prison, or underground."

"What you want is to be dead, I guess."

"Yeah, well, you know what they say about madness and genius: they look very much alike." He stepped forward then. Leaned over the judge's desk. "Remember: I've seen the other movies. I have a very good fucking idea how high up this goes. You don't know where those tapes are, and you never will. Until it's too late. And add to that fact, Judge," he added with a smile, "I'll always have something on *you*."

Reynolds's face turned red from his seething rage. He was barely able to control himself as he spoke. "You don't understand," he said. "If I give you *her*, then *I'm* dead. You don't understand what you're going up against. You have no conception."

"I don't give a fuck about you. What I want back is the mother of my child. And you'll give her to me, or I will—repeat, *will*—get every last federal agency I can find to go after you. Once the public sees these tapes? There will be a shitstorm. There will be nowhere you or your sick friends can hide, no matter how rich they are."

Reynolds's cell beeped, and he picked it up. Glanced at the screen, then put it back. Looked across his expansive desk at Mallen. Shook his head. "Like I've said already, I can't make this decision on my own. I would need to talk to some people. See how they feel about it."

The way Reynolds said it was what set off alarms in Mallen's head. The even modulation was back. There was a sudden assuredness in his words. He snatched Reynolds's phone before the judge even knew what was happening. Checked the incoming text list.

ON WAY.

He tossed it back to the protesting judge and made for the door.

"You won't be able to find a hole deep enough for all the crap that's going to be falling on you, and your ex-wife!" Reynolds said as he left.

Okay. He now had to figure Reynolds had called immediately, then kept him waiting five minutes. Add onto that another ten while he was in the office. They'd probably arrive just as he was leaving the building.

He quickly moved down one of the side staircases. All he needed to do was make it to the truck, and the gun.

At the lobby exit doors, he stopped. Checked through the glass. Nothing. Everything looked ordinary. Pushed them open and stepped outside. What should he look for? Guys in suits? *Good fuckin' luck with that one*, he thought, *this is San Francisco.*

Made his way quickly back to the plaza across the street. After he gained that, he figured it would be more prudent if he ran the rest of the way. Reynolds would give the goons his description.

He'd never been happier to be inside a vehicle. The truck felt like an armored car at the moment. The first thing he did was retrieve the gun. Then he geared up the engine, drove to the end of the block, and made a left on Grove. As he crossed Van Ness, he spied a black SUV with smoked windows up ahead of him. It began to prowl along the front of City Hall. Had to be them. That had become the "bad guy's" car in his head. Watched as they tried to locate him, probably knowing it was in vain. Maybe the gods were with him after all? Giving him this little bit of good luck? Kept a couple cars behind them and sent up a silent prayer for Chris and Anna because he suddenly wondered if he'd live through this to see them ever again.

He laid back, playing it easy. Let them do as many circuits as they liked. *Tail the guys on the tail.* He smiled. Changed lanes. Anything to not get them used to seeing him in their rearview. Hated tailing people in cars. It was the worst job to do on your own. Was bad enough in a nondescript vehicle, but in an old Toyota Land Cruiser? Hell . . .

The sedan turned south on Van Ness, but he didn't get the light to follow. Watched as far as he could. After a long and agonizing moment, the car in front of him turned right. Scanned ahead. Couldn't find them. He'd have to guess. Turned on Grove. If they figured he was gone, maybe they'd head to Central Freeway. He drove quickly down the block, almost slamming his brakes when he came up on them stopped at the light. They hadn't made for the freeway. Mallen followed their turn onto Franklin, where they headed north. For the better parts of town.

The car turned left on Broadway, and Mallen kept the truck as far back as he dared. The SUV stopped when it got to the border of the Presidio park. There was an old stone staircase there. Two men got out. The bald one looked like a cookie cutter cutout of a Darkstar employee; the smaller guy with the cigarette in his hand looked like any other guy in a suit. Both men walked to the stone staircase and started down it.

Jesus, Mallen thought, *we're moving into rarified air now.*

A state senator lived along those stairs, along with a couple of the wealthiest men in the city. He got out quickly and followed.

Mallen slowed at the top of the stairs. Watched as the men walked casually down, one talking on his cell. Just as they got to the foot of that section of stairs, they turned. Went through tan ornate, rod iron front gate that led to an expansive mansion. He thought he knew that house, had seen pictures of the gates in some classy magazine in a waiting room, and when he remembered, goddamn it if his heart didn't skip a beat in fear. That was the house that belonged to the new mayor's top advisor, Brett Nolan.

How many of Goldman's staff were involved in this? Were they all there just to keep Goldman in line? Keep the mayor from going off the deep end? If so, then Mallen figured he was probably as good as dead, and so was Chris. Had to get word to Gato. Went and stood in the shadows of a nearby tree. Pulled out his phone and dialed his friend. Gato answered immediately.

"Mallen!" Gato said. "Where you been? Been wonderin', bro."

"Later for that, G. Look, I'm at the top of the stairs, the ones on Broadway by the Presidio. I tailed a couple Darkstar guys here. They went into Brett Nolan's place, man. That's the mayor's advisor."

There was a silence on the other end for a moment, then, "Mallen, get away from there, bro. I'll call that Oberon guy and tell him what you found out. You can't do this on your own, bro. Get the fuck outta there!"

"It's cool, G," he replied. "I'm chillin' at the top of the stairs. Do what you said: call Oberon. Tell him we need backup. There's got to be *someone* he can trust to give us help."

"I gotta come and help you, man. If Oberon says he's sending backup, I'll tell him to send them here, and then I'll burn rubber to you. You hear me, bro? You. Stay. Put."

"Why, Gato," Mallen said with a joke in his voice, "I didn't know you cared so much."

"Shut up with that shit, bro. Stay safe and wait it out. Someone will be there. Somehow." Gato ended the call then, and Mallen knew he was probably already speed-dialing Oberon. It was good to have friends, and that was a fact. He put his phone in his pocket. He wanted to see better if anyone went in or went out. Moved down the stairs for a closer look …

That was when he heard someone jump out of the bushes behind him and his world turned upside down. Something that felt like a boulder slammed onto the back of his head, and then he was falling down a long tunnel of blackness, tumbling through space, realizing briefly that he was going to die.

———

Oberon sat at his desk in Homicide's bullpen, going over what he'd learned from George Septemberson, the operations chief at Darkstar. Funny how he'd begun to think of the company as just Darkstar, not Darkstar Security. Like it was something out of a movie. Well, he had to admit, it fit. Septemberson there had given him the runaround, then stonewalled him, then given him the name of the company's lawyers.

Basically, the man had told him to fuck off.

So he'd come back to home base and started doing some research. The company had indeed given money to Mayor Goldman's campaign. There were rumors in the press about that, but nothing was for certain. There were also rumors about some of the company's men using excessive force while on security detail. But that was it. A few more odds and ends, but nothing to write home about.

He pushed his chair away from the desk and rubbed his eyes. Had to wonder again, for the umpteenth time, what Mark Mallen had thrown in his path. He'd been sitting there for the last hour, trying to figure out what to do next, but nothing came. Knew that when he'd left Mallen outside of Westbrook's flat that he would probably just turn around and go back inside. Of course he would. But now Oberon was concerned. He hadn't heard from Mallen, and yes, that worried him many times over.

His cell rang and he yanked it out, hoping it was Mallen, feeling it probably wasn't. Mallen only seemed to call when Oberon was standing over a newly discovered dead body. He didn't recognize the number. "Detective Kane," he said.

There was a moment of dead space, then, "This is Gato. Mallen's friend?"

That got Oberon's attention. "I remember. What's happened?"

"I got a call from him only a minute ago..." Oberon listened as Gato filled him on Mallen's call. About where he was calling from, and what he'd seen regarding the men going into Nolan's house. "I need to get over to him, man," Gato said, "but I can't leave his daughter here all alone. He said you could send backup. Can you, man? I think my friend is in trouble."

Knowing Mallen like he did, Oberon replied, "You're probably right." Who could he trust to watch the house where Anna was?

Wracked his brains for a moment. Came up with a couple rookies he'd seen around. Rosen and Guilders. He'd talked to them once or twice after they'd each sought him out, telling him they wanted to make Homicide. They were eager, looking to make points. Probably not around long enough to have become tainted or jaded. If they were available, they would be his best bet. If they were off duty, all the better.

"I think I have backup for you. Just stay there until you hear back from me. Should only be a few minutes." Gato replied in the affirmative, and Oberon ended the call. As he began tracking down Rosen and Guilders, he tried to wrap his mind around the revelation about Nolan. Mallen wasn't given to crazy stories or wild accusations. Oberon started to get the feeling he could make a very good guess as to why Gato had called him but Mallen hadn't.

THIRTY-THREE

THE WORLD STARTED TO make itself known by a rude slap across his face. The sting brought him back from dreams about Anna and Chris. They'd been at the park, flying kites. Then they were gone and he was left alone, bleeding from a thousand pinpricks.

Opening his eyes hurt. Throbbing pain behind his right ear. He was vertical, legs and arms tied to a beam in what looked to be a large basement. Not the basement belonging to a business, but to a house. It was fitted out with a wet bar, pool table, leather couches, and a big-screen TV. Some fucker's man cave, for Christ's sake. Tried to move his head. Difficult, because there was something tight around his neck that made breathing hard. He was suddenly really fucking angry with himself. He'd walked right up and given himself to them. No way to tell how long he'd been out. No way to tell where he even fucking was.

Mallen heard footsteps behind him. One of the men he'd seen entering Nolan's house now walked into his field of vision. The bald one. Was bigger up close. Had a knife scar that ran across his right cheek and down under his jaw.

"Do you know me?" the man asked. Mallen shook his head as best he could. The man slapped him with a folded leather belt he'd kept out of view.

"Fucking answer when I ask questions. That's lesson one, fucker."

"Ask my mother. She'll tell you I've always been a slow learner." Was slapped again across the face. Like being hit with a ball of needles. "No, I don't know you," he answered.

"Really? Because I felt that maybe you wanted to marry me, what with you following me all over town."

"Sorry, pal," Mallen replied, "you're a little short for me." That drew a punch in the stomach. His body wracked with cramp, but he couldn't bend forward, being tied. Sweat broke out all over his body. His mind went into overdrive, frantic to set up walls and barriers against the coming agony. Kept reminding himself the golden rule of being tortured for information: They don't want you dead, they want what you know. They won't kill you unless they fuck up.

Please don't let them fuck up.

The other man he'd seen walking down the stairs, the smoker, strolled over. Hair pulled back in a tight, black ponytail, eyes slightly slanted, like maybe grandpa or grandma had come from Asia. Black goatee trimmed to a point you could draw blood with. Looked a little like an Asian Mephistopheles. He carried a metal folding chair with him, one that he set up and sat in about eight feet away. Then he lit a cigarette and calmly crossed his legs. Like he was getting ready to watch a movie. Regarded Mallen through a haze of gray smoke, then spoke to Scarface. "Where's his phone?"

For an answer, Scarface pulled Mallen's broken cell out of his coat pocket and threw it on the floor with a clatter of plastic. "Fucking piece of shit here owned a fucking piece of shit. Must've broke when he fell down the stairs."

Goatee nodded, some concern there in his eyes. Looked at Mallen, and Mallen figured the asshole was probably working the odds on whether to even bother asking if he'd made a call or just get right down to the business at hand. The answer was soon in coming. "Where's the stuff Teddy gave you when he died?"

"Teddy? Don't know him."

The man grinned. Nodded at Scarface. Scarface slammed Mallen again in the stomach. Breathing was a severe challenge. Had to work hard to not lose control of his bladder. Could not show he was scared. *Take the pain. Endure… but do not show fear.* He concentrated on keeping the information they wanted hidden away, compartmentalized in a nice, safe nook of his mind. Concentrated on staying alive. Had to do that for Chris. For Anna. Tried to focus on their faces. At least he'd gotten clean before he died, if that's what was going to go down.

"Where's the stuff Teddy gave you?" Goatee intoned as he took a drag of his cig.

"Too late," he breathed, "gave it to the police."

"Really? Then Reynolds lied about what you told him in the office?"

"Yeah. He's a big fucking ugly liar." For an answer, Scarface hit him in the groin, and his world exploded in agony. Wasn't even conscious of being untied and dragged over to the folding chair as Goatee got up. Barely felt his feet get restrained. Then his waist. Like wearing a belt three sizes too small. His arms were left free.

"You right-handed, Mallen?" Goatee asked. *Shit.* He hated questions like that. Fifty-fifty chance you'd get it wrong.

"Yeah, see?" he said as he flipped off the man with his right hand. Scarface punched him in the mouth and he tasted blood. Scarface then went to a dark corner of the room, returning with an old fashioned folding table. Almost identical to the one Mallen had back in his old apartment in the Loin. The man methodically opened out the legs. Set it squarely right in front of Mallen, pushing it right up to his stomach. Scarface grabbed his right hand, a hand still in pain from the knife slash he'd gotten from Carpy, taping it down to the table with heavy, red duct tape. Used a lot of it. No way to move that paw anymore.

If Mallen was sweating before, he was drenched now. Tried to keep his breathing even. As normal as possible. Kept telling himself that it was the *threat* of the pain, not the pain itself, that was key in all this. These guys must know, would know, that once they started in on the pain they had to gamble: was he telling the truth or lying to make that pain stop? Tried to keep that little gem of wisdom forefront in his mind. *Fuck that,* a part of him answered, *this is gonna fucking kill.* Well, at least they'd fallen for him being right-handed. He would still be able to hold the gun that would shoot their fucking heads off when he got the chance. And he would get that chance. He would make it through. Had to, for his family. For Oberon. For Gato. And for himself.

Took a deep breath…

Scarface brought out a hammer and what looked to be concrete nails. Big, long, and sharp. Strangely, Mallen wondered if this is what Jesus felt like. Laughed loudly.

"What is it, you fucking loser?" Scarface said, looking a little nonplussed at Mallen's outburst.

"Sorry. Reminded me of this joke I saw in a movie is all. About Jesus, three nails, and an innkeeper."

"Just fucking do it, will you?" Goatee said to Scarface. The man nodded, put a nail in the soft flesh between the pinky and ring metacarpals. Right between where the bones flange out. Mallen tried to float his mind away from the pain that was coming, focused on how he was going to fucking kill these two pricks first chance he got.

"Where did you put the stuff Teddy gave you?" Scarface intoned.

Shook his head. "Go fuck yourselves."

There was a sharp, gunfire-like sound as the hammer came down. He couldn't help it: he screamed as loud as was humanly possible.

———

Mallen was brought back to consciousness by someone putting a cigarette out on the side of his neck. He cried out, the smell of burning skin acrid in his nostrils. His right hand throbbed beyond agony or any word he could think of. Glared down at the hand. Took a moment to realize there were now two nails there, the second one between the ring and middle finger. And with the visual, the pain came alive and overrode the adrenaline, which finally just couldn't keep up.

The smell of his burned skin made him cough. He hacked up a bloody wad of phlegm. Only afterwards did he wish he'd remembered to spit it at Scarface. That wasn't to say he wasn't fucking scared. He was ... but fuck them, his anger was still bigger than his fear. And he knew he had to keep it that way.

"Glad you could visit some more," Goatee said as he lit another cigarette. Flicked the match at Mallen. "You're pretty tough, for a junkie."

"Ex-cop ex-junkie, man. Get it right," he rasped. Was awarded with another punch from Scarface, this time across the jaw. Probably just lost another tooth. He spit just to make sure. Didn't want to die choking on his own blood. This time he remembered to spit at Scarface's feet.

The room was still. His captors stood like statues, and he noticed a slight look of bewilderment on Goatee's face. They probably figured he would've caved by now. They'd forgotten about the man who'd existed before the junkie.

Goatee just smiled then. Got up. Came back rolling a TV and VCR on a cart, like it was movie day in class or something. Put it right in front of Mallen. Smiled again as he turned on the VCR, then hit a button on the remote. "You sure you don't want to tell me where the tapes are?"

His breath caught in his throat. A deep fear and dread welled up inside him. He could guess what would appear on the screen. *Oh sweet Jesus, let me be wrong*... But he knew he'd be right. He shook his head at Goatee. If he gave up the tapes, he knew he'd be killed outright. As long as they didn't have the tapes, they wouldn't kill Chris. It was a desperate chess match now.

The screen went black, and then it was filled with an image of Chris, strapped nude to a chair, a cart of medical instruments next to her. A man walked into the frame and Mallen forced himself to watch the entire thing. He had to make sure she was alive at the end.

"She's got a hot pussy, Mallen," Goatee said. "Why the fuck would you want to fuck up your shit with that hotbox? You're more stupid than shit in a bag, man."

But Mallen didn't hear him. All he could hear now were Chris's whimpers of fear and screams of pain as the man in the mask cut a symbol into Chris's stomach.

Then, at the end, as the man held the knife up to Chris's neck, her entire body covered in sweat and her stomach and legs covered in her blood, the screen went black. Goatee said, "That's some good shit, right, Mallen?" Goatee looked at him seriously as he said, "Where are the fucking tapes, asshole?"

Mallen just shook his head. He wanted to tell them. So bad. But he couldn't.

Scarface picked up the hammer and another nail, but Goatee halted him with a look. Goatee then went over to the bar. Reached behind it. Came back with a small leather case. Like a man's toiletry case. Put it on the table and opened it. Brought out a hypodermic needle and a couple vials. Mallen knew what was in those vials, as he'd bought ones like them for years. Wished now he'd remained a junkie. At least his family would be safe.

Goatee smiled, seeing the look in his eyes that he just couldn't hide. Fear, mixed with longing. All Mallen could do was watch as Goatee cooked up a shot, then nodded over at Scarface. The big man came over. Mallen's left sleeve was ripped open, his arm held down.

"No man, please," he muttered. Couldn't help himself. He was clean. Had to stay that way! "No!" he yelled.

"Okay, you don't give a shit about your whore. I get it. No worries. You're just a piece of shit. I told them that, you know? That you were just a piece of dog crap. Easy to scrape off. Well, here you go.

The scraping begins now, asshole," Goatee said. He then rested the needle just on the flesh of Mallen's left arm. He could feel the pressure of the needle's point...

"Where are the fucking tapes?"

A doorbell rang upstairs. Mallen barely registered the fact that it was an expensive one. Chimes, ringing out. He must be in the house at the bottom of the steps. The house of the mayor's assistant.

He was about to yell out when Scarface leapt at him, clamping a massive hand over his mouth. It smelled of blood. Mallen's blood. Goatee went behind him somewhere, probably to the door that led out. The door to freedom. He tried to bite at the hand, but he couldn't get a good enough angle on any of the meat.

Heard the door behind him open. Hushed whispers. "Come on," he heard Goatee say, and he was immediately clocked good on the side of the head. The blow dazed him, but he managed to wonder if they'd meant to knock him out while they dealt with the situation upstairs.

Knew he had only minutes. Tugged and tugged at the tape keeping his left hand to the chair. It was a little loose from the river of sweat he'd poured. Realized then he'd sweated right through his clothes. Yanked and tugged and pulled ... was finally rewarded with freedom for his left hand. Scooped up the hammer. Looked down at his right hand.

Jesus fuck ...

He placed the fork of the hammer under the second nail head. The one between his ring and middle finger. Luckily, his hand was numb, or this was going to fucking kill.

Mallen began to yank out the nail ...

Oberon stood at the curb outside Nolan's home, leaning against a black and white parked there. Looked over at the fire engine parked nearby. No one knew it, but he'd called in a 911 to this address. Man down, heart attack. He hated, positively hated, to waste resources, but he couldn't come up with any other plan. Knew that if he was wrong, Mallen would probably die. Also knew that Mallen had a nose for solving cases when he was still a police. Had earned his Distinguished Service Medal. He glanced back down the block, to where Gato sat on the hood of his Falcon. Oberon was learning to like the young man and how he truly regarded Mallen as a friend. Gato was obviously sharp, though quite the hot-head. After Oberon had gotten Rosen and Guilders to sit on Mrs. Netter's steps, he explained to Gato what his plan was. Gato had grasped it immediately, and after following Oberon over to Nolan's, he'd hung back waiting to see Oberon, and hopefully Mallen, exit the house.

Oberon pushed himself off the patrol car. Decided it was time to put in his appearance. Play it for all it was worth. Walked up the carved, granite path to the front door. What if Mallen were really still inside this house? What then?

"No, there is no medical emergency here," Nolan was saying with some annoyance as Oberon walked through the tall, dark oak doors and into the palatial foyer. "There's no emergency, at all. You sure you have the correct address?" Nolan was smaller than he appeared on TV. Wore a white shirt, open at the neck and cuffs. Khaki pants and loafers. Typical rich man's at-home casual.

One of the uniformed cops checked his notebook. Nodded. "Yes sir. This is the address we were given. Are you sure that—"

"Hi, Tom," Oberon said to the uniformed policeman, "I was driving by and saw your car. What's all this about?"

"It's about nothing," Nolan replied. Two more men joined them, coming from somewhere else in the house. He knew one of them by sight, having seen his face around the department's Bunco Unit. Wong was the name. Winston Wong, so nicknamed for his love of Winston red packs. The larger man he didn't recognize, but the man's red, raw knuckles told Oberon everything he needed to know. Mallen was indeed inside this house somewhere, and in trouble. There'd been bad rumors circling around Wong from the first day he'd been promoted to plain clothes. It was certain now: what Mallen had told him was true. They were indeed treading in very deep waters.

"Excuse me, you're Brett Nolan, aren't you?" Oberon asked, smiling and extending his hand. "Detective Kane, SFPD. I've seen you on TV, many times. How's the new administration going?"

"Well, thank you," Nolan responded, off guard.

"Great, really great." He then looked at Wong. "You work Bunko, don't you?" Oberon asked him. "I could swear I've seen you about. You're Wong, yes?"

Wong nodded, blowing smoke out through his nose. Eyes slits. Oberon knew he'd have to be careful with this one. The tension in the room ramped up into the red.

Nolan came forward. Now playing the indignant bureaucrat. "Look," he said to the uniforms and firemen, "there's obviously no emergency here. So, please … I'm busy on a proposal for a new youth program the mayor is hoping to introduce next week."

Oberon knew then he would lose this fight. He wondered what else he could do. He hadn't expected Wong and his friend to be here. He'd played the wrong hand, and now Mallen would probably pay. He couldn't believe he'd have to just leave, but he had no other cards to show.

"Can I use your restroom?" he asked, clutching at anything to stay inside the house. "Too many beers at lunch you understand," he added with an embarrassed smile.

Nolan glanced at Wong. Wong kept his eyes on Oberon as he lit a fresh cigarette. "Yes, of course officer," Nolan replied. "There's one down the hall, on your right."

"Thank you," Oberon said as he moved off down the hall. He knew that even if they didn't follow him down that hall, he had only a couple moments to look for Mallen.

———

The small basement window on the side of the mansion opened, and Mallen crawled out, using only his left arm and his legs. Rolled down a slight hill of grass to a wall made of rough stones. Fresh air had never smelled so good. *And for this, I gave up shooting smack?*

Quickly glanced around as he cradled his right hand. It'd been bleeding pretty bad, so he'd quickly wrapped it in some of the duct tape that had been used to tie that hand down to the table.

Pulled himself to his feet, knowing every moment was precious. Checked his bearings. He'd come out on the west side of the house and had rolled north. The garden wall looked about seven feet high. He took a couple steps back, then launched himself at it. Hooked his left arm over the top. Kicked with his feet, gripping the uneven stone. Had to throw his right arm over the wall, trying to grip as best he could with his index and middle fingers. His arms cried in agony as he hauled himself up and over, falling to the sidewalk, slamming down onto a bed of newly planted flowers and shrubs. Struggled to his feet. Had to lean against the wall for a moment until the world reassembled itself.

In the street, he could see the back end of a fire truck, a couple black and whites, and what he swore was Oberon's car. Could *that* be what caused the interruption? Mallen took a deep breath and forced himself forward. Staggered along the street side of the parked cars, keeping as low as he could without falling over. Got to Oberon's car unseen. Tried the back door. Locked. Tried the front passenger side. Also locked. Was too tired and spent to do anything else. He propped himself up against the car, out of sight of the house, and hunkered down to wait.

———

Oberon came back out of the hall. His insides were numb. He'd done as much as he'd had time to do. All he'd found was a locked door at the bottom of the stairs leading to what was probably the basement. He'd tried to open it, but the lock was very high end. Not easy to pick. Wondered as he walked back down the hall to where Nolan, Wong, and the firemen were just how much time he'd have to get a search warrant for Nolan's house. He almost laughed out loud at that. Who would give him that warrant? The only chance he had at saving Mallen was to barricade the house: him at the top of the stairs, Gato at the bottom. At least they'd be able to tail the men and try to take Mallen back from them, assuming they ever left the place. Hopefully it wouldn't be with Mallen's corpse.

He said his goodbyes to Nolan and Wong, tried to smile briefly as he was bum-rushed out the door. Oberon sighed, hating to be defeated. Walked slowly back to his car, pulling out his cell phone to call Gato and let him know the new plan.

———

After what felt like a lifetime to Mallen, there was the crunch of shoes on the street as someone approached the car. He managed to angle into a squatting position, hand screaming pain waves into his body. The driver's side door opened and he tapped on the opposite rear glass. That door lock clicked opened almost instantly, and he scrambled into the back as Oberon peeled away.

Mallen groaned as he tried to move his right hand. Oberon glanced back at him. Did a double-take.

"Good lord, if your mother could see you now, son," Oberon said. "You need a hospital?"

He looked down at his hand. Nodded. "Yeah, that would be prudent."

"I can't believe you made it out of there."

"On my own?"

"Well…"

"Thanks for coming after me, Obie."

"It seems to be that karma thing at work again." He glanced back at Mallen. "It's certainly blown up in our faces, hasn't it, Mark?"

The laughter hurt. "Thank you, Captain Obvious. Gato still with Anna?"

"I got some good men, some trustworthy men, to sit guard duty." When Mallen began to protest, he said with a look to his rearview mirror, "Your friend wouldn't just stand to the side, Mark. That's a young man who is more loyal than just about any other man I've ever met."

Mallen pulled himself up. Smiled when he saw the Falcon behind them, running rear guard. "Yeah," he said, "he is."

Oberon turned onto California Street. "I'm taking you to Cal Pacific."

"Anywhere they can sew up the nail holes."

———

The emergency room wait wasn't too long. Gato met them at the door. He kept staring at the mangled hand as they went inside, shaking his head, mumbling angrily. Mallen had given both men a quick rundown of what had happened in that basement room. He'd never seen Oberon so angry. Gato was silent. Stone silent, and Mallen thought that was worse than any outburst the man could've given.

Later, in the room with the doctor, Mallen avoided answering any questions about how it'd happened. He just kept repeating that he'd lost a bet. They sewed up his hand. Told him he might need some physical therapy; they were unsure about the long-term effects of such damage. Whatever the outcome, the hand would be out of commission for a while. The only thing he could think of as he sat there, wincing every time the doctor sewed another suture in his skin, was about how it all was going to end. He'd have to trade the tapes for Chris. He knew that now. They'd tried to get them from him, and failed. They didn't seem like the people to repeat a plan that hadn't panned out. They would move on to the next one.

Wondered if there was another way. Could he hand the stuff over to Oberon? He could go to the press, maybe someone higher up on the force who Oberon felt they could trust. But would that get Chris back? Force their hand? No, he figured, that probably wouldn't work. These guys didn't seem like the "force their hand" types. The doctor then came back into the room. Started to write a prescription for painkillers.

Mallen shook his head. "Sorry, doc, but no can do."

"Excuse me?"

"Long story. I'll just have to tough it out."

The doctor studied him for a moment, then shrugged. "Okay. If the pain gets too great and you change your mind, get a message to me." He then got up and left. After a moment, Gato and Oberon came in. Gato again looked at Mallen's hand, and then at the beating he'd take.

"We need to fuck their shit up, man!" he said. "We need to burn their houses down. Chop ears off, *vato.*"

Oberon shook his head. "I understand the sentiment, trust me. But we can't do that. Chris would suffer the consequences, I'm sure."

Gato took a moment to cool off, but he still paced back and forth. "Fucking *pajarones!*" he mumbled under his breath, obviously frustrated. "What do we do, Mallen?"

He hesitated a moment before answering. "We go get the tapes."

THIRTY-FOUR

"Well, at least now you know you can take a punch," Oberon said as the three men walked to the Falcon.

"Yeah, guess so." When they got to the car, Mallen hesitated, glanced up at the sky. It was now approaching morning, the sinking moon barely visible through thin cloud cover. The wind that blew in from the ocean was very cold. It never looked so beautiful. He was flooded with a great wave of truth: it could all be swept away in a split second. One blink, and poof. He would need to remember that for the rest of his life. His hand was throbbing, his right eye swelling up. Would be a hell of a shiner. Ribs ached. Jaw was on fire. It hurt to breathe. "Obie," he said, "thank you for saving my life. Again."

Oberon just nodded. "Like I've said, it's all part of my karma in this life, Mark."

"And that's a fact," Mallen replied.

Gato started up the car. "Come on, man. Let's get these guys."

"So," Mallen said to Oberon, "you'll follow behind us as backup. It's the post office express next to the Outer Richmond Safeway."

"Okay," came the reply. Oberon went quickly to his car and Mallen crawled into the Falcon.

Gato took a look at him. "There's nobody tougher than a recovering junkie. You prove my point, *vato*."

"Well," he replied, "let's hope it's tough enough. Let's go, G."

———

Mallen and Gato drove in silence down Balboa Street to the storefront where the tapes had been sent two days ago. Mallen would check behind them from time to time to make sure Oberon was still there. He was. Hung right on their tail.

Mallen thought over again what they were about to do. The only way to move this to the real end-game and get Chris back was to play it like they were going to play along. Like fishing, he would have to bring them to the surface. His mind raced over all the alternatives, all the variations. Just like a person playing chess. He figured the blowback from it, the retaliation, could be devastating. He knew that. But there was only one course. All Mallen could think about as they drove was Chris and Anna—he had to ensure his family's safety. He would always have the two tapes he'd sent to Bill at the Cornerstone. He could use that as a chip.

"What about you, man?" he asked Gato as they rolled through the park, the pale reddish streetlights casting eerie glows in the fog.

"Me?" came the answer. "What do you mean?"

"What if they come after you? Or your mother? What if they find Lupe before you do?"

"Then they do. My *padre* always said that if we pussied out over the hard shit, then what kind of men could we call ourselves? It's not the easy shit that makes us who we are, Mallen, it's the hard. You know that, just like I do, right?"

"Very true, G." After a moment he said, "I'm gonna owe you a lot by the time this is over, man. I already owe you more than you know."

"No way, *vato*. Family doesn't owe family. Not ever."

They arrived at the mailing center. A few campered trucks lined the perimeter of the otherwise empty parking lot. They parked right in front of the mailing center's door. Oberon pulled up behind them and killed the engine. Mallen looked over his shoulder just in time to see Oberon get quickly out of his car and go to the trunk. He opened it, then closed it and came over to Mallen's side of the Falcon. Mallen got out to meet him. Oberon came up to him silently and handed him a snub .38 in a worn, leather clip holster.

"I know you might have quite the collection," he said dryly, "but I also know you're unarmed right now. I do not like doing this, but I feel it would be best if you had something on you to help keep your enemies at bay."

"But Oberon, if I use it? It's tied to you, yeah?"

"Well ... it is. And it isn't."

"Jesus, Obie. You have an illegal weapon?"

"Not illegal. It's registered to a cousin of mine. He gave it to me when he drove out from New Orleans last year. I think it was reported missing, but you know ... I just can't remember." He glanced around the lot. "Would you like one of us to accompany you inside?"

"No, man. It's only a two-minute operation."

The box of tapes was indeed there. Crammed in with just enough room for him to get them out. He figured it was a sign; if he'd not taken out two and mailed them to Bill, the box wouldn't have fit.

Shut the mailbox door and left quickly. Gato was out of the Falcon, scanning left and right... smiled at Mallen when he saw the box of tapes under his arm.

The gunshots exploded the night sky just as Gato reached for the door handle to open it for Mallen. A huge boom and Mallen watched in horror as Gato fell to the ground, the front of his shirt turning red fast. Mallen checked his friend's pulse as another shot was heard and the driver's window of the Falcon exploded. He could just hear Oberon call into his radio: "Officer Four Seven! Ten-forty at the Mail Boxes Plus on La Playa. Ten-forty!" Another round of shots rocked both cars, a tire on the Falcon going flat. Mallen peered over the trunk.

And there was a black BMW. Out on the street. The same one or another, he had no idea of knowing. A muzzle flash exploded only thirty feet away, near a large dumpster.

"Just hold on," Oberon yelled at him as he crawled back out of his car. "Help's on the way."

"Fuck that! We need to get Gato to a hospital," Mallen yelled and returned fire. He'd always been good with a gun. It was a natural thing with him. It was like he could see a laser line to his target. Could just point and know when to pull. Maybe it was all those years playing video games, who knew? He got off three shots at the location of the muzzle flash. Was rewarded by a yell. Saw two men lumbering away, one helping the other as they made for the BMW. Registered that neither appeared to be Goatee or the man who'd driven nails into his hand.

"Look after Gato!" he yelled as he bolted for the driver's door of Oberon's car. He ripped the door open and slid inside, tossing the tapes onto the passenger seat. The car screamed around in a U-turn.

Mallen knew that every available cop in town would be burning rubber to that Mail Boxes Plus, since Obie had called in that a cop had been shot at. The BMW swerved and entered the park. Mallen figured they'd ditch it and continue on foot. That was what he would do. He got ready to leap out.

The BMW swerved onto a dark road near North Lake, then ran up the curb and over a grassy knoll, where it was momentarily lost from sight.

"Shit," Mallen yelled as Obie's car took the curb. The heavy sedan sailed over the hill and there was a huge crash and shattering of glass as it slammed into the rear of the parked BMW. The two men had gone over the hill and bailed the moment they were out of sight.

Mallen leapt out and ran to the BMW. Viewed it to make sure no one was inside. Bolted to his right, looking for signs of passage. There was just enough reflected light, coupled with the park lights, to be able to see. Everyone seemed to be wearing black these days. That would hurt. Ran as fast as he could, knowing the enemy would do the same. They'd shot at a cop, and if they did indeed know the troops had been called, they just might run all the way to Sloat Boulevard to get the fuck away.

He was at Chain of Lakes and JFK Drive when he spotted them. One of the men was jogging fast, limping. The man he'd hit. The other Darkstar man kept looking over his shoulder from time to time for signs of pursuit. Mallen bolted over the grass, his body in agony from its recent trials. But there was no fucking way he was going to let both of these fuckers get away. Ran as fast as he could, pumping every last reserve, getting as close as he dared. Then he stopped, aimed, cradling the butt of the gun with his right wrist under his left. Fired.

The shot echoed over the park. The limping man yelled as he went down, sliding across the wet ground to a stop, like a guy sliding into home headfirst and missing by a yard. Mallen had aimed for the back of the leg, and hit pay dirt. Gave a silent thanks to his old man who'd made him spend hours on the shooting range as a kid. The other man turned on a dime and fired blind, the shots ricocheting off some trees to Mallen's left. He returned fire but knew he wouldn't hit anything. The other Darkstar fucker had by this time run off into the night and disappeared.

Mallen walked over to the man he'd shot. He was curled up in agony, clutching at his blown-out knee. As Mallen approached, the man reached into his jacket, but too slow. Mallen kicked the hand away. Frisked him. Pocketed the Taurus 941 he found. Drove the muzzle of his gun into the man's cheek.

"You're never going to walk right again, you son of a bitch," he said. "And every time it rains, that knee's gonna fucking hurt, asshole. You shot my friend, and I hope you always think of that, too, as you sit there rubbing that knee, missing the fact you can't run or whatever anymore." Pushed harder on the muzzle, intent on leaving a tattoo if possible. "Who's giving the orders? Who's behind you? Is it the head of Darkstar? Who?"

His only answer was a glare that would freeze lava. This man wasn't scared; he was pissed. Just like the guy he'd corralled mid-piss outside the dock parking lot. Mallen had to hand it to the people at the top of the food chain: they recruited only the best.

"Who sent you?" he asked as the sounds of sirens filled the air. Time was running out. Pistol-whipped the man in the face. The man looked shocked.

"I'm not a cop," Mallen said quietly. "Not anymore. So I have no rules to play by, and I'm really pissed. You have maybe two minutes to make sure you don't have to take your food through a straw for the rest of your life. Who sent you? Who?"

The man looked at him. Could see that Mallen would do exactly as he said. Shook his head. "Do what you gotta do."

"Really?"

"Yeah. You're way outta your league, needle man."

"And you're out the rest of the game." Punched the man on the side of the head with the butt of his gun. The guy groaned and went out.

The sirens got louder. Flashing lights appeared from around the bend on his left. He had to get the hell out of there, find out if Gato was okay. He would need wheels. Had to get back to Gregor's truck, still parked by the Presidio. Ran off back to Obie's car and grabbed up the tapes, then dashed away into the bushes. It was easy to not be seen in the dark. Ran until he made it to Lincoln Way, then walked across the street to a gas station, where he found a payphone and called for a cab.

———

Mallen had the cabbie drop him near the Land Cruiser. He strolled quietly up the street, hands in pockets as he spied the other parked cars. Didn't want any fucking surprises. The street appeared dead. Only the occasional light on in a few windows. His breath wooshed out in relief when he saw the truck. Got in quickly and drove off, keeping one eye peeled to the rearview mirror. Shifting was both painful and difficult, having to do so with just the thumb and index finger of his right hand. He chose side streets for quite awhile, not heading toward any real destination; it would be easier this way to see if anyone were on his tail.

Wondered about Gato as he drove. Then called General. Asked after his friend. Yes, Eduardo Calderon was there. He was currently in the operating room and was he a relative? Mallen hung up instead of answering, and made good time over to SF General.

———

By the time he'd gotten to the hospital, Gato was out of surgery and in the recovery wing. Oberon stood near Gato's bed like a sentry. Gato looked pale, his right arm and shoulder wrapped up in a lot of gauze and bandages. "How is he?" Mallen asked.

"Doctors say he should pull through. Lost a lot of blood. They got to him in time."

Mallen looked down at his friend. This man had helped him so much in a very short time. Had helped keep him clean. Had cared about other recovering addicts remaining clean. But the man was a study in contrasts. He could quote the bible, then slam a man in the face with brass knuckles. *Well*, Mallen thought, *bottom line: thank fuck Gato is a friend and not an enemy.*

Oberon had been eying the box under Mallen's arm. "That them?"

"Yeah."

"What do you want to do next?"

"I don't know. What happened in the park? Do you know? The man I shot?"

"Police picked him up and brought him in. Took him to UCSF. Seems that Darkstar Security has a good medical program."

"So he works for Darkstar?"

291

"Yes. All he would say was that he and his partner were on a security detail for a VIP. They were attacked in the park by some muggers and it all went wrong. They pleaded Darkstar policy of anonymity regarding their clientele."

"What about the gun he used to shoot Gato?" But he thought he knew the answer to that.

"There was no gun. They're combing the woods around the two cars."

"A cop took it," he said with conviction.

"Yes, I'm afraid you're right. I had to call in a couple markers regarding my vehicle, which was found one mile away. I told them that there had been two men, one of whom took my car and drove off in the ensuing fire fight."

Mallen put his hand on Oberon's shoulder. Gave it slight squeeze. Winced with the effort. "Obie, thanks."

"Thank me when this is over and we're all still alive."

"Yeah, good idea." He was more tired than he'd ever imagined possible. Needed down time. Time to regroup. All he could do was go home and try to rest. The next move was theirs. He wondered how long it would take them.

———

Turned out it wasn't long at all. He'd said goodbye to Oberon. Looked one last time at Gato, then took the tapes and left the hospital.

As he approached the Land Cruiser, he noticed there was a piece of paper stuck under the driver's side windshield wiper. Probably a fucking parking ticket. Maybe a note from someone about his lousy parking job. He felt as he approached that he was wrong on both counts.

And he was.

The piece of paper was a note. A torn page from a day planner. The message had been neatly typed on it, before it'd been ripped out. There was only a location on it: *Palace of Fine Arts*, along with a time: *4 AM.* He tried to tell himself that if they wanted to meet in public, then maybe it wasn't going to be a hit. Sighed then, wishing again he lived a very different life.

Got in the truck and pulled away from the curb, feeling very vulnerable.

———

Mallen went to his house, figuring if the meet was set, they wouldn't try to kill him beforehand. Not under the current combat conditions. The drive home was uneventful. That was a plus. Made it to the door of his house, wondering how Chris would make it through the ordeal she'd been subjected to. *She has to still be alive*, he told himself over and fucking over again. Otherwise, why the meet? They could whack him any time they wanted. They'd showed him how large the organization was. He'd managed to bob and weave so far, but eventually his luck would run out and he and Chris would lose. *Christine. Anna.* Would he ever be able to live with himself, involving his family in this? He hadn't meant to, yeah … but that didn't count for shit. It'd happened. Maybe, he thought as he drove, he'd be able to get a few hours of shut-eye before the final curtain went up. He was at the point where he was having a hard time remembering what sleep felt like.

When he was inside his place, Mallen put the tapes in one of the cabinets in the kitchen, the one below the sink. Someone had replaced the wood down there really badly, leaving a large open space under the drainpipe. Large enough for him to shove the shoebox through and push it out of sight. It reminded him of the small space in the floor trim of his Tenderloin apartment, where he used to hide his dope. At that thought, he promptly got the bottle of whiskey from the cupboard, along with a stained coffee mug. Sat down at the table. Poured a drink. Took it all in one gulp. He set the alarm on the old wind-up clock he'd found when he took over the place, then laid out on the couch, trying for just a moment to not think about it all. But he knew it wouldn't work.

All he could think of was Chris.

THIRTY-FIVE

HE ENDED UP GETTING no sleep at all. Time seemed to tick by slowly, but eventually it was time to leave. Took one last look around at his house. He was happy here, and had looked forward to many days of listening to the water slap against the hull. Hearing the seagulls cry as they flew above. He hoped he'd have the chance to come back here, to this place he now regarded as home.

Mallen rolled his window down as he drove, drinking in the foggy night air. Made him feel a little more alive, and he needed that right now. As he drove, there was again that wish that he'd never gotten clean. At the moment, shooting his life away seemed the better alternative. But a voice inside him told him that was the easy way out. That taking the hard road, doing those things that tore at you but in the end made you stronger, was the only road worth taking at all.

———

He turned down Baker and drove along the lagoon next to the Palace of Fine Arts. Built in 1915 for the Panama-Pacific Exposition, it was still one of the most beautiful places in the city. Couldn't count the times he'd brought Anna here to watch the swans or fly a kite. Hopefully he'd be able to do that again, one day. He parked in the empty lot next to the old Exploratorium building. There was no point in playing this on the sly, or quietly. He knew he should've asked Oberon to accompany him. Oh fuckin' well. It was a question of Chris's life. He just couldn't run the risk of them seeing he had some form of backup. The only precaution he'd taken was to leave the .38 Oberon had given him and take the Glock from his file cabinet, along with the spare clips. He'd also shoved the knife he'd used on Westbrook's neck back into his left boot. But with all that, his only goal was to get Chris and get away. He had no idea what they'd try once the box of tapes was in their hands; he had to be prepared to shoot his way out. Once out of there, the two tapes he'd kept back would hopefully act as a shield for him and his family. In perpetuity.

The dome loomed above him. As he advanced, he perceived a group of men standing in the shadows close to the lakeside. Seven, maybe eight. Couldn't be sure. Two of those men detached themselves from the rest of the group and walked toward him. One was Goatee—who Obie had revealed was the policeman named Wong; the other a man he'd never seen before. Older, maybe sixty. Thinning hair. Tall; six feet and some change. Healthy-looking, and his suit fit like a glove. Newspaper nestled casually under his right arm. They must be feeling very sure of their position if this guy was here, because that meant management was in town. That made him nervous. Couldn't help glancing at the shadows, wondering how many hidden enemies might be there.

"How's that hand?" Wong asked as they came up. He gestured with his cigarette, a smile on his lips.

296

"Enough," the man scolded. "And put that cigarette out." Wong did as he was told. The man turned his attention back to Mallen. Eyed the box under Mallen's arm. "Thank you for coming," he said.

"You bastards have my wife," Mallen replied.

"And in the biblical sense, too, junkie," Wong said.

"*Ex*-junkie. Thought I told you that."

"He's lying, of course. Officer Wong here has a desperate sense of humor," the man said as he shot Wong a deathly look that made Wong step back and put his hands in his pockets.

The man then turned back to Mallen. "Taking her and then making the tape was meant only as a warning, I assure you," the man said. "We had to be sure you knew just what this encompassed. We didn't think you did, until it was too late." He then looked over his shoulder at the group of men and made a gesture much like a man calling for a waiter. A figure moved forward from the midst of the group. It walked stiffly and as it came closer, Mallen saw that it was Chris. She was dressed in a dirty, torn linen sun dress. Had mental hospital flip-flops on her feet. She saw Mallen and tried to run to him, but was intercepted by Wong who grabbed her by her wrist and held her back.

"Mark!" she cried out as she struggled.

"Chris! I'm here. It'll be all right! I'll get you home and back to Anna, I swear." He then said to the man: "No, I guess I didn't know what this was really about. Not right away. Not until the night you guys iced Teddy in the warehouse."

The man nodded, scratched at his chin—Mallen wondered if that was a sign. He kept his hand gripped around the gun in his pocket, waiting to hear a shot that could come from anywhere.

"No, we're not going to kill you," the man said, like the guy could read minds or something. "What we have here is—what was that cute phrase from the seventies? Ah, yes: a *détente*."

"Yeah, *détente*. What do you mean?"

"Well, it has gotten a bit out of hand, hasn't it? A lot of people are nervous. I'm sure that some of those tapes are still out there somewhere. You're obviously that smart and cautious. And it's a big world, correct? You know, there's been quite the discussion on how best to handle you and your ever-growing army of friends. Friends such as Detective Kane, or that 'Gato' gentleman. There's also the question of your family, yes?"

Mallen thought of Chris and Anna. Chris, horribly abused, almost killed. His family's safety. His family's future. "What's your offer?" he rasped out.

For an answer, the man handed Mallen the newspaper tucked under his arm. He took it and read it. The *San Francisco Chronicle*, dated today. He knew that it had probably just hit the stands. Read one of the lead stories. Seemed that Judge Toland Reynolds, mayoral assistant Brett Nolan, and head of security John Westbrook had been killed while flying to Tahoe for the weekend. The small plane had gone down in the mountains during the night. The reason for the crash was still under investigation.

"Take that," the man said, "as a sign of good faith. We'll never find those other tapes. We know that. However, you'll never give them to anybody, either, because you know your family will then die. You'll die, too, but only after watching *them* shuffle off this mortal coil in a very bloody manner. Might make a great movie, who knows? And maybe we'd throw in your friends, for good measure. Your in-laws? Every person you've ever known or spoken to. So, you see? Stalemate."

Mallen forced the word from his mouth, the taste bitter: "Right."

"So," the man continued, "we go our way, you go yours. You don't give the remaining tapes to anyone. Ever. We let you and yours go your own way unmolested. Agreed?"

Mallen looked at Chris's face. At the tears that ran down her cheeks. "What guarantees do I have you won't change your mind?" he said to the man. "Like a couple months, or years, down the road? When my guard is down, yeah?"

"You don't. But then, neither do we. You could disappear, your family could go into the witness protection program. Look, neither side is *ever* happy with *détente*, correct? That's what makes it *détente*." After a moment, he added, "So? Do we have a deal?"

Mallen stood there and gazed at the man, then at Wong, and then over at the dark group of men whose faces he couldn't see. And that was the perfect image for him: a group of men whose faces he couldn't see. As long as he had a family, he'd never be able to take these guys down. Never. The fact they were talking to him like this meant they'd probably really come to a place where they felt they could live with this fly that refused to buzz away. He thought of the women on those tapes, already beyond his help. It was for his family, he told himself.

"Deal."

The man smiled, and Wong let go of Chris. She came over to Mallen and threw herself into his arms, shaking. He hugged her tightly, as tight as he dared, not wanting to hurt her more than she'd been. Chris looked into his eyes and he looked into hers. In hers, he saw her strength. Saw her pain. It would be a very long time before she was over it, but he knew she *would* get over it. She was so strong. He stroked her hair, just like he'd done in the old days.

"I'm so sorry, Chris," he said, his voice almost a whisper.

"You look like shit, Marky," she answered, a tired smile playing over her mouth for a moment.

Wong came over and held out his hands for the box. Mallen gave them over. "I'm sure I'll be seeing you again," Mallen said to him.

"I'll bring the hammer and nails. Good luck with that hand," Wong said and then turned and walked back to the group of men.

The man in the suit seemed ready to reach out to shake hands but then thought better of it. "Hopefully we'll never meet again, Mallen." He turned and then walked away.

Mallen watched them go, feeling like he was watching a part of himself go too. Even though both sides had called a truce, he'd failed. No one went down, and no one was going to pay for all the bodies he'd seen in the last week. He wasn't sure he'd be able to look at himself in the mirror tomorrow morning. Maybe not ever. He couldn't ever remember wanting to shoot some horse so badly in his life. Just fly away from the whole shitty world.

Then he felt Chris's hand on his shoulder. "Come on, Mark. I want to see our daughter."

THIRTY-SIX

HE SPENT THE FIRST couple nights after it was over at Chris's. Wanted to take care of her as best he could until her mother arrived to help out. What the hell Chris would tell her, he had no idea.

He'd told Oberon what had happened, about the choice he'd made. Oberon's only reply was, "You did the right thing, Mark. There was nothing else for it. You did the right thing." It was nice of him to say, but Mallen didn't feel that. Probably never would.

On the third night at Chris's house, he overhead a conversation she was having with someone on the phone. At first he thought it was her mother, announcing she'd landed at the airport early, but then he heard Chris's tone. It *wasn't* her mother. Not at all. It was obvious the person on the other end of the line wanted to come over, and right away. He got it. Wasn't surprised when Chris came limping into the room and told him he looked tired. That he should go home and get some rest. She'd call, she said. It was all good, he told himself. He needed to be reminded of the boundaries. Had to remember the size of the playing field, and its rules.

He got it.

Mallen said goodbye to Chris, her again telling him she'd talk with him soon. He gave Anna a big hug. She clung to him for a moment, very tightly. Told him she didn't want him to go. He told her he'd be back, that he'd finally have that kite too.

"Promises, promises!" Anna said, in her best Cockney accent. Mallen had no idea where she'd picked that bit up, but it was so *Anna* that it made his eyes sting.

He hugged Chris again. Whispered to her how sorry he was about how it'd worked out. Felt her nod her head, then say, "You're still the knight in shining armor, Mark. Better than a man with a needle in his arm, right?"

———

Gato was doing better already. He'd be all right. Had woken up long enough to smile at Mallen and squeeze his good hand. Mallen wondered how long his friend would put up with this interruption to his search for Lupe. Probably crawl out of the place, Mallen figured, IV still attached to his arm.

———

The next week, he picked up the tapes from Bill at the Cornerstone and moved them to a much more secure spot. Bill had given him a worried look when he'd come for the envelope, but he'd assured the barkeep it wasn't a drug thing. Told him with a clear smile that he was now fighting on the side of the angels. Bill understood, smiling back as he made Mallen a drink, on the house.

He took the tapes to a safe deposit box up in a Santa Rosa bank under a fake name, prepaid far into the future. Mailed an envelope to Oberon's home address, with instructions on the outside to only open it if Mallen ever failed to appear.

Obie would know what to do.

THE END

Photo © Dawn Vail

ABOUT THE AUTHOR

Robert K. Lewis has been a painter, printmaker, and a produced screenwriter. He is also a contributor to Macmillan's crime fiction fansite, Criminal Element. Robert is a member of Mystery Writers of America, Sisters in Crime, the International Thriller Writers, and the Crime Writers Association. *Critical Damage* is his second novel. Visit him online at RobertKLewis.com and at needlecity.wordpress .com. He lives with his wife in the Bay Area.